The Grey Dog

Part Two of the Godyear Saga

By Jason Malone

Copyright © 2022 by Jason Malone
Map copyright © 2020 by Elizabeth Barlow-Hall

All rights reserved.

This edition first published in 2022

Cover design by Lena Yang
Map illustrated by Elizabeth Barlow-Hall

ISBN 978-0-473-66591-3 (paperback)
ISBN 978-0-473-66592-0 (Kindle)

Published by Jason Malone
authorjcmalone@gmail.com

*This tale is for Pops,
who was always a role model.*

The Black Coast
Fyrdun
Glacier Cape
N
Swelenda's Sound
Key:
* The Capital
1 Oldford
2 Edward's Home
3 Henton
4 Everlynn
5 Beglen
6 Winterhome
7 Tidegate
8 Hariton
9 Greensted
10 Mudhill
11 Tillysburg
12 Giant's Rest
13 Oarsley
14 Aedside
15 Carol's Fortress
16 Nellip
17 Kingshowe
18 Waterhold
19 Mudbank
20 Applehall
21 Bellthrop
22 Willosted
23 Bullhorn
24 Grovebury
25 Brimhaven

The Northern Realms
and Kingdoms
The Northern Alps
Ard River
15
11
12
Lakeland
ARDONN
9
10
8
13
4
5
Beglen
Heights
erlynn Forest
3
Aed River
22
14
1
2
21
20
Broken Firth
19
23
16
Cris River
Crisan Ranges
The Borderland Moors
ERILA
24

1

Wolf

I could feel the beast approaching.

The great hall was almost empty. Six of us sat around the small fire we had built in the centre of the hall, and its crackling echoed throughout expansive room. That fire was our only source of warmth and light, while around us was total darkness. Neither stars nor moon decorated the sky that night.

They say this place was once the home of the Edan, the giants, who had built it in an age long since passed. Now it felt inhabited only by ghosts. Not even rats seemed to linger in these halls.

Yet before that night it had been full of people. People from Tillysburg, mostly, but many from other parts of Ardonn too. They sought to make a new home here — at least until their old homes had been rebuilt — but after several weeks people started to disappear in the night.

Then, bodies began turning up in the dark pine forests nearby or in the streams that flowed down from the mountains. One night, the entire fortress was haunted by the sound of roaring and the deathly screams of a dying man. Someone — or something — was angered by our recent arrival.

We were not welcome.

After those horrifying cries echoed through the fortress, the people decided they had had enough, so the king resolved to solve the problem for good. He ordered the people to leave and make camp outside the fortress' walls. Then, he sought the help of his Royal Godspeaker.

That was me: Edward of Oldford. Carol knew that whatever plagued this ancient fortress was not of this world; thus, the only person who could solve such an unnatural problem was one whose purpose was to deal with all things Otherworldly.

And so, six of us remained inside the fortress' great hall, in the dead of night, to wait for this horror to strike again.

We did not know when it would come, or even if it would. Would it sense our trap? Was it smarter than us? We tried to ignore these questions and remain confident, but each of us believed there was a high chance of failure.

What if it attacked the common folk out in the camps? I suspected it would not do that. This creature guarded the fortress. It had no quarrel with any who did not set foot in its lair.

One thing was certain: the fiend had a thirst for blood. That is why we had tied one of the horses to a post right outside the great hall. If the poor beast had known its fate, it would not have been so calm.

"How much longer, Edward?" Carol asked.

The other men stared, awaiting an answer.

"I cannot say," I said.

"Helpful," said Dughlas. Dughlas was my oathman, and my closest friend. He had fought with me in many battles, had even lost an eye for me, and we were close as brothers.

My apprentice Philip — the little Lurian, as the men had taken to calling him — sat beside Dughlas. Usually I would not allow a boy of only eleven to partake in such a task, but he needed to see me work, and what better way to learn our trade than to witness the horrors of the Otherworld first hand? There was only so much books and lectures could teach a person.

Nevertheless, I made him promise to do nought but observe, and remain at a safe distance from the coming fray. He was scared, I knew, but that only meant he was wise.

Far wiser than Sigg, the great lord from beyond the mountains, who had come for his daughter's wedding. He was the most renowned warrior from the Northern Realms, and that showed in his fearlessness. He was confident, cocky even, and thought that the terror we would soon face would be "no more frightening than a fox raid on a chicken pen." If only the brave fool knew what danger awaited.

Of all the men there, it was perhaps William who knew best the threat this being posed. Aside from me, of course. William, who was both my friend and hostage, had once been possessed by a mara — a powerful Otherworldly being. He knew the horror and hopelessness one experiences when dealing with such things.

The pretender-king Carol had had his own run-in with the Otherworld, though of a different nature. In the winter of that year, Carol's army went head to head against a horde of immortal horsemen led by a millennia-old king. It was a fierce battle, one we almost lost, and Carol suffered a grievous blow to the head.

Yet he lived to tell the tale, and he frequently boasted of his encounter. The Immortal King Emrys had fled the field that day, and was still out there somewhere, but he had shown no signs of warmongering since his defeat near Tillysburg, so our attention was turned to the monster that had been attacking Carol's people.

The night drew on, and the six of us spoke little. We wondered if our plan would even work.

But strike it did. In the late hours of the night, when all sane folk slept, we began to feel cold. It was always cold that far north, but not like this. It was unnatural.

That was the first sign of the beast's presence.

The second sign was the chill down my spine. The knot in my stomach. The racing of my heart. My senses were alert. My Gift, bestowed upon me by the Gods, was screaming at me. *Danger*, it said. *Danger, danger, danger, danger!* As a Godspeaker, I was trained not to fear these warnings, for I was one of the few that could do anything about what caused them.

The third sign was the restlessness of the horse. We heard it stamping its hooves at first, and snorting and huffing, but it quickly began to whinny. It was afraid.

William stood, but I held up my hand. We needed to wait.

We all felt terrible leaving the horse tied up out there. We knew what would happen if we did not go out to it, but we could not kill the creature and also save the horse. It was one or the other.

And then the horse screamed. It kicked and bucked and shrieked. Then we heard the roar. Deep. Long. Almost pained. Sigg believed it to be little more than a bear, but no bear makes noise so horrific. I cannot put it into words. Pray you never hear a sound like it.

The horse went silent.

"Now," I said.

The six of us stood and grabbed our torches and weapons. I had advised the others to use spears so we could pierce the creature from a distance, but Sigg insisted on using his axe and Dughlas favoured his bow.

We rushed outside. Sigg and William pushed open the great double door and we ran through, finding ourselves face to face with the horror.

And what a horror it was. It must have been twice the size of the horse that now lay on the cold ground with its belly torn open. Its thick grey fur oozed with blood, mud, and some kind of slime. Its eyes glowed a cloudy white, and as we burst from the hall it snapped up its enormous head to snarl at us with its terrifying maw. Blood and saliva dripped from its fangs, and a low, long growl echoed from deep within its chest.

Sigg was wrong. This was no bear. It was a wolf. A great, fearsome grey wolf.

"Plough me backwards and call me Buttercup — *that's* a wolf," said Dughlas.

"And the bastard will die like a wolf," declared Sigg.

Before I could stop him, the great northern warlord threw himself forward and brought his axe down at the fiend's neck. The wolf only stepped to the side and then in one swift motion pushed itself into Sigg. The man toppled to the ground, but before the beast could finish him, Dughlas loosed an arrow at its side and earned the beast's attention. He shot another arrow, and the wolf snarled back at him.

"Those arrows won't pierce its flesh!" I yelled. "It's dead; we need to spear it."

"Dead?" said Philip.

I yelled for him to back off and then, letting out a cry, I charged at the wolf. It turned to me, and with two hands I used all my strength to lunge at the creature. It dodged, but my spear's blade scraped against its shoulder.

Carol charged too, followed by William and Philip, but the wolf evaded each lunge and snapped and roared at its assailants.

We all stepped back, and Sigg crawled to his feet. The wolf backed up, slowly, keeping its eyes locked onto mine.

"It's going to run," I said.

"We must not let it," said Carol.

"No, we must not."

As I said those words, the wolf proved me right. It spun around and then sped off away from us, fleeing into the night.

"Horses, get your horses!" Carol cried. We had prepared for this, and so had our horses hidden in the stables on the edge of the courtyard. We all rushed over there and mounted, and I kicked the side of my strong stallion. He was a black warhorse named Brand, and we had been friends for some time now. He had served me faithfully and never failed me, and I prayed he would not fail me then.

The six of us rode off through the courtyard and through the fortress. The wolf was wounded and so it was slowed, and we were gaining on it. We chased it out of the fortress' gate, over the bridge, and past the camp made by Carol's people. I held Brand's reins in one hand and my spear in the other as I raced past the tents. The wolf growled and panted as it sprinted away from us, but it would not be able to outrun us forever.

The air howled past my face and my ears hissed. I kicked Brand, urging him onward, faster and faster and faster. The wolf fled into the woods, clearly hoping to lose us in there. We followed, dodging trees and leaping over roots and ducking under branches. A twig sliced across my cheek, but I kept on riding.

I could hear the snapping and thumping as the wolf ran through the forest, but I could not see it in the dark. I followed my senses. I heard the other men shouting, but they were distant, and when I turned I could not see them. They must have gone off track and lost the wolf, but my senses were much stronger than theirs.

And then I saw it. It was up ahead, barging past large trees and toppling small ones. I pushed Brand onward and came closer and closer to the wolf. I could smell it, and wanted to vomit. As I drew nearer, the wolf kept turning its oversized head to see me, and that only increased its resolve. It ran faster and faster. I held my spear tight under my arm, ready to thrust it into the wolf's back once I was near enough.

But then I heard the sound of running water. No, *rushing* water. Not far up ahead there must have been a river, and not a calm one. If that wolf were what I thought it was, it would be able to cross it with ease, but would Brand? I could not take that risk. If the wolf reached that river, it would likely have escaped, and we would have lost our one chance to kill it. It would not be baited so easily again.

I put the spear over my shoulder and squinted at the dark mass moving swiftly through the trees. I whispered a prayer. I gripped the shaft tight. I focused. I held my breath. Time seemed to slow down.

And then I threw it. I jerked my arm forward and opened my

fist, and the spear hurtled ahead of me. It whistled through the air, and then, with a loud thud, the wolf rolled and rolled. I heard the spear snap and the beast rolled some more until it smashed into the trunk of a pine and let out a ferocious roar.

I skidded Brand to a stop and threw myself from his saddle, then went to stand over the wolf. Its breath was heavy, and it stared up at me in pain with its dead, white eyes. It groaned and growled. I held what was left of the spear with both hands, and with great effort pulled it from the wolf's side. It howled, and before it could run I brought it back down and buried the shaft into its chest. The wolf sighed, then its eyes went dark.

"Good hit, Wightman," Sigg said. He appeared behind me, sitting atop his large brown warhorse.

"You can credit the Gods with that. I'm terrible with spears, and would never have been able to do that without their help," I said.

Sigg laughed, and soon the other four arrived alongside us.

"What in the Heavens was that thing?" William asked.

"A revenant," I said. "The soul of a dead man who refuses to die, or who by some curse cannot. Bound to flesh, ever hungry, ever thirsty for blood. His body must have been destroyed, but his spirit possessed an ordinary wolf. The anger and hatred within the dead man would have twisted and corrupted the poor beast, giving it unnatural size and strength."

"And ugliness," said Dughlas.

"We should burn it then, before the spirit possesses a beast more fearsome than a wolf," said Carol.

"No, we must bury it," I said.

"Why?"

"If we burn it the soul will possess a new beast, or perhaps even the forest itself. But if we bury it properly, it should be bound to its grave, or at worst be harboured only by worms."

Carol nodded, then ordered the others to head back to the fortress to retrieve some spades. Carol and Philip stayed with me, and the three of us dragged the corpse to a suitable spot for burial.

We laid it down and I stared at it for a while. It reminded me of something, but back then I did not know what. It looked sad now that it lay there empty and lifeless. I like wolves. They are beautiful animals, and seeing one made wretched by wrath pained my heart.

The others took their time, but eventually they arrived with spades and we got to digging. I wanted the grave to be deep, and the men were not happy with that, but they trusted I knew what I was doing. Once the hole was dug we pushed the wolf into the grave and watched it fall and then thud at the bottom. The smell was awful.

"William, your spear," I said. William gave me his spear and, pointing it downwards, I thrust it into the hole and pierced the wolf once more. "That should bind it. Come, let's fill the grave."

We spent the rest of the night shovelling dirt back into the hole. Then, just to be safe, I had the men gather sticks and leaves and other dead forest matter so we could disguise the grave. Once we were finished, the ground appeared untouched. I was satisfied.

I said some prayers, asking the spirits of the forest to guard the grave, then we all mounted up and returned to the fortress. Dawn was approaching, and I was eager for food and sleep.

The people would rejoice to know that the horror that plagued their nights was now dead and gone. They would be glad to pack up their camp and head back inside the great ruined fortress.

It was Seeding, the final month of spring, and a wedding was about to be had in Giant's Rest.

The sun was creeping up over the mountains that backed the fortress in the east when we arrived from the woods. People from the camp crowded to watch us pass, and Carol pulled his horse to a halt.

"The beast is dead," he announced. The crowd clapped and cheered, and Carol held up a hand for silence. "It was slain by the hand of my Godspeaker, Edward of Oldford. You have him to thank for this."

At that, the crowd began chanting my name. I looked over them from atop my horse and saw a mass of people smiling up at me and offering me praise. My heart surged with pride.

Then I saw in the crowd my dear friend Matilda. She stood with Arne, one of Carol's oathmen, and she carried one of his puppies. They had grown a lot in the weeks since Tillysburg. Matilda gave me a wave, and I nodded to her.

Carol blew his warhorn and pointed his sword toward the fortress, then the six of us moved onward. The crowd began packing up their things and followed us toward the great bridge that crossed the moat surrounding Giant's Rest.

Giant's Rest was an ancient fortress abandoned long ago, and now sat in ruin at the foot of the eastern mountains amid a vast pine forest. I call it a fortress, but in truth it was more like a city — a great city of stone. After Tillysburg had been sacked and burned by the Immortal Horde a month before, the survivors took refuge in that ancient city and now it was Carol's base.

Already efforts had been made to rebuild the city with wood and stone, to clean up the dust and cobwebs, and bring life back to the dead ruin, but no matter how hard we tried we would never be able to live up to the grandeur of the ancients. They built in ways long lost to us. Perhaps it was built by giants after all.

We crossed the bridge and approached the huge walls of the fortress and under the massive gate, into the streets where the fortress' inhabitants once lived. Those streets were now the homes of Tillysburg's refugees. Further up the hill was another great wall, and behind that wall was the fortress proper. I assume this higher part was established first, and then the town below was built after as people began to gather around the centre of power. [I imagine Giant's Rest was once the seat of an ancient kingdom now long dead.

The six of us dismounted, then entered the enormous keep that rose high above the rest of the old fortress. It felt much less eerie now that the revenant was gone. During the wedding the great hall, which was now empty and cold, would be full of song and dance and laughter. Everyone was looking forward to it. These times were grim, and a wedding would be a pleasant change, even if only for a moment.

Everyone in Giant's Rest would be celebrating, for it was no ordinary occasion. This was a royal wedding, held in conjunction with the springtime festival of Petalsong. Carol, the pretender-king and rightful claimant to Ardonn's throne, was getting married.

That is why Sigg was there — to witness the union between his daughter Amalie and the true king of Ardonn. I suppose he hoped to gain an ally if Carol regained his throne. In exchange, Sigg would pledge some of his warriors to Carol and support his efforts.

Carol was at peace with the usurper Stephan for the time being, but we all knew that peace would never last. Once the Immortal King Emrys was dealt with, Carol would surely rise up against Stephan in rebellion. Supporters were flocking to him from all over the kingdom after news had spread of his victory over Emrys, and Carol had received secret letters from nobles across the land who promised to support him should he try to reclaim his birthright.

We went to stand around the remnants of the fire we had made the night before, and Carol thanked us all in turn.

"Most of all, we have Edward to thank. If it were not for his abilities, we would never have killed that wolf," he said.

"Aye, the lad has talent," said Sigg.

"Indeed. I will reward you, Edward, in time. I owe a lot to you. I can give you land, money, titles — all you need do is ask."

"Thank you, Lord King. I will think about it," I said.

"She has only seen nine winters, but perhaps when she comes of age you would like my sister's hand in marriage? She is fond of you, I have noticed."

"A childhood fancy, Lord King, nothing more. Clodild only likes that I talk to elves."

Carol laughed. "That is true. Ah, but I forget you have your heart set on another woman. Am I correct, Edward?"

"I have no idea what you are talking about, My King."

"Right." Carol smirked. "Anyway, gentlemen, I am tired and in need of rest. I must retire before it is too late in the day. I will see you later, I hope."

We bid each other a good night and headed off to our chambers. We were all tired. Most of us had had little sleep the past few nights on account of that revenant and I was eager to rest.

I followed the corridors through the keep until I found my room, threw myself onto the bed, and fell asleep almost instantly.

I must have woken around midday. Most of the people had already moved back into the fortress and occupied the stone houses they had been living in for the past few months. Carol's court moved back into the great keep and life was coming back to the place. Torches and braziers were relit, and the large fireplaces were roaring once again.

Servants resumed their cleaning of the great hall and continued with their preparations for Carol's wedding. It would not be for another week, but there was a lot of work to be done before it. A bard played a merry tune on his lyre while the servants worked, and I gave him a nod as I made my way through the great hall and into the courtyard.

It was there that I found Matilda, wearing men's clothes and with her long black hair tied in a bun. She was with Arne, and the two of them were sparring with wooden swords. Since her arrival in Giant's Rest, Matilda had wanted to learn to fight properly. She had learnt some sword skill during Winterlow, but it was far from satisfactory, so Arne was kind enough to teach her. She practiced with Arne every day that spring. I did not like that a lady was learning a man's skill, but Matilda was a free woman, and I could not stop her from doing what she wished.

Carol's heir and younger sister, Clodild, sat nearby on a stool watching Arne and Matilda train. She was flanked by two armed housecarls, and Arne's two puppies, Bark and Bite, lay at her feet. Clodild noticed me emerging from the hall and waved at me with both hands, a smile on her face.

"Hello, Edward!" she called.

Matilda turned her attention away from her fight for a moment, and Arne struck her on the arm. She let out a cry and Arne shook his head.

"No distractions! In a real fight, you'd have been cleaved in two," he said.

Matilda rubbed her arm and handed her sword back to Arne. She ran over to me, grinning. "I am getting better," she said.

"I've noticed. But Arne is right: focus on your opponent," I said.

"Yes, I know. Anyway, I hear you killed the fiend last night. Did it give you much trouble? Are you hurt?"

"I've not a scratch on me. It gave us quite the run-around in the woods, though."

"Well, it was doomed the moment you decided to hunt it. I knew you would be the one to slay it."

"I was lucky, that's all. How are you?"

"I am well. Would you like to go for a walk? So you can tell me all about last night, of course."

"Later, perhaps. Have you seen Dughlas?"

Matilda nodded. "He is with Philip and William at the river. I think they are fishing."

"Thank you, Matilda. I will see you later."

"I hope so. You seem happy here, Edward. I am glad of that."

I did an awkward nod, unsure of how to respond, then bid Matilda farewell for the time being.

I headed off down through the fortress, crossed the bridge, and headed into the woods. I loved those woods. They were truly awe-inspiring, and nothing like the forests anywhere else in the kingdom. The trees were tall, strong, and ancient — great mountain pines, firs, and spruces — and they spread in all directions, blanketing the countryside and creeping up the slopes of the mountain ranges flanking Giant's Rest in the north and east.

These woods were happy, full of life both worldly and Otherworldly, and largely untouched. Few resided in these parts of the kingdom, but those who did lived in harmony with the forests, preferring to survive on the foods provided by the wilds than to clear the land and grow food themselves. They rarely starved, for these woods were ripe with game. The arrival of the rightful king and his people did little to anger the forest, and as I wandered among the giant conifers I felt the trees whisper a warm welcome.

I did not wander far. A short walk along a track led me to a spot we had discovered that was perfect for fishing. The river here was flat and calm, and shallow enough to stand up in without being swept away or freezing to death, though not far upstream were some violent rapids, and further up it got colder and colder as it stretched further into the mountains.

Downstream, the river came to Giant's Rest, where it hugged the front of the fort, creating a natural moat, and then it continued on through the woods. The locals had no name for it, but Carol's people had taken to calling it 'River Trout,' after the abundance of trout that could be caught there.

Fishing for trout is what my friends Dughlas, William, and Philip were doing then. They did not notice me as I stood among the trees on the riverbank. I watched them for a time. The three of them stood in the water, their pants rolled up, holding their rods as they waited for a trout to catch.

It did not take long. Philip's rod jerked and he let out a cry. "I've got one, I've got one!" he said. He tried to pull it in, but the fish must have been too strong, for the rod shot forward and Philip fell face-first into the river. William and Dughlas laughed, as did I, and then my friends noticed me.

"You're too weak, Philip!" I called.

Philip stood back up, soaking wet, and he waded back to the shore grumbling.

"Oh, leave the poor lad be," Dughlas said.

"He is doing well for his first time," William observed.

"It looked like it," I said. "Did you learn anything last night, Philip?"

"Yes," said Philip. He had climbed up on the bank and was now jogging on the spot.

"Good. We will talk more about it tonight. Dughlas, I need to speak with you alone."

"Aye, Boss," Dughlas said.

"Dry yourself off a bit and get back in the river, Philip. I want you to catch me a nice big trout for my supper."

Philip rolled his eyes. "Yes, Master," he said.

William chuckled as he reeled in a fish, and we gave each other a nod.

Dughlas came up onto the bank, pulled on his boots, then followed me into the woods. We walked for a bit, talking about the fishing and our hunt the night before, until we were out of earshot of the others. Dughlas and I sat down on a fallen tree, and he looked at me with his one eye, waiting for me to speak.

"I feel uneasy," I said.

"Uneasy?"

"Yes. I have not felt this way since the battle of Tillysburg, but after we killed that revenant I began to sense a growing threat. It is not overwhelming, but it bothers me."

"What could it be?"

"I have my suspicions."

"Emrys?"

I nodded. Since Emrys was defeated in battle we had known that he would not hide forever. He was gone for now, but everyone knew he would eventually emerge again and the fragile peace of the past weeks would be broken. This was merely a break in the war.

But then, after the revenant had been bound, I felt a sense of foreboding. A warning. Was that feeling always present, only I could not notice because of the presence of the wolf, or was something terrible about to happen? Was the wolf even connected?

"You should tell Carol," said Dughlas.

I shook my head. "I don't want to dampen his spirits with ill news. Not before his wedding."

"That's fair. You'd also be wise not to give King Sigg any second thoughts about marrying his daughter to Carol."

"I'm not sure Emrys would bother him too much. I'm told Sigg has dozens of daughters."

Dughlas laughed. "And thrice as many sons. Look, after the wedding I would tell Carol what you feel. He trusts you, and I am sure he'll do all he can against this threat. But there is another issue we need to address," he said.

"Oh?"

"What are you going to do with William?"

I had been trying to avoid that question. It was always in the back of my mind, and in truth I did not have an answer for it. William's father, Lord Odo, had betrayed Stephan during the battle of Tillysburg and fought against him alongside Emrys. Odo had fled the battle and returned to Everlynn, but William had surrendered to me and so was my hostage.

To those who did not know him, though, he would not have seemed like a hostage. He was a nobleman and was treated as an honoured guest, yet I could tell he longed to return to his wife and home. We were friends. We enjoyed our time in Giant's Rest, dining, hunting, fishing, sparring, and talking together. However, there was no denying that William longed for freedom once more. He could feel the weight of his invisible bonds.

"A smart man would ransom him back to his father. On top of the gold Odo owes me for helping with that mara, the ransom would make me rich, and I could rebuild my hall near Oldford thrice over," I said.

"And still have enough to retire," said Dughlas.

I nodded. "I do not want to ransom him. If I did, William would be at Stephan's mercy. It is only a matter of time before Odo's petty rebellion against the usurper fails. What will happen to William when it does?"

"You mean to release him when Lord Odo is defeated?"

"Yes. I will not let William be charged with treason. His freedom would mean his death."

"You're a better man than most, Edward. Many would just take the money and leave his fate to the Gods."

"Thank you, Dughlas. You're a true friend."

"Only 'cause I swore an oath to you. Daft idea if you ask me," Dughlas said. He grinned. "Come on, join us in the river. There's plenty of fish today."

Dughlas was right — there was a lot of fish. We went back to William and Philip and the four of us spent the next few hours bringing in trout. Once the day grew late we brought our haul back to the keep. We would have a feast that night to celebrate the fiend's defeat, and Carol's guests would be grateful to us for our catch.

Before we left, I tossed a few lumps of silver into the river as thanks to the water spirits for their gifts, and then we headed off back through the woods. Dughlas and William sang while we walked, and the four of us told jokes and stories, but despite our jovial hike back to the fortress I could not shake off that feeling of unease.

Why did that grey wolf feel so meaningful?

2

Wedding

If you could have seen Giant's Rest on the day of Carol's wedding, you would not have thought that the fortress had been an empty ruin only a month ago. The whole place was alive, filled with excitement and cheer.

Some of the locals from the surrounding areas came to see the ceremony and partake in the celebrations, as did many merchants and travellers from across Ardonn. I even noticed a few nobles disguised as commoners so as not to reveal their hidden support for the pretender king.

On the morning of Carol's wedding, I sat with William outside a makeshift tavern that one of the refugees had set up right by the fort's gate. We drank ale while watching the arrivals come into Giant's Rest, making guesses about who they were and where they came from.

One of the visitors came in through the gate pulling a wagon full of barrels. The big-bellied man looked tired and messy, his brown hair and beard tangled and knotted. The cart was too heavy for him. William and I laughed as he tripped over the uneven stone road and stumbled forward while his wagon flipped onto its side. His barrels tumbled out onto the road, and some of them smashed open, spilling wine everywhere. The man grumbled and looked around for help as he tried to lift one of the large barrels, but everyone seemed to ignore him.

"Oh, let us help the poor man," William said.

I chuckled. "Alright. He does look like he could use it."

The two of us pushed through the crowd and we flipped the wagon back upright, then went to help load the barrels.

"What's your name, merchant?" I asked.

"Thorry, lord. I'm from Beglen. Thank you, lords, for your help," said the merchant.

"Ah, Beglen. And how is Lord Edric these days?"

"He is well, lord."

"What brings you to Giant's Rest?" asked William.

"Wine, lord," said Thorry. "I've brought my father's wine hoping Carol would like to buy some for his wedding. But now the barrels are all mixed up."

"Mixed up? They all look the same to me," I said.

"Oh, well, yes. But I know which is which."

"Indeed. The wine for Carol's wedding feast has already been brought, but bring it to the king anyway. I am sure he'd like a taste.”

“Thank you, lord. Forgive my rudeness, but I haven’t asked your names.”

“This is William, son of Lord Odo of Everlynn. My name is Edward, and I’m Carol’s Godspeaker.”

Thorry’s eyes grew wide. He bowed, then went down on one knee. “Pardon me, my lords, had I known I was in the presence of such high men I would’ve shown more respect.”

“No pardons are needed, Thorry of Beglen,” I said. I placed the last of the barrels back into Thorry’s wagon. “Just keep going uphill till you come to the second gate. Tell the guards you wish for Carol to taste your wine, and say Edward sent you.”

Thorry thanked us, then made his way through the fortress to the keep. William and I returned to our table, where we remained until evening drinking, eating, and enjoying the Petalsong festivities. We were allowed to have some fun on the day of a royal wedding. Everybody up at the keep was frantic in their efforts to make everything perfect, but there was little use for a Godspeaker and his hostage, so the two of us stayed out of everyone’s way at the tavern.

Carol would have been in the keep readying himself for the marriage, as would his betrothed and her father. Matilda spent the day shaving, washing, and prettying herself up with the other ladies of the court, while Dughlas and Philip too had a pampering far more luxurious than what they were used to. William and I had already been washed and tidied earlier that morning.

As evening approached, a great horn was sounded from the inner wall surrounding the keep. It echoed throughout the ancient city and into the forests and mountains, signalling that the wedding was about to begin.

William and I were late — and slightly drunk — so we missed the beginning of the ceremony. The guards ushered us quietly into the great hall and we came to stand at the back of the crowd just as Amalie was finishing her oath. I looked around, trying to spot my friends.

I saw Matilda standing near the front. She looked beautiful. Before I rode to join Carol in the battle near Tillysburg, Matilda had kissed me — though we had not spoken of it — and ever since then I viewed her as perhaps something more than a friend. I had often caught myself staring at her since our arrival in Giant's Rest. William noticed and elbowed me, smirking.

"Ask her to dance tonight," he whispered.

"She is a noblewoman. It wouldn't be proper," I said.

"And my father swore an oath to King Stephan. Breaking that oath was not proper, but did it stop him?"

"Stupid comparison."

"You are Gifted, my friend. The laws of caste and class do not apply to you."

Before I could respond, the woman beside me hissed at us to be quiet. Amalie had finished her oath, and now it was Carol's turn. William and I watched as Carol swore to defend his new wife, provide for her, love her, honour her, and all that. He promised to lead their marriage well, and make Amalie into a queen who would be remembered for eternity.

They were beautiful words, and now Carol was bound to them. I wondered then if I would ever marry. Carol wanted me to marry his sister so that we could become brothers and he could grant me land without his nobles complaining, but Clodild was still too young and a lot could happen before she came of age. In those days, I did not want to marry.

After the oaths were sworn, five servants entered the great hall bearing three chests — two large, and one small. The two heavy chests were placed at the feet of Carol and Amalie, and Carol bent down to open one. It was filled with gold and silver.

"I offer this gift to you, Sigg King, son of Rolf King," Carol said. "May it prove my worth to your daughter."

Sigg, who stood behind his daughter, nodded and said a word of thanks. Carol then opened the next chest, also filled with silver and gold. "I offer this gift to you, Lady Amalie, daughter of Sigg King. May it prove my worth to you."

Amalie smiled, and accepted the gift. She turned and nodded to her father, who came and stood before Carol. The warlord towered over the pretender, but the shorter man looked far more regal. Sigg handed Carol a sword sheathed in leather lined with the fur of a snow fox, then bowed. Carol drew the sword and held it up to the crowd. He was smiling, and we could all see why. The blade was beautiful — a blade fit for a king.

The sword was sheathed and Carol placed it down on the table beside him, and then the final gift was presented. This was a gift that was not present at most weddings, but today it was necessary. The small chest was held out to Carol, and the hall was silent as he opened it. No one wanted to even breathe.

The click of the lock as the box opened echoed throughout the hall. Carol reached inside with both hands and pulled out a circlet of immeasurable worth. It was the circlet that for centuries had been worn by Ardonn's queen. It had once belonged to Carol's mother, who died a decade prior during the assault on the Capital, and his grandmother before her. For a decade, that circlet had been worn by none, but now it was placed carefully on Amalie's golden head. The priest said a prayer, and then everyone cheered. The ceremony was over.

The sacrifice happened next. Everyone moved out into the courtyard while the great hall was rearranged for the feast, and there stood nine boars. The rite was performed by Carol's High Priest, a young man he had recruited from the temple in Tillysburg, but I assisted him with the slaughter of pigs.

I opened their throats one by one with a long ritual knife and poured their blood into large wooden bowls. The priest invoked Hefencyn, the god of kings, and Lufi, the goddess of love, and asked them to bless the marriage. Nine priestesses poured the blood bowls out before two tall idols as the newlyweds prostrated themselves before them.

Once the ritual was over, the feast could begin, which was a sacred rite in itself. Everyone moved back inside just as the sun was setting and took their places at the long tables in the great hall. The fires were roaring, the bards were playing cheery songs, and servants brought out food and drink to all.

It was a great feast. The tables were stacked with trout and wild game, along with breads, cheeses, sweets, and wild berries and mushrooms. All sorts of wines were passed around, and it did not take long for the guests to become drunk.

I sat beside Princess Clodild and Matilda at the high table, while Carol sat between Clodild and his wife. Carol and Amalie seemed oblivious to everything else that was going on, their attentions turned entirely to each other. They had not met before the wedding, only corresponding through letters, but now that they had met they were completely enamoured with each other. It seemed then that it would be impossible to ever pry them apart.

I spied Dughlas and Philip sitting on the lower tables with Arne and some of Carol's other oathmen.

"Who are you waving to?" Clodild asked me. She was eating the leg of a wildfowl with her hands, ignoring her cutlery completely.

"My friends down there. You've met them, my lady," I said.

Clodild spotted them and held up her greasy hand to wave. "They helped you rescue me?"

I nodded. Clodild grinned up at me with her wide eyes, and I remembered the day she received the long, gruesome scar that ran across her cheek from ear to chin — a scar she would bear her whole life. Clodild's blood had been used as an offering by William's uncle to free the Immortal King from his prison. Every time I saw the scar, I felt a pang of guilt. I should have done more to stop Hakon, but instead an innocent child paid for my failure.

Matilda must have sensed my regret, for she placed her soft hand on my arm. "She will never forget that, Edward. You are her hero," she said.

I gave her a smile. Matilda was acting strange that night. She was always shy and awkward, but that night she was more so than usual. She enjoyed wine, though at that feast she drank only water. She also spoke little.

Matilda turned to watch the crowd of people dancing to the bards' songs. They were enjoying themselves. The songs were merry and quick, and the drunken dancers kept tripping and stumbling with their partners as they spun around the hall. William was dancing with two of Carol's courtiers, but in his drunkenness he fell backwards and pulled them down with him.

Matilda giggled. "That does look fun," she said.

"What, falling over?" I asked.

"No, dancing. I have always wanted to dance at a royal wedding."

"Well, tonight's your chance."

"Edward," someone said. I looked around to see Carol, Amalie, and another girl I did not know smiling at me.

"Edward," said Amalie.

"My Queen," I said.

"This is Solvi, one of my good friends. She wanted me to ask you if you would like to dance with her, as she does not speak your tongue."

I smiled at Solvi. "Don't worry, I speak yours," I said in her language.

Solvi's face lit up. "How?" she asked.

"I had an oathman from your lands, and he taught me."

"I am impressed. Would you like to dance?"

I looked at Solvi, and thought about it. She was perhaps a few years older than Amalie, and unlike most of her blonde-haired people, Solvi's long hair was fiery red. I admit, she was attractive, and we were at a wedding. Weddings are a time for love and courtship, so where was the harm in it? It was only a dance.

"I would be honoured," I said in the northern tongue. Solvi smiled, and I climbed over the table to take her hand. She led me to the crowd, taking my hands in hers, and we began to dance. Solvi gazed into my eyes the entire time, except when she tripped on occasion. We danced, and sang, and laughed, and when the songs were not as lively we talked.

"Why did you come to Giant's Rest?" I asked.

"I wanted to see Amalie become a queen. I also wanted to meet the Hero of Tillysburg," she said.

"The Hero of Tillysburg?"

"That's what Amalie calls you. Amalie said King Carol said that you single-handedly defeated both your king's enemies in battle."

"His Lordship likes to exaggerate. I was beaten to a pulp that day."

Solvi laughed. "You must be very brave."

One of the dancers fell back onto Solvi and pushed her into me. I steadied her, then she put her hands on my shoulders, I put mine on her waist, and we continued dancing.

"Bravery is rare among men. Most just fear oathbreaking more than they fear death," I said.

"True. I think you are just too humble."

"Is that why you wanted to dance with me? Because of Tillysburg?"

"Possibly."

We continued dancing as the night went on. I had fun, more than I had in a long time. While I danced with Solvi I noticed Matilda still seated at the high table chatting with Clodild, but she had moved on from water to wine.

Carol and Amalie were flirting with each other again, apparently in their own world, and the two were now clearly drunk. At one point Amalie turned away from her new husband and vomited on the floor, then turned straight back to him as if nothing had happened. Sigg, who sat beside his daughter, shook his head and stood up to enjoy his meal elsewhere. Solvi and I were in hysterics.

"I cannot watch her embarrass herself any longer," Solvi said. "Let's get some air."

Solvi led me out into the keep's courtyard, where it was much quieter. We could still hear the music and shouting and laughter from inside the hall, but now we did not need to yell to hear one another. There were others outside as well — dancing, talking, fighting, flirting — but only a few. The sky was clear, and Solvi looked up and admired the stars.

"Aren't they pretty?" she said.

"Aye. Hefenstea's jewels. One of Fyrwald's greatest creations, in my opinion," I said.

"Fyrwald?"

"You call him Smithi. The forge-god who created this world."

"Oh. Some people say the stars are windows into the Heavens. Is that true?"

"I would not know. I've never seen them up close."

Solvi laughed at that, then pointed up at the abandoned watchtower at the front of the courtyard. "We can get a little closer up there."

"That's off limits. Apparently it is unsafe."

"Come on, Edward. Going to war is unsafe, but you men still do that anyway."

Solvi ran off to the tower, giggling, and I ran after her. When she got to the door she looked around to make sure no one saw, then the two of us pushed it open. Solvi took the torch from its sconce outside and we went in. A spiral staircase lined the tower's walls, leading to the top. We climbed the steps and came to a small, empty guardroom filled with cobwebs and rubble from the gaping hole in the tower's roof and wall. Solvi gasped in awe.

"You can see the whole world from up here," she said.

I stood beside her and looked out into the night. You could see the dim silhouettes of the trees stretching for miles, and far off into the distance the line where the stars disappeared and met the horizon. Faint orange lights dotted the landscape, revealing the small settlements that surrounded the fortress. Solvi shivered, then handed me the torch.

"Can you light a fire?" she asked.

"I can."

I started a small fire in the middle of the room, then Solvi joined me beside it. She sat as close to me as she could and the two of us looked out at the stars.

Solvi turned and kissed me. I kissed her back, then Solvi began removing her dress. The two of us got to know each other better, by the fire, in an ancient watchtower high above the rest of the kingdom.

The feast was still lively when Solvi and I returned. We slipped in through the hall's main door, then Solvi turned to me and grinned.

"Where is the wine kept?" she asked.

"In the cellar," I said.

"Of course. Shall we go and get some?"

"There's plenty out here already."

"I know, but it's better straight from the cellar."

I laughed, already far too drunk to need more wine, but I was having fun with Solvi and I did not want that to end.

But end it did. I led Solvi to the back of the great hall to the corridor that would take us through the keep to the cellar. We ran hand in hand down that corridor, but then we bumped into Matilda and Clodild, who seemed shocked at our appearance. Clodild smiled at me, holding Matilda's hand, and Matilda just stared.

"The princess wanted to find you," Matilda said. Her speech was slurred. "Where have you been?"

"Exploring," I said. We spoke in our native tongue; thus Solvi could not understand us.

"With this red-haired harlot? I do not even want to know what you mean by 'exploring.' Princess Clodild, when you are older and ready to marry, make sure to avoid men like Edward."

"Why?" Clodild asked.

"You will be grateful for that advice one day. Come, my lady, Edward is busy."

Matilda pulled Clodild away towards the great hall, and the princess turned and gave me a wave before Matilda pulled her around a corner.

"What was that about?" Solvi asked.

"Don't worry; let's find some wine."

I led Solvi to the cellar and the two of us descended the steps, talking and joking and laughing. I tried to forget about Matilda, but that encounter had struck something, and I felt less enthusiastic about being with Solvi.

The cellar was enormous, filled with barrels, kegs, and crates of all sorts of food and drink. An open barrel sat on a table at the edge of the room, and at the foot of that table lay two men in a pool of their own vomit.

Solvi giggled. "Looks like they had the same idea as us," she said.

I smiled and went over to the men, but my heart dropped as I approached. "No," I said. "They're dead."

Solvi gasped, and then noticed what I already had. Their faces were a horrible purple, their eyes wide open and bloodshot. Their lips were black and swollen, and blood dripped from their ears.

I pried the cup from one of the dead men's hands and sniffed it. "Poison," I said. "Solvi, go back to the hall and find Arne. He speaks your tongue. Tell him there's been two deaths, but that he should not make a fuss."

"But—"

"I'm sorry you had to see this, but Queen Amalie may be in danger. Also, tell Arne to make sure no new barrels are opened up there."

Solvi nodded, and ran back up the stairs. I pulled out a knife I had been hiding in my boot and searched the cellar for any signs of tampering. Nothing else seemed out of the ordinary.

"You sorry fools may have saved your king," I muttered.

Arne rushed into the cellar with two warriors behind him. "By the Gods!" he exclaimed, halting as he saw the scene.

"This wine was poisoned," I said, thumping the barrel. "These servants must have wanted a taste before they brought it up to the feast."

Arne and his men stared in shock.

"Is the king safe?" I asked.

"You would know if he wasn't," Arne said. "He and his wife went to their quarters a while ago."

I nodded. That was a relief. That wine was intended for the king, no doubt, but it had failed to reach him. "More barrels might be poisoned. Tell your men to bring all the wine down into the cellar and then lock the door."

Arne gestured for his men to do as I said. "I will make sure the fortress is locked down, and I'll send scouts to search the area. We will find who did this," he said.

I thought for a moment. "Look for a man named Thorry of Beglen."

"Thorry of Beglen?"

"He is a wine merchant. He arrived today to sell wine for the wedding feast."

Arne nodded, then headed upstairs. Something had reminded me of Thorry, and upon inspecting the barrel further I recognised it as one of his. Whether that man's name was Thorry, and whether he actually did come from Beglen, I did not know. It was possible he had nothing to do with the poison and that another had tampered with his wine, but I had my suspicions. I knew to trust my Gift.

Thorry of Beglen was brought before the king in chains the next morning, battered and bruised. Carol sat on his makeshift throne in the great hall while his new wife stood next to him. He was furious.

"He tried to fight us, My King," Arne said. "He panicked the moment we approached his little camp."

"Please, Lord King, I beg you. Show mercy on a poor wine merchant," Thorry said. He was on his knees, tears streaming down his chubby face.

"Mercy? Why would you need mercy? Have you done me wrong?" Carol said.

"What? I—No, Lord King."

"Last night, two of my servants died in my cellar after drinking wine from a barrel that *you* sold me. If you are not responsible for this, then why leave my fortress the same day you arrived, and why attack my guards when they approached you?"

"Do not lie to him, merchant," Arne warned.

Carol shot him a glare, then turned back to Thorry. "Do you know how much danger you put my guests in? My wife? Two men — *good* men — now feast with the Black Hostess. Confess to everything, tell me who sent you, and I may show you mercy."

"Oh, thank you, Lord King. Thank you," Thorry sobbed. "I confess. I confess I knowingly sold you poisoned wine."

"Were any other barrels poisoned?"

"Just one, Lord King."

Carol nodded. "Why did you do it?"

"They made me, Lord King. The men dressed all in black. They came to my father's vineyard and burned our vines, then took my father hostage! They put poison in one of the fresh barrels and told me I would not see my father again until you're dead, Lord King. They told me to deliver the barrel to your wedding."

"You are from Beglen?"

"Yes."

"Where did these men come from?"

"I don't know, Lord King. South, maybe? I overheard them speaking of their leader hiding in the woods, and they said they'd restore the true king to his throne."

At that, Carol spat and then waved for his guards. "Get this wretch out of my sight and lock him in the cellar. If he gets thirsty, there is an open barrel he is welcome to."

My stomach churned as Thorry was dragged out of the great hall. *Restore the true king to his throne.* Unease began to grow in the back of my mind again.

"Men, it seems our enemy has made his first move," Carol

said. "I will march my army to Beglen and demand Lord Edric support my claim and lend us his aid. Then, we will find Emrys and crush him."

"My King, might I suggest a more…pragmatic approach? Edric's walls are strong, and we don't even know if Thorry spoke the truth," Arne said.

"Oh, he did. What would you suggest?"

Before Arne could speak, I interrupted. "Lord, let me go find these men."

"Nonsense, Edward. I need you here."

"I am your Godspeaker. If Emrys is indeed responsible for the poison, who better to deal with him than me?"

Carol thought for a while, and none in the room spoke. After some time he spoke up again. "You do not plan to kill him. You think you can break his curse."

"I do," I admitted.

"Do you think Godwin, and all the others who dealt with Emrys, did not already try to break that curse?"

"I am sure they tried, Lord King."

Carol nodded, and pondered again. "Very well. But Edward, your top priority is your own survival. I will not accept death as an alternative to victory."

"Thank you, Lord King."

"I will send that wine merchant with you. Perhaps he can help you find those who wanted me dead. But once his use has diminished I want you to carry out his execution. Traitors die in my kingdom."

I bowed, then headed to my quarters. I did not know what I hoped to achieve, but if I could end Emrys's curse then hopefully he would cease his campaign to reclaim his crown. I guessed, after a thousand years of life, one would lose interest in politics. If I could find another way to break Emrys's curse, I would save many lives.

I would be a hero.

I had grown comfortable in the past month. Giant's Rest was a beautiful place, and I was happy there. We had peace, but Carol's enemies would see the power and legitimacy brought about by his marriage as a threat. They knew they would need to act fast, so we needed to be faster.

I would need to leave behind my new life and happiness, and set off once again to stop the Immortal King from bringing doom upon our kingdom.

3

Beglen

"Where is Beglen?" Philip asked me. He was packing his bags with all that he would need for a long journey, for I was planning to bring my young apprentice with me on the mission.

"A city about a week's ride to the south. His Lordship is sending me there to see what I can do about Emrys," I said.

"You are leading an army?"

I laughed. "No. It will just be me, you, and Dughlas. Oh, and Carol's would-be-murderer."

"And how are *we* supposed to defeat Emrys?"

"We aren't. I am hoping to free him from his curse."

Philip looked up at me, confused. Emrys had done terrible things in the short amount of time he had been out in the world, and Philip had witnessed his brutality first hand. Why I would want to help Emrys rather than simply kill him would have made no sense to him.

We heard a knock at the door, and Dughlas entered the room without invitation. His sword was at his belt, his bow and arrow bag slung over his shoulder, and he carried his shield and a large bag under his arm. He wore his travelling gear, and a thick woollen cloak was draped over his shoulder. "I'm ready. When are we heading off?" he asked.

"Once Philip has packed his things," I said. "Though at this rate we will be here till nightfall."

I looked down at Philip rummaging through the mess in his room. "I can't find the knife my pa gave me," he complained.

"I'll help you find it," I grumbled. "Go and ready the horses, Dughlas. We will not be much longer."

"Aye," he said. "Have you spoken to Her Ladyship yet?"

"Who?"

"You know who I mean."

"Matilda has decided to spend this morning with Arne and Clodild. Apparently I am not allowed to interrupt her training."

Dughlas shook his head. "I'll ready the horses. Don't take too much longer, Philip."

I knew why Matilda was being sour. I cared about Matilda, and so for her own sake I had been pushing her away since our kiss before the battle of Tillysburg. We had spoken little the past month because I feared that she would fall in love. It was for her own good, I told myself.

I helped Philip search for his knife, then we headed out when he finally finished packing. I had wanted to leave as soon as possible, so two nights after Carol had assigned me that task, we were ready to set off.

I planned to ride south across country for about a day till we came to a small river heading down from the mountains, where we would abandon the horses and hire a boat to take us downstream as close to Beglen as possible. Thorry would then lead us to his vineyard, and from there we would find Emrys. I did not have much more of a plan than that.

Philip and I were stopped by Solvi before we left the great keep. "Were you planning to leave without saying goodbye to me?" she asked. She spoke in her own tongue, so Philip would not have been able to understand her.

"No, I was coming to find you, but it appears you've found me."

"Shall I walk you to your horse? It is custom for the women among my people to kiss their men as they mount their horses for war."

"I am not your man, nor am I going to war."

Solvi held out her arm and smiled. "Still, a lady needs to see you off so you have good luck."

I took Solvi's arm, and the three of us headed out into the courtyard where Dughlas and Thorry were waiting. Matilda was sparring with Arne at the yard's far end, and Clodild watched the two. I gave the princess a wave and she waved back, but Matilda ignored me.

"Good luck, Edward!" Arne shouted as he parried Matilda's jab. "We'll write your name in songs when you return."

Matilda slipped and Arne knocked her to her knees. She jumped back to her feet with impressive speed and swung at Arne, striking a blow against his side. Clodild giggled, then waved at me again.

Thorry bowed to me when we reached the horses and I noticed his hands shaking. He was nervous, or maybe even terrified, but I did not tell him I would need to kill him once he had served his purpose. I needed him to cooperate, so I had to be friendly.

"Carol says your hands must be bound while we ride through the fort," I said to him. "But once we cross the bridge, remind me to cut your ties. I want to work with a free man, not a slave."

"Thank you, lord," he said.

"Just call me Edward. I'm no lord."

As I helped Philip mount his pony William came to bid us farewell. He was disappointed that he could not come with us, but he understood. He was a good warrior and, as I had discovered in the past month, an excellent tracker. Yet he was more valuable as a hostage and I could not risk him escaping or being rescued on our journey — though in truth, my real fear was that he would return to his father, willing or otherwise. I did not want to lose my friend.

"I am leaving Matilda in charge of you while I'm gone," I told him. "She is to ensure you remain safe and sound in Giant's Rest."

"She will be a tricky one to escape, though as long as I am allowed to hunt I promise I will remain a hostage," he said with a smile.

"Take her hunting with you. She used to go with her father and brother in Henton; it might lift her spirits."

"I will, my friend."

"Thank you, William. I have told her she is in charge of you, but admittedly I want you to keep a close eye on her. Don't let her do anything stupid."

William laughed. "I will try, but you know how she is. Farewell, Edward, and good luck on your quest."

We embraced and said one last goodbye before he returned to whatever he was doing beforehand, then Dughlas whistled for me. The morning was passing us by, and Dughlas wanted to reach the river by nightfall.

"Come back soon, Edward," Solvi said. She then leant in close and whispered in my ear something I probably should not repeat.

My face went red, and I grinned. "I will hurry. Goodbye, Solvi."

"Goodbye, Edward."

Solvi took my horse's reins and then closed my fist around them. She moved in closer to me, stood on her toes, and we kissed. Dughlas cleared his throat and Philip retched. Solvi and I laughed, I bid her farewell once more, and pulled myself up onto the horse.

She was a spotted grey mare called Ren whom Carol was

lending to me for the ride south to the river. Carol insisted we borrow his horses because they were, supposedly, the fastest in Ardonn, though I still believed that my warhorse Brand was swifter.

We turned our horses and made our way from the courtyard and into the streets below the keep. Folk watched us as we passed by, some cheering my name and others hissing and jeering at Thorry. I told the Beglener to ignore them, and he nodded. I pitied the man.

As we crossed the bridge, I looked back up at the fortress behind us. I sighed, for I was leaving a place I had grown fond of in the past month. I hoped I could keep my word to Solvi and be back within its cold walls and her warm embrace before the coming summer's end, at least. If all went well our journey should not have lasted more than a few weeks.

As I admired the fortress I noticed a woman standing up on the inner walls surrounding the keep, her jet-black hair blowing in the breeze as she watched us leave. She looked so small from where we were, but I could tell it was Matilda. She stood beside Clodild, and I waved up at them both. The princess held up her hand, but Matilda only stood there, arms folded.

"You should've said goodbye," Dughlas said. He noticed I had stopped and came to sit beside me.

"I know," I said.

"You want to go back up?"

I hesitated, then shook my head. "No. We're running out of

day."

"Treat her better when we return. The girl is quite mad for you."

"It is a childish infatuation, nothing more. It is the Gift she loves. Mark me, by the time we're back in Giant's Rest, Matilda will have eyes for another."

"Stick to talking about the Otherworld, maybe. You're a dimwit when it comes to everything else."

Dughlas turned and kicked his horse, then the four of us crossed over the bridge. We headed south. Emrys had sent a gift of wine to Carol's court, and we were his response.

"Are you cold, Philip? Tired?" Dughlas asked as we rode through a wide meadow under the light of the moon. I smirked.

"Yes," Philip replied.

"Good. We're late because of you," said Dughlas.

"If my master were a better teacher, my things would be more organised."

I laughed. "Don't bring me into this, little Lurian. If you're sick of Dughlas nagging you, you can always challenge him to a hazeling," I said.

"I'd win," said Dughlas. Philip said nothing.

We rode until about midnight, and Gods was it cold. The sky was clear, but a light breeze came down from the mountains to the east and chilled us to the bone. Eventually, we saw a few dim lights at the base of a hill reflecting off running water.

"Let's hope the innkeeper is awake," I said.

We made our way downhill to the river's banks, then rode along it until we reached the little town where we would find a boat. Oarsley, the place was called.

"What a shithole," Dughlas commented.

We wove our way through Oarsley's narrow streets until we found the inn at last. It was shabby and did not look comfortable, but we were cold, tired, and hungry. That inn beat sleeping under the stars.

The innkeeper was awake, and he welcomed us enthusiastically. He did his best to treat us like kings — partly because I assume he saw few customers, but also because we wore expensive mail and carried weapons of war. The four of us took a seat around a low table, and the innkeeper brought us a big plate of fish and bread, and four pints of awful ale. He told us we need not pay, but I insisted.

"You're going to kill me, aren't you?" Thorry said once we started eating.

I stared at him, and licked the grease off my fingers one by one. There was fear in his eyes. "His Lordship has sentenced you to die for treason," I said.

"Please, lord. You have nothing to gain from my death."

"It is not about gain, Thorry. I swore an oath to serve Carol. I have a duty."

Thorry gulped, and I smiled.

"If you prove your worth — and your loyalty — I may be able to convince the king to pardon you. I see no sense in killing you."

Thorry sighed. "Oh, thank you. I will prove myself. You have my word."

"Good," I said, biting into a piece of fish. "You did what was necessary to save your father. I do not blame you."

We finished our food and our drinks, then the innkeeper showed us to our rooms. He only had two available, with two beds in each, so I shared with Philip. The ceiling was low and the room was cramped, and Philip noticed the walls were slightly on angle. The bed was hard, and my feet hung over the edge, but after a day of hard riding it was not too difficult to fall asleep.

I drifted off into a dream in which I was hunting. I rode on horseback, riding through the woods as the air gushed past me. I was chasing something, but I could not see it. I rode for a while, as fast as I could, until I finally caught sight of my prey.

It was a wolf. A big, grey beast with black eyes and blood dripping from its fangs. It was the size of a horse, and could easily have overpowered me if it wanted. But it did not want to. Instead of turning to fight, it ran from me. Why? I brushed the question aside, for all that mattered was the hunt. The kill.

I gained on the wolf, slowly. When I was close enough to smell its rancid breath, I gripped my spear in my hand, held it over my shoulder, then jerked my arm forward. The spear hurtled toward the beast, whistling through the air, and when it buried itself in the beast's hide I heard a resounding bang, followed by a woman's scream.

I shot up in bed, my breath heavy, and looked around the room. Light streamed in through the small window, and Philip was rubbing his eyes. I heard the scream again.

"Philip, wake up," I said.

"I am."

"Did you hear that?"

Before he could answer, the sound of a horn filled the room, followed by the shouts and cries of many men.

"What's going on?" Philip asked.

"Get up," I commanded.

Philip made no argument, and the two of us jumped out of bed and quickly dressed. In that moment, our bedroom door burst open and I drew my sword. Dughlas stepped in, his sword drawn, and he looked at me in confusion. I shrugged. Outside, we could hear the sounds of steel beating against steel and wood, the screaming of men and women, the churning of water, the hiss of arrows, and the roar of fire.

"Sounds like battle," I said.

"You're kidding?" Dughlas laughed. "Let's get going, then. We'll see if we can slip away before they burn all the bloody boats."

Dughlas grabbed Thorry by the arm, and the four of us gathered our things and made our way out of the inn. The innkeeper was nowhere to be found, but I left some coins on the counter in case he returned.

The streets were muddied outside, beaten down by dozens of heavy boots. Men and women were running in all directions, but the sounds of battle were coming from the river. Our horses were not tied up where we had left them, so I hoped they had been freed and managed to find their way back to Giant's Rest. We pushed past the crowd and headed through alleyways to the water.

"Can you fight, Thorry?" I asked.

"I make wine, lord!"

I chuckled. "Find a weapon you can swing. You might be crushing more than grapes today."

Thorry found a club, probably used by a fisherman to put his catches out of their misery, and gripped it in both hands. He was frightened, and I could tell Philip was too, though he tried to hide it. He had a short sword made for him by Carol's blacksmith, and he carried a small shield in his other hand. It was painted red with a gold wolf, which he told me was the banner of Luria, his homeland.

We came to the edge of the town and stopped as we saw a line of peasants forming a shield wall along the riverbank. A boat beached right in front of them, and its crew threw themselves overboard and charged at Oarsley's defenders. Some stayed aboard the boat raining spears, stones, and arrows onto their enemies. Behind us a great plume of smoke billowed from the town's northern edge; I assumed Oarsley was being attacked there too as another boat had been beached further upstream.

The fishermen here stood no chance. The attackers were menacing. Their hair was long and wild, and they wore big beards braided in different styles. They decked themselves in glass and wooden beads. Some wore mail, but most wore fur and leather. They wielded spears, axes, and strange, leaf-shaped swords. They snarled and bore their teeth, which were stained red or blue with paint, at the villagers.

"Are you going to help them?" Thorry asked, pointing to the shoddy shield wall along the bank.

I shook my head. "No. Carol gave us our task, and we would be foolish to endanger our lives defending this place," I said.

"But these are your king's subjects!"

"Then the king can deal with them," I snapped back.

Thorry flinched, then I pointed to one of the jetties sticking out into the river. A small boat with a little sail was tied at the end. "That will do. We can come back here later and reimburse its owner."

The four of us made for the jetty, dodging the arrows and other projectiles that the raiders shot our way. Dughlas loosed a few arrows back, and managed to hit a couple of the archers and send them tumbling off their boat and into the river.

Just as we neared the jetty, Dughlas pointed to the river. "Another fucking boat!" he cried.

A third boat filled with raiders came gliding downstream and smashed into the jetty ahead of us. Splinters went flying as the boat crushed the jetty's rotting wood, then it ground to a halt against the riverbed beneath it. Three grinning warriors climbed out onto what was left of the jetty, swords in hand. Our path was now blocked.

"Are we killing the buggers, or finding another boat?" Dughlas asked.

"I want that boat," I said.

"Gods help us," Philip muttered.

The warriors laughed as they charged at us, and Dughlas and I stood side by side as we braced against our opponents. Dughlas and I had fought beside each other many times before, mostly against robbers and raiders who came to my old home expecting easy loot, so we were confident we could beat these men.

One of the raiders threw himself at me with a great yell. His hair was like wildfire, and his teeth were red. I could smell the stench of his breath and his filthy clothes as he smashed against my shield. I pushed against him, then he pushed back and tried to swing his axe around at my side, but I parried with my blade and jumped backwards. He swung at me again and I knocked his axe down, thrust my shield at his face, and sent him tumbling into the mud.

The second warrior lunged at me. I smacked his sword to the side with the rim of my shield, then thrust my own blade forward and buried it into his gut before he could stop his charge. He gurgled and let out a scream, I kicked him back, then turned to face my first opponent once again.

He slashed at me, I ducked, then cut at him and felt my sword tear through cloth and flesh. The man stepped back, his eyes red with rage, then he threw himself at me. I sidestepped, turned, and brought my blade down his spine, cutting him open.

"More coming," Dughlas warned. I turned to see he had finished his man, but more warriors had climbed out of the boat and onto the jetty.

"Dughlas, stand with me. Philip, look after that blubbering merchant. Stay close: we'll take that fishing boat or die," I said.

Dughlas stood beside me, then with a yell the two of us charged at the raiders on the jetty.

We clashed. Shield against sword, sword against axe, and body against body. We fought with our weapons, our feet, and our fists. It was savage. There was no technique, no strategy, no style. We had no room on that narrow jetty to make a show of the fight. We just kicked, punched, hacked, slashed, and stabbed. We screamed, we yelled, we cursed, and the pirates died one by one. The river turned red.

Philip and Thorry followed close behind, and whenever I glanced back at them I saw Philip fighting well. I had him trained at Giant's Rest, and before that he was trained in Oldford. He learnt fast, and it showed. He even managed to drive back a couple of men. Philip was a boy of nearly twelve years, but that day he became a man.

The defenders on the bank were not faring as well as we were. Their wall had broken and those without the courage to fight ran for their wealth, their families, and their lives.

Many of the warriors on the boat that had rammed the jetty were jumping overboard for a chance to pillage the town, which I suppose was more profitable than fighting us, but a few still sought glory above wealth. That glory was to be found in slaying warriors, not in robbing fisherfolk.

Dughlas and I jumped aboard the raiders' boat and fought with those remaining. "Philip, Thorry, get aboard that boat and make ready to sail!" I shouted.

Philip nodded, led Thorry along the jetty and over the boat we were now fighting in, then helped him into the little fishing craft still tied up at the end.

Once Philip and Thorry were ready, Dughlas and I finished the last of our opponents, then climbed out of the boat and back onto the jetty. Dughlas glanced up at the bank and swore. "We forgot our stuff," he said. He was right. Before the fight we had dumped our bags on the ground, and in the heat of it all we had forgotten about them. That was our food, our clothes, and our belongings.

"Wait with the other two; I'll get the bags," I said. I sheathed my sword and handed Dughlas my shield.

"Don't die."

"I don't plan on it."

I leapt over the raiders' boat and sprinted for the shore. Most of the pirates had their attention turned to the town, but one saw where I was running to and he made for it as well. He was grinning, and I sprinted harder.

He reached the bags first and threw himself on top of them. Before he could defend himself, I pulled the blade from my belt and dived at the man. For his trouble he earned a dagger in the back before I pushed him to the side. I left the blade deep in his flesh, hoisted the bags up over my shoulders, and ran to the boat as fast as I could.

Dughlas, Philip, and Thorry were yelling at me but I could not make out what they said over the screaming and burning and fighting from the town behind me. I ran, panting, heaving myself forward with every breath. I stomped along the jetty and heard more stomping behind me.

"Behind you, Edward!" Dughlas yelled. I urged myself on faster. The jetty seemed to stick out into the river for miles. I felt like I was running forever, and time seemed to slow. My shoulders and back were aching. A rhythmic throbbing echoed inside my ears. I could hear the breathing of the man behind me and I could smell his sweat. He was gaining on me.

Dughlas notched an arrow, drew his bow, and loosed. I leapt over the boat in the jetty and as I did I heard — no, I *felt* — Dughlas's arrow zip past me. I heard a thud and a wail behind me, followed by a splash, then I tossed the bags aboard the little fishing boat my friends occupied. I let out a groan of relief.

"I hope none of you have anything fragile in those," I said.

"There's more coming," said Philip.

I turned to see three more warriors running to the jetty.

Without hesitation I untied the boat and kicked at its side. It floated away, and just as the pirates chasing us leapt over their own boat, I jumped into ours and fell on my behind.

But one of the warriors on the jetty was bold. His beard was little more than stubble, and he was evidently young. He wanted to prove himself. Perhaps that was his first battle. The young man stepped back, then ran forward and threw himself from the jetty towards our boat, sword in hand.

He almost made it, but I grabbed the tiller and jerked the boat sideways. He missed, but only just, for he managed to grab onto the side of the boat and nearly tipped us over. He held on and tried with all his might to climb aboard.

I drew my sword and Dughlas reached for his, but to our surprise it was Thorry who dealt with the nuisance. He thumped the warrior over the head with his fisherman's club, but the man kept hold of the side of our boat. Thorry clubbed him once again, harder this time, and blood went everywhere — over the deck, the sail, and over Thorry himself.

Thorry screamed, the warrior vomited, and then went limp and slid into the river. He did not emerge again.

I grabbed the tiller and turned the boat south. The sail filled with air, and we were taken swiftly downriver with both the wind and the current. Thorry sat back in shock, his hands and face covered in blood.

Dughlas laughed and clapped, shouting insults at the two men who stood staring at us from the jetty. Philip joined in, and he pulled down his trousers and bent over to show his rear to the raiders before turning back around to shout insults at them again. We were happy. We were relieved.

Oarsley quickly faded into the distance, yet we could see the smoke billowing above it for the rest of the day. As we sailed downriver I saw people fleeing up the hill that we had come down the night before, only to be chased down and killed by the raiders who had sacked their village.

"Lakelanders," Thorry said once we were a few miles downstream.

"Sorry?" I asked.

"They came from Lakeland, lord. Every spring they cross the mountains and raid Lord Edric's lands. Some by river, others by road."

"Have you seen this before?" Dughlas asked.

"No, not me. They never come as far west as my father's vineyard. But I've heard stories from friends who have witnessed their raids, and those men match their descriptions. They go from village to village, taking slaves and wealth as they go before the local lords have time to assemble their warriors. Then they simply sail back upriver and go home, following the mountain streams."

"Cowards," Dughlas said. He spat into the water.

I stared up at the great plume of smoke that rose over the trees and felt a sharp pang of guilt. I should have done more to protect those innocent people. I was reminded of the raid on my own home the previous winter, and how I had failed to defend my people there, too.

"So, you two," Dughlas said. "What was your first scrap like?"

"It was horrible," Thorry said.

"Exciting," said Philip. "I felt invincible."

Dughlas laughed, and Thorry leaned over the side of the boat and threw up his supper from the night before. He tried desperately to wash the blood from his face and hands, but when he tried to clean his clothes he lamented over them being stained. Thorry was born and raised a merchant — he was used to wine stains, not blood stains. He was no killer.

I sat by the tiller and steered the boat downstream for most of that day, and although the river was calm and flat, we travelled fast. When Dughlas was not manning the sail he passed food around and we filled our bellies eagerly, except for Thorry, who had no appetite that day.

The trip along the river was peaceful, and we admired the tranquil beauty of the surrounding lands. The forests were thick and green as new life blossomed after the cold winter snows. The fields and meadows were lush, flowers dotted the land, and peasants were already sowing the first harvest.

Livestock had been brought out into the fields once again, too. Philip would low at the cows we passed and counted how many times he won a response. We passed the occasional farming or fishing village, and sometimes the people along the riverbank would wave at us.

I made a silent prayer to the Gods and whatever spirits guarded this river asking that they protect the people who lived there. I hoped the Lakeland raiders would stop at Oarsley, but I doubted that poor village would satisfy their thirst for blood and gold. We shouted warnings to those we passed who were within earshot with the hopes that they might prepare defences or flee.

Thorry told us that the river would run southwest towards Beglen, then enter the forest where he thought it took a sharp turn east as it made its way to join up with the River Aed. He said if we followed the river it would take us straight to Beglen, and from there it was only a half-day's ride to his father's vineyard.

"How far downriver is Beglen?" I asked him.

"A few days if you flew, I think. But the river slithers like a snake, so the journey would be more likely a week."

That was good enough for me, for I enjoyed travelling along that sleepy river. We sailed through the night on the first few days, with Dughlas and I taking turns steering while the others slept. I admit I much preferred being on the tiller than sleeping. The river was always calm, so when the skies were clear it seemed as though we sailed across a sea of sparkling jewels.

The nights were quiet aside from the soft sound of our boat gliding across the water, the sails gently flapping, and the occasional hoot of an owl or the low of a cow. I would sometimes forget to wake Dughlas as I sat by the tiller mesmerised by the stars in the night sky. I forgot about everything in those moments.

We had to make landfall after the third night because the boat had sprung a leak and we were low on food. We beached where the woods met the river on its southern bank one morning, and I took Philip out to look for food while Dughlas and Thorry mended the boat.

I tested Philip on his knowledge of the various forest spirits, both good and evil, that one might encounter in the wilderness. I then had him find a natural sacred place — a spring, in this case — and let him propitiate the forest's guardian with prayers and an offering of silver. Only a few moments afterwards we were approached by a doe who showed no fear of us. The four of us feasted well that night beside the river.

We set off early the next morning, and after Thorry had a thorough wash he was feeling much better. The wind had died down, so Dughlas and I had to sit either side of the boat and row while Philip steered. He was jerky at first, but quickly got the hang of it. We travelled this way for a few more days, camping in the trees at night and floating downriver during the day until eventually, just as Thorry had promised, Beglen emerged over the hills.

"There's Beglen," Thorry said as the city grew nearer. "Isn't she beautiful?"

Thorry was right — Beglen was beautiful. Originally a fortress sitting on a wide hill, it had grown wealthy from its wine production, and the buildings showed it. They looked like those in Oldford, a mix of wood and stone, though much of the timber was newer.

The old city, where Lord Edric had his keep and where the city's wealthiest individuals lived, rose above the rest of the city and was surrounded by ancient stone walls. The new city formed a ring around the old. It was the larger part of Beglen, and was where the rest of the citizens lived. That was surrounded by a grand wooden wall with a stone base, which was then encircled by a wide moat.

The city rose above the low, green countryside around it, and from miles away you could see the rich red banners of Edric's family flapping in the wind. Every second building seemed to have one flying above it so that it appeared as though a great flock of red birds flew above the city. The sight filled us with awe.

"I've never seen so many banners in my life," Dughlas said.

Thorry grinned. "The people love Lord Edric. He is a just man. A good man."

"Let us hope he's on the right side," I said.

We docked our boat at a small town just a few miles from Beglen, which acted as the city's port for loading barges with barrels of wine to be sent downriver, to Oldford and then the sea.

We bumped into one of those barges as Philip tried to steer the boat toward the jetty, earning us some bitter looks from the barge's sailors. I paid the toll for keeping our boat there, and told the port master that if we did not return in a month's time to collect it, he could do with it what he wished.

We then hitched a ride aboard an empty cart heading back to Beglen. As we made our way to the city, Thorry was excited to tell us all about what lay within its walls. We almost forgot we were here to prevent a war. All we could think about now was the wine, the women, and all the other wonders Thorry told us that Beglen had to offer.

4

Heat

The tight streets of Beglen were a maze, but Thorry knew his way around. He showed us the best alehouses and taverns, took us past some shops run by his friends, and gave us a tour of the city's sights. He showed us the temples and the town hall, then took us right up to the inner walls around the old city.

"We cannot pass these walls," he said. "Lord Edric keeps them locked up most of the time these days, and only those with an invitation can get through the gates."

Guards stood on the high walls, watching us from above. They wore mail, and had cloaks dyed a deep red draped over their shoulders.

"Edric's men," Thorry explained. "You don't want to meet one of those red-cloaked warriors in battle, I have heard."

As the sun set Thorry led us to his favourite tavern. The

innkeeper, Hilbert, was a good friend of his. He treated us well. He was a round-bellied, bald-headed man with a great brown beard and puffy cheeks. "Welcome to The Grapevine," he declared as we entered. Thorry introduced us simply as friends he had met on the road. He did not reveal our true identities, nor our purpose.

"You have found some well-armed companions, Thorry," Hilbert said.

"It's just as well. After what happened to my vineyard, I need protection," said Thorry.

Hilbert glanced at us and our swords, then he grinned. "I suppose you warriors are in need of something to drink."

"That would be nice, Hilbert," I said.

"We've been hearing about Beglen's fine wines all day," said Dughlas.

Hilbert laughed. "Aye, trust a wine merchant to talk highly of wines," he said. "Go, take a seat. I'll tap a barrel for you four."

Thorry led us to a table by the fireplace at the rear of the tavern, close to the bard who played a cheery tune on his lute. The smell of smoke, wine, and roast meat filled the air. Hilbert emerged from the kitchen shortly afterwards carrying a barrel of wine, flanked by two servants carrying plates stacked high with meats, breads, and fruits.

Hilbert slammed the barrel onto the table and grinned. "I bet they don't feast like this up in Edric's hall," he said.

The servants placed the food in front of us, took our bags

upstairs, and we dug in.

We feasted very well that night, eating and drinking to our heart's content. We would deal with Emrys tomorrow, we told ourselves, but for the moment we enjoyed what could potentially be our last night alive.

The food was delicious and the wine was superb, and Thorry boasted that it had come from his vineyard. Dughlas put his hands to his throat and pretended to choke, then fell to the ground in a fit of laughter. We were all laughing, and we quickly grew drunk as we emptied the barrel. It did well to distract me from the reason we were there.

The bard soon joined us, playing and singing joyful songs about heroes and maidens and all that fill men with laughter and cheer. As the night passed, more and more of The Grapevine's patrons came to join our little feast, bringing with them their drinks and their food. Soon the whole tavern was in a state of drunken revelry as we sang, danced, boasted, and cheered with each other.

People poured in from the streets and crowded the place, and Hilbert thanked us again and again for drawing in so many patrons. In my drunkenness I put my whole coin purse in his hands and told him I would pay for everyone's drinks for the rest of the night.

The whole tavern cheered and chanted my name when they heard the news, and soon enough I was the centre of attention. We caroused well into the night. Men and women danced with each other, some people brawled, bottles were smashed, and the bard's fingers bled as he strummed at his lute.

At some point in the night a pretty, pale, black-haired girl found herself a comfortable spot on my lap. She fed me and poured more wine down my throat while Thorry climbed up onto a table with his shirt off and his belly hanging over his belt. The forest growing on his chest was matted down with sweat and his short beard was soaked with ale. A crowd stood around him and cheered as he sang and boasted of how he valiantly slew a hundred Lakelanders at the battle of Oarsley with nothing but a shaft of wood.

"But do you know what the greatest honour that day was?" Thorry shouted. The crowd roared with excitement, waiting for him to share the answer. "The greatest honour was to fight beside Edward of Oldford, the Godspeaker, the Hero of Tillysburg. That man right there is a legend!" Thorry pointed to me, winked, then raised his cup. The crowd turned to me and cheered, while those who still had drinks shouted a toast.

Thorry was a daft fool, but in that moment I thought nothing of it. The girl on my knee had me lose all sense, and all it took for me to forget the meaning of 'danger' was for her to look me dead in the eyes and say, "Show me how legendary the Hero of Tillysburg really is."

I took her to my room upstairs, my duties a distant memory. Once we had exhausted ourselves we collapsed in each other's arms and I quickly fell into a dreamless sleep.

I leaned against the window sill and stared out at the streets of Beglen late the next morning. The street below me was bustling with activity, with men and women moving back and forth as they went about their business. A girl selling river snails and mussels pushed her cart through the throng of people, shouting as she went. I watched her for a while, though my mind was elsewhere.

The black-haired girl I had met the night before stirred in the bed beside me and stretched her arm over the space where I had slept. "Come back to bed," she mumbled.

I turned to her, and her eyes were clenched shut. "It's late," I said.

Her eyes opened and she shot up. The girl was naked, and I quickly looked away.

"Oh Gods, my da will have my head if he hears about this," she said.

"He will not hear about it."

She rubbed her eyes. "What if I am with child?"

"I can send you silver," I said. I forced a smile, then turned back to the window.

"We could marry. My da will definitely approve of that. He's wealthy, and he can buy us a home by the river, and—"

"Forgive me, but I have duties, and we barely know each other." My head ached, and the talking only made it worse. "I don't even know your name."

The girl pulled the covers up to her chin. "It's Retta. I told you last night."

I sighed, and faced Retta. I did pity her. As I looked into her beautiful blue eyes, I saw a soul in despair. She reminded me of someone else, and guilt surged through me. "Do you pray, Retta?"

"Sometimes. Why?"

"You should visit the temple more often. It will do you good." I stood up, pulled on my boots and buckled my belt, then made for the door.

"Where are you going?" Retta asked.

"I don't feel so good, so I'm going to stretch my legs. I will return soon, I promise."

"Oh. Okay. I'll be waiting."

I left Retta and most of my things in the room and made my way downstairs. The Grapevine's ground floor was almost empty and appeared entirely different to how it had been the night before. Still, the place was a mess, and the servants worked tirelessly to clean it up before the patrons poured in again after sundown. Hilbert stood behind the counter washing plates, and he called over to me.

"Your friends are waiting for you outside," he said.

I gave him a wave, smiled — though it probably looked more like a grimace — and tossed him a gold coin as a tip. "Thank you, Hilbert. I feel miserable, which is only evidence of your grand hospitality."

Hilbert nodded, and watched me as I headed for the door.

I walked out into the street and took a deep breath of fresh air. Without warning, I was grabbed from behind by two men, and a third came to stand in front of me. He wore a grin on his rough, pox-ridden face, and was dressed in a black tunic with a black cloak draped over his shoulders. He jabbed me in the gut with a black, studded glove. I spewed over his feet, then he hooked me across the jaw. I struggled against the men gripping my arms as the third man pulled a sack over my head. Then I was hoisted over one of my assailant's shoulders and thrown into the back of a cart.

The men climbed aboard, shouted an order, and I heard a whip crack. The cart started moving but the sounds from the streets seemed distant. We must have been under cover.

"That you, Edward?" a man groaned beside me.

"Dughlas? What happened?"

"Cork it, you two, or I'll cut your tongues out," said one of the thugs. I was flipped onto my belly, my arms were pulled behind my back, and my hands and feet were tied.

We had a long journey ahead.

For much of the day we travelled in silence, through countryside and then, as evening fell, through woodland. That peace was broken as we neared our destination. The sound of hooves and the laughter of drunken men grew louder. Then, when it was all around us, we were pulled from the cart and tied with our backs to a post.

The sack was pulled from my head and I squinted. My eyes adjusted to the light of the campfires and I assessed my surroundings. I was in a large camp, deep in the woods. There were tents all around, and men gambled and talked around small tables as they filled their bellies with ale. One man several yards away from me played a flute.

They were warriors, for many wore mail and all carried weapons. Some were dressed all in black, but others wore a cloak of deep red. A dozen or so horsemen sped past me.

"You alright?" Dughlas asked. I turned to see him tied up beside me. Next to him, Philip was also bound. To my left, Thorry sat with a blank stare.

"Where are we?" I asked.

"No idea, but we're definitely not in Beglen. Cursed fucking city," Dughlas seethed.

"Those are Edric's men," I said, nodding to the ones with the red cloaks.

"Aye, and the black ones are Hakon's, I reckon."

"Hakon's, or Odo's? I wish I had killed them both."

A man in black approached us and held out a long knife. He pointed it at each of us in turn. "Which one of you is Edward?"

"I am, you slimy cunt," Dughlas spat.

"I'm Edward. It's me you want," I said.

The man turned to me and snorted, then approached. I held my head back and closed my eyes, awaiting death.

But death did not come. Instead, the man cut the ropes around me and pulled me to my feet. He sheathed his knife. "You're wanted. Come with me, and don't make my job harder by trying to flee."

I followed the man through the camp, trying to ignore the stares and jeers from the men we passed. We arrived at a section of the camp with no tents. It smelled like horse manure, but I saw no horses nearby. There was only a clearing with a grand tent in the middle. A pillar of smoke rose from the hole in its centre. At the tent's entrance the man grabbed my arm and pulled me close. "Don't do anything stupid, or he'll have both our heads."

"Who?" I said.

He said nothing and pushed me forward. I entered the tent. It was hot inside, uncomfortably so. An enormous bonfire roared in the centre so the place felt like a great oven. A tall shadow stood behind the fire, but I could not make out what it was. The tent was empty aside from that. I stood still, unsure of what to do. Should I move? Should I speak?

Before I could answer that the shadow turned, and I could make out the shape of a man on a horse. He moved slowly from behind the fire and came into view. Despite the immense heat my blood ran cold.

For the man atop that big, grey stallion was Emrys.

He was draped in thick grey furs, and in the saddle with him sat the same grey puppy that had been with him when we first met. His grey hair was combed and braided, and the tip of his long beard touched his horse. He wore black makeup around his grey eyes, and when they met mine his cold, sharp face smiled.

"Greetings, Edward Godspeaker," he said in his own, ancient tongue. "I did wonder when that boy-king would send you to me. Does he offer fealty?"

I said nothing. Fear gripped my bones. I could only stare.

Emrys turned his horse to face the bonfire. He pondered it. "How do you feel?" he asked at last.

"Hot," I said.

Emrys grunted. "That is what all my mortal followers say. Despite this mighty fire, and all this fur, my bones still feel like ice." That last word came with a hiss. Emrys turned and smiled before walking his horse over to me. "They say men speak highly of you, Heir of Godwin. 'Hero of Tillysburg,' they cheer. And yet you slew none of your king's enemies."

"We routed you."

"A temporary setback." He spoke hauntingly, hollow, and every word sent chills through my veins. "I am wise enough to know that you did not come to Beglen to drown in decadence. You were sent here to kill me."

"Carol wanted to lead his army here. I convinced him to send me instead," I said.

Emrys almost laughed. "Tell me, child, what can you do against me and my horde that Carol's warriors cannot?"

"I can free you."

"Ah." Emrys moved back to the fire, facing away from me. He stared into the flames for a while, deep in thought. Then he sighed. "You sound just like him."

"Like whom?"

"Godwin. They tell me you are unrelated to him, merely adopted by his descendant, but I would beg to differ," said Emrys. He shrugged. "You are clever, Edward, but you are not wise. Only my crown can free me from this curse."

"I can try," I said.

"Hubris!" He reared his horse, turned, and trotted over to me. My heart froze as he pointed his sword at my chest. The very breath was driven from my mouth. "I should kill you where you stand and be done with it."

I took a deep breath and calmed myself. "You won't."

Emrys stared at me, his eyes ablaze with cold fury, then he sheathed his blade. "Do you know what I long for most of all, Edward Godspeaker?"

"Your crown?"

Emrys laughed. "No. I long to feel the grass beneath my feet once more. To feel the warmth of a fire, or of a lover. To dig my heels in the dirt. I miss feeling. I miss *life*. No, Edward, I care little for crowns and kingdoms, and yet Fate has decreed that the only way I can live once more is if I wear that wretched ring of iron. Or if this accursed creature gets down from my saddle. And so, I prepare my men for war."

I stepped away from Emrys, and walked towards the fire. I could feel its heat embracing my flesh, and in that moment I pitied Emrys. He was a man once, and he craved the things all men crave. He wanted to be a man once more, and if giving him that would save our kingdom, I knew I should do all I could to break his curse.

"All I need is a chance," I said. "Give me one chance to free you from immortality and save my kingdom from destruction."

Emrys thought. "Godwin begged," he said.

"I will not beg."

Emrys exhaled, and brought his horse up beside me. "Very well. But should you fail in this quest, I will unleash my horde upon your kingdom and reclaim what is mine. The petty lives of your people are insignificant to me, but because of the respect I feel for your predecessor I do this for you, Edward Godspeaker."

"Thank you. I will do all I can," I said. A wave of relief washed over me, and I felt how much I had been sweating.

"Ride south-east until you come to where the River Aed leaves the forest's southern border. A cliff rises above the river there, and at the base of that cliff on the western bank is a cave. Enter it as the last rays of sunlight creep over the horizon and you will receive the hospitality of the dwarf lord Wilere. Do keep your wits about you, for the dwarf is cunning and treacherous. That is all the aid I shall give you, Godspeaker. Free your friends and go." He bowed his head.

I nodded, then marched from the tent. The man who brought

me there stopped me as I left and demanded to know what had happened.

"Bring me my things and let me go," I said.

"Why should I do that?"

"Do you want to defy the Immortal King? Do as I say!"

The man sensed the truth in my words, or perhaps he was just as frightened as I was. He did not argue. My heart was racing, and a tide of emotions were washing over me. I was filled with pride, fear, relief, and foreboding. I did not know what to feel.

I cut Thorry, Philip, and Dughlas's bindings and our things were brought to us. We were led from the camp, told the way back to Beglen, and the four of us headed north the way we had come. The other three kept asking what had happened and why we were allowed to go free, but I said nothing. I was deep in thought.

My companions bombarded me with questions. It was just as we were leaving the woods that poor Thorry asked about his father, and that tipped me over the edge. I spun around and drew my sword. Thorry froze.

"Forgive me, Thorry, but I did not think to ask. When I was standing beneath a ruthless warlord from legend, my body being roasted by the heat of that blasted fire he had in his tent, your father was the last thing on my mind. I had a hundred other things scrambling through my head at the time," I barked.

Thorry opened his mouth to speak, but I interrupted him.

"In all honesty, your father is likely dead. Those men in that camp do not care about you or me, and keeping him alive would have been a waste of food and drink. You were going to poison Carol regardless."

Thorry fell to his knees and began to weep. I looked upon him with pity, while Dughlas and Philip stood emotionless behind him. An owl hooted in the distance, and I watched Thorry cry for some time. Eventually he wiped his eyes and gazed up at me. "Are you going to kill me?" he asked.

In that moment, I certainly wanted to. Carol had charged him with treason and commanded me to carry out his execution once his usefulness had expired. I had found Emrys's camp, so I no longer needed the burden of a fat merchant.

But, since we left Giant's Rest I had grown somewhat fond of him. Did he really deserve to die? I looked down the length of my blade at the man who knelt at its tip, and I made the decision. That was the first time I broke my oath to Carol.

"I am sorry about your father, Thorry. I spoke out of turn. You should leave Ardonn."

Thorry's eyes went wide. "But, but your orders…"

"Carol commanded me to execute you once your use had diminished. I believe those were his words," I said. "So long as you have two feet fit to crush grapes, and two hands for picking them, I believe you still have a use. But not here."

What Thorry did next surprised me. He unhooked his fishing club from his belt and held it out to me, then bowed his head. "My vineyard is burned and my wealth is gone. I have no grapes to make into wine, so I put these hands and these feet in your service, lord. I swear, from this day forth, to defend all that you own as your housecarl and oathman."

Dughlas and Philip both raised their eyebrows. I admit, I did not expect that. I sheathed my sword and pulled Thorry up onto his feet, then looked him in the eyes. I pushed his shoulders back and lifted his chin.

"You're a warrior now, Thorry, whether you like it or not. You have just sworn an oath to me — an oath I would rather not receive — but once the words are spoken they cannot be taken back. Will you fulfil this oath?"

"Yes, lord. I will."

I grunted. "Good. I do not know how I'll explain this to His Lordship, but we can cross that bridge when we come to it. You're a shit warrior, and stupid for swearing that oath, but it's done now."

"We'll need to get him a proper weapon," Dughlas said.

"Aye. A mace or an axe, perhaps," I said. "But first we need to get back to Beglen. Once there, I will tell you all everything, and we will plan our next move."

We headed north, back to the city of wine. We found a village on the way with a small inn, and we bought rooms and spent the last few hours of the night there. We spoke little, and once we woke in the morning we ate a short breakfast before continuing on our way back to Beglen. We reached the city around noon, and I decided to pay Hilbert of The Grapevine a visit.

Hilbert was less than happy to see us return, which only confirmed my suspicions.

Apparently, when Thorry had drunkenly revealed my identity the night before we were kidnapped, a spy in the service of Emrys went and informed his comrades, who threatened Hilbert the next morning demanding that they be allowed to take us away.

When he did not give in, they resorted to bribery and Hilbert took their coin eagerly — but told them instead to snatch us when we left The Grapevine so his reputation was not harmed. Hilbert begged me to spare him, and proclaimed how sorry he was.

I did not take his life, but I did take what I had paid him during our stay, and some more on top of it for good measure. We used that money to buy new provisions and gear for the road, an axe, shield, and helmet for Thorry, and four horses.

We stayed the night in Beglen at a different tavern, where I revealed everything that had happened in Emrys's camp. At dawn the next day we took the road south-east through the countryside and toward the woods.

"Now that nobody is eavesdropping," Thorry said, once we were well on the road, "I should tell you all what you probably already suspect."

"Lord Edric had men at Emrys's camp," I said.

"Yes, lord. I think Edric has betrayed the king."

"Which king?" Dughlas said.

Thorry glanced at him, then back at me. "My loyalties lie with whichever king Edward serves."

"Lord Edric, for whatever reason, has decided to pledge his forces to Emrys — that much is clear," I said. "Though if I can free Emrys from his curse, that may not matter."

"We're being followed, master," Philip said.

I turned to see where Philip was pointing, and for a split second saw a man on horseback disappear behind the hill to our right.

"Good spotting, Philip. Stick to the road, everyone. Whoever it is, we will lose them in the woods," I said.

"That didn't work out so well in Everlynn," said Dughlas.

"Remind me, Thorry. If we were going to Lakeland, what would our journey look like?" I said.

"We would go east through countryside, lord, till we reached the foot of the mountains — Beglen Heights. If we followed the mountains south, we would come to the Aed, then following that upriver would take us to Lakeland," Thorry said.

I smiled. "You know this land well."

"It is a merchant's business to know the land in which he sells his wares."

"Indeed. We'll head east, and hopefully throw them off our trail."

I turned my horse eastward and we carried on, with Thorry as our guide. We rode across country again, through hills and pastures, and fields of wheat and barley. We passed through the occasional village or hamlet, and made it clear to the people there that we were heading east to Lakeland. Hopefully, whoever it was that followed us would ask where we went and hear a lie.

As we travelled through that day we caught sight of our followers a few times. There were at least two of them, and they were dressed as warriors with mail and steel helmets, and shields on their backs. We thought that they were likely Emrys or Edric's men, perhaps ensuring I kept my word. If they were not, however, I hoped we could lose them.

We rode through the evening until the darkness concealed us. When I was certain we would not be seen, we made camp among the trees at the edge of the woods. The four of us took turns to keep watch throughout the night. While I guarded our camp I saw no sign of those who tracked us, and wondered if we had lost them. I hoped so.

The next morning, instead of continuing eastward to Beglen Heights, we went south, deeper into the woods. We waded across a river at midday, and after that the forest became much denser and much darker. Philip had to keep climbing trees to make sure we were heading in the right direction, using the sun and the mountains as his guide. There were no tracks or paths through this part of the woods. We were truly in the wilds.

Our journey through the forest lasted a week. At night we would make camp, propitiate the spirits, and take turns keeping watch. On the second night, Philip said he saw elves deep in the woods, and while the rest of us slept he followed them for a while until he came across a pool surrounded by stone statues, with a grand fountain in the middle.

The elves bathed and played in the pool, while others sang songs, and Philip watched for a while mesmerised by their beauty.

I asked him to show me the place the next day, and he traced his steps and led us to it. When we arrived at the place he swore he had been to, all we saw was a murky pond surrounded by overgrown shrubbery. I tossed a lump of silver in the pond and we continued on our way.

On our sixth day we heard the sound of rushing water, and we followed it till we came to what we assumed was the Aed. The river ran fast at this point, churning and gushing over the boulders and fallen trees. It was violent.

Traders from the east would often sail down this river on their way to Oldford, Aedmouth, and out to sea, and I wondered at how they could possibly navigate the waters here. It would have taken great skill to steer a boat through those rapids, weaving around the rocks and debris. An old, broken sailboat lay rotting on the bank opposite us as proof that not all had the skill to pass that way.

We followed the river for another day or so. As we moved south, the land rose higher and the river went further and further beneath us. The sounds of it roaring between the cliffs on either side echoed up to us and we could barely hear anything else. We had to shout just to hear each other at some points.

Finally, after a week of marching through dense woodland, we came to the forest's edge. Ahead of us was a sheer drop, and several hundred feet below us was a vast meadow. Further in the distance could be seen farmland, and a few miles downstream we could see the thatched rooves of a village peeking up from behind a hill. The river poured out from the cliffs in a great torrent, and then it calmed again. It was a beautiful place.

"The cave is at the base of the cliff, by the river," I said.

Dughlas peered over the edge and whistled. "How do you plan on getting down there?"

"Rope."

"You're joking? I'm sure we could find a safer way down if we followed the cliff westwards."

"We don't have time. We could end up walking for days, even weeks, if we go that way. We have a war to prevent."

"Alright, but if you fall I'm not following your body downriver to retrieve what's left of it."

The sun was setting, so we tied the horses and made camp. The next morning I would scale the rock, climbing down as the river roared beneath me. While Thorry tried to light a fire, and Dughlas and Philip searched for food, I lay on my belly and peered over the edge.

There was little light left in the day, but I thought I could make out a narrow ledge at the base of the cliff, just above the river. I assumed that was the entrance to Wilere's cave. It curved around to the south face of the cliff and appeared to slope towards the ground. Perhaps it would have been better to find a safer way down, then simply walk up to the cave along that outcrop. I considered it, but urgency pushed the thought from my mind.

Dughlas and Philip returned with some berries and a few rabbits, which we skinned and roasted over the fire Thorry had managed to start. The other three talked and joked, but my mind was elsewhere. I stared off into the distance and let my thoughts wander.

"Someone's coming," Thorry said. My mind snapped back to reality, and I heard movement in the trees behind us.

"An animal?" Dughlas said. "There's no way those people tracked us through the woods."

"Ready your weapons," I said.

We took our shields and our weapons and stood close to each other by the fire. Dughlas drew his bow and awaited whoever — or whatever — was following us to emerge from the trees. The bushes rustled, a twig snapped, and soon we heard footsteps. They neared, crushing sticks and leaves beneath them.

Dughlas saw movement ahead of us, asked who was there, and after receiving no response he loosed an arrow. It whistled through the trees and was followed by a sharp yell.

"No!"

"State your business or I'll give you another," said Dughlas. He notched another arrow.

"It is William. William of Everlynn. We wish to share your fire."

Dughlas turned to me, confused, and I shrugged. Before we could respond, a man with twigs stuck in his mail, a helmet on his head, and fur draped over his shoulders tumbled out of the shrubbery and fell on his hands and knees. He climbed to his feet and smiled, brushing himself off.

"We have been following you for weeks," William said. "Gods, you gave us a good run around."

"We?" I asked.

William looked over his shoulder as another mail-clad warrior stumbled out from the bushes. He also wore a fur cloak, carried a sword and a shield over his shoulder, and his black hair fell loose from beneath his helmet.

Except he was not a man — *she* was a woman. She came to stand beside William and held up her hands. Her eyes and nose were hidden behind a visor, but I recognised her.

"Thank the Gods you two're here," Dughlas said. He made his way over to William, arms outstretched. "Maybe you can talk some sense into Edward."

Dughlas embraced William and his companion, who looked over at me and gave a shy smile. I stood there, dumbfounded. Had they really come all this way to find us? Why?

I should have known Matilda would do something foolish while I was away.

5

Wilere

"What are you doing here?" I demanded. Matilda's smile became a frown. "You were supposed to remain in Giant's Rest."

Matilda stammered, but it was William who answered my question. "We needed to find you, Edward. Matilda regretted the way she had acted towards you, and it grieved her to think you might die without saying a proper farewell."

"I thought I asked you to ensure she did nothing foolish," I said.

William sighed. "She said she was going to follow you with or without company. I could not refuse."

"Is this true?" I said. Matilda nodded slowly. "How witless of you — you could have died. Do you know how dangerous the roads are in times like this? And take that stupid helmet off, it's too big for you.”

Matilda removed her helmet and let the rest of her hair fall messy and loose. She clenched her jaw and stared at me.

“She came all this way for you, Edward,” William said.

“No. Matilda came here for none but herself. She’s a weepy little puppy that cannot go a day without clinging to my arm.” I shook my head and turned to Matilda. “You are a burden, my lady. Henton is not far from here, actually. Go home.”

Matilda stood there agape, and said nothing. Her eyes began to water. The others looked at me dumbfounded, and Dughlas shook his head. I pulled on my boots, picked up my sword, and stormed off into the woods. None tried to stop me.

I walked until I could hear my companions no longer, pushing through the dense undergrowth until I came to a small clearing illuminated by the light of the moon. I sat myself down atop a fallen tree, closed my eyes, and tried to meditate.

My eyes were shut for only a moment when I heard movement in the trees behind me. I turned around, but before I could react, Dughlas lunged out of the bushes and threw himself onto me. He tackled me to the ground with a yell, pinned me down, then backhanded me across the face.

“You selfish, heartless bastard,” he said.

“My parents were married.”

“Don’t give me your cheek, you icy piece of shit.”

He slapped me again. With all my strength, I heaved Dughlas off of me and threw him to the side. I rolled over, straddled his chest, then punched him square in the jaw. He spat blood back at my face and grinned. I lifted my fist to strike him once more. "You swore an oath to me, you insolent—"

"Stop!"

I turned to see Matilda standing at the edge of the clearing. She was still dressed in mail and fur, and her eyes were red and wet. "Please, both of you. Just stop fighting."

I looked back down at Dughlas, then rolled to the side and sat beside him. I looked up at the moon while Matilda came over to help Dughlas up.

"I'll leave you two alone." Dughlas wiped the blood from his chin, then stumbled back into the trees.

Matilda came and sat a few feet away from me, and for a while the two of us just stared up at the moon. It was almost full that night, and we could see clearly in its light. It was beautiful as it sat up in the sky, floating in a sea of stars. I have always loved the moon. After what seemed like forever, I broke the silence.

"The Moon-God Efenled once loved an Edin woman called Nihta," I said. "He came down to the World to be with her, but when they united his light was too much for her to bear. She was blinded. After the Split, when the Gods invited the Edan back to the Heavens, Nihta desired to join her beloved at last. Yet blind to all light she could not find the way. Still she searches for Efenled, who tries in vain to guide her with his light. They cannot be together yet still Nihta struggles to feel his love once more."

"I know how she feels," Matilda said.

I looked away from the moon to see her facing me, cross-legged. There were tears in her eyes and her jaw was clenched shut. A tear fell from her cheek and landed on the steel links she wore.

"I am sorry I reacted the way I did. I don't deserve your forgiveness," I said.

"I forgive you anyway. I always do."

I sighed. "I did not mean to yell at you, or say any of those things. I use anger to conceal my fear."

"What are you afraid of?"

I stared back up at the moon and hesitated, then bowed my head. "Everything. Tomorrow I must descend a rock face hundreds of feet above a torrent of water, then enter the Otherworldly realm of a powerful dwarf. It is not death I fear, however, but failure. Failure to protect my friends. Failure to protect Ardonn from Emrys's wrath. Failure to make my father proud."

"But—"

"And failure to keep you safe. If harm were to come to you, my lady, I would not be able to live anymore. I also fear to break your heart."

"Why would you break my heart?"

I hesitated. I had never spoken of it before, but in that moment, I felt I could tell Matilda anything. "Do you know of the Leech of Oldford?"

"The witch you defeated some years ago?"

I nodded. "Before she died she bound me to her, and cursed me, that all those who love me would know endless pain. I fear what may happen should I let you fall in love with me, my lady."

Matilda smiled. She was deep in thought. "I hate when you call me 'my lady'."

"Why?"

"Because to you I want to be Matilda, not Earl Harold of Henton's second daughter."

I nodded, then looked back up at Efenled's cold, white face. He appeared to be smiling down at us. I felt Matilda squeeze my hand, then she let out a deep sigh.

"I love you, Edward of Winterhome."

I turned to her, but before I could say a word she took my face in her hands and kissed me. That was the first time we had kissed since the battle of Tillysburg, and in that moment a wave of calmness washed over me.

I realised that ever since that first kiss on the hills outside Tillysburg I had felt a piece of me was missing, but in that moment that piece had fallen back into place. I ran my fingers through Matilda's hair, then pulled her closer to me. We kissed for a long while, and despite the chill of the night, I felt a warmth I had never felt before.

Without breaking the kiss Matilda moved to sit over my lap, a leg on either side of me, and I held her waist tight, digging my fingers into the chain links. She rubbed herself against me as we kissed some more, then she pushed my chest and I fell back onto the dirt. She started to unbuckle my belt, but then I grabbed her wrists. Matilda frowned.

"No," I said. "You are not like them." I took her cold hands in mine, then rested them against her chest.

"What did I do wrong?"

Matilda climbed off me then lay down at my side. She rested her head on my shoulder. Her breath was heavy, and I could feel her heart racing. I lay there beside Matilda and gazed up at the moon.

"Why are you dressed like a warrior?" I asked.

Matilda laughed. "William said that knowing how to fight is useless if the smallest scratch can kill me."

"I suppose that is true, though I hope a blade never touches that mail while you wear it."

"One almost did."

"What?"

"We were ambushed by robbers on the way south. They looked almost ready to kill us, but William just paid them to go away."

"I would have killed them all."

Matilda smiled. "I know."

"I should probably get back to camp," I said. "The others might be worried."

Matilda nodded. After a few more moments we got up and headed back to where we had made camp. Dughlas gave me a nod upon our return, and I begged forgiveness from each one of my companions. They were all just happy that Matilda and I were friends again, though we did not tell them what had actually happened in that clearing.

We sat around the fire together and I introduced Thorry properly to William and Matilda. They asked how he had come into my service and why I had not executed him as Carol had commanded, so I told them the whole story from the morning we left Giant's Rest right up to when we arrived at that cliff.

William then told us that after supper on the day we had left, Matilda had come to his room and demanded that he take her south and help her track me down. They argued for a long time, but eventually William caved. He wanted to leave the next morning, but Matilda insisted they take two horses and leave immediately.

So, they rode through night and through day, trading horses for fresh ones at each town and village, only taking a break for a few hours every night to sleep. They arrived in Beglen the same night we did, and in the morning they tracked us to The Grapevine, but they arrived shortly after we had been kidnapped. Hilbert told them he had no idea where we went, and Matilda became depressed.

They stayed another night in Beglen, but Matilda stayed in bed all morning the next day, so they stayed yet another night. As they were about to leave the next day, William heard news that we had returned to Beglen and had only just left again, so they followed us some more. Thanks to William's excellent tracking ability, they did not lose sight of us.

Matilda wanted to wait until the perfect moment to reveal herself to us, but after they had to abandon William's horse after it broke its leg in the woods, they decided it was probably time to show themselves.

After William told his story we decided it was getting late, so we tried to get some sleep. I offered to take the first watch, because I could not seem to shut my eyes, and I stayed awake for most of the night looking out over the countryside below us and admiring the beauty of the stars.

Matilda slept beside me. Every so often she would mumble in her sleep and I would feel a surge of warmth run through me. Dughlas eventually woke, and we whispered to each other for a bit about nothing important, before he urged me to get some sleep before morn.

I lay down and tried to close my eyes again, and drifted off to sleep with Matilda at my side, thinking how fortunate I was to have met such a lady.

I tugged at the rope as hard as I could, trying to pull it free from the tree it was tied around. It was bound tight. "Are you sure this will hold?" I asked Dughlas.

"I am almost certain," he said.

"I don't want you to be *almost* certain. I want you to be

completely certain."

"It'll hold."

I pulled at it one last time. Dughlas was probably right — the rope was holding fast. We had tied it to a strong tree rooted a few feet away from the cliff's edge. Dughlas and William would hold it and slowly extend its length as I climbed down, but the tree would act as an anchor.

We measured the rope about a dozen times to make sure that, should Dughlas and William slip, the rope would be just shorter than the height of the cliff. If I fell into the torrent below I would surely die. I leaned over the edge and looked down at it, gushing from between the narrow gap between the two rock walls. I sighed.

"You don't have to do this," Dughlas said.

"I do. It's the only way."

"It's a pity my slap didn't smack some sense into you last night."

I ignored him. Matilda stood back with Thorry and watched us. She had her arms folded over her chest and was biting her nails. Philip had just returned from the woods with William, and he came and handed me a dirty piece of oak root. I thanked him.

"Do you know why I had you collect this?" I asked.

Philip nodded. "When men enter the Otherworld, they are in danger of losing themselves there and being trapped for centuries."

"So what is the root for?"

"To keep you rooted in this world."

I ruffled his hair and smiled. "I've taught you well."

"You sure have, Master. But I have not finished my training, so please do not die."

I nodded. "Alright, William, tie me up."

"I bet he's been waiting a long time for you to ask that," Dughlas said. William shot him a glare, then we all laughed. Nervously. We were all worried about what might happen. There was so much that could go wrong, and not just during my descent. I had dealt with Otherworldly beings for nearly thirteen years, but those were spirits that had entered our world. I had only once before entered theirs, though not alone. I was afraid.

William took the other end of the rope and tied it around my waist. He secured the knot, then put his hands on my shoulders and looked me in the eyes. "Mark me, my friend. If you fall in that river and drown, the men who bury you will never loosen that knot."

I smiled and pulled at the knot myself. The rope was very tight — uncomfortably so — but it needed to be. I let out a deep breath. "Let's get this over with."

I tied a piece of string around the bit of oak root, then hung it around my neck. Matilda ran over and wrapped her arms around me. She pulled me as close to her as she could, and I had to pry her off me else she would have held on forever. Tears were welling up in her eyes, and I wiped them away. She smiled. "If you do not return by twilight tomorrow, I will be coming after you.”

“I believe you. But I will return,” I said.

Matilda nodded, then stepped back. I turned and slowly walked towards the edge of the cliff. Dughlas and William took hold of the rope, I turned around, and then nodded to them. They nodded back, I gripped the rope in both hands, held my breath, and then, before I could change my mind, I leaned back and felt myself tipping back over the side.

I slid down a few feet and found my footing against the cliff face. I turned my head to look down below me, then immediately looked back up at the sky. I swallowed. I could hear no other sound but the rush of water beneath me. Only a few hundred feet to go.

“Edward! Are you okay?” William shouted.

“Yes, let me down. Slowly!”

The rope began to loosen, and my feet skidded down the rock face. I slowly, carefully, lifted one foot and lowered it, planted it against the rock, then did the same with the other. I made progress little by little, edging my way down the cliff. Little pebbles and bits of dirt fell as I stepped and scraped against stone, and the rope creaked. My knuckles were snow-white and the palms of my hands were burning. As I moved slowly down the rock, the storm below me grew ever louder.

The descent seemed to take all day. I climbed down for what felt like hours, but when I looked down it seemed I had made no progress. I called up to ask how long I had been descending, and

Dughlas told me it had only been about half an hour.

I kept going, despite my body aching and the fear growing within me. I would take breaks every so often, but eventually I was too far down for the others to hear me shout over the sound of the river, so I could not tell them to stop. There were no more breaks after that.

The raging river appeared to be slowly rising up to embrace me, and I admit, there were a few moments when my mind told me to give up. To cut the rope. It would be a lot easier that way. But I kept going, descending step by step.

And then I saw it. The cave. I was right about the ledge being its entrance. It was narrow, a small crack in the rock face. It was there, as the warlord had said, and a wave of relief washed over me.

The descent was not yet over. I still had a few more yards to go, but it was then that I heard a shout from above. A sound of distress. The rope went loose. I kicked and scraped at the rock and in my panic I let go of the rope and lunged for the cliff, but found nothing to grab onto, so I fell.

The roaring torrent rushed up to swallow me and the rage rose to a crescendo. Time seemed to slow and my memories flashed before my eyes. My heart lurched from my chest and felt as though it was leaping from my throat. I tried to scream, but no sound came out.

All this happened in a second, then the rope tightened and I stopped falling. The rope cut into me and I yelled, but it held fast. I was suspended mid-air, hanging only a few feet above the river. I could feel it spraying against my back.

A second later the rope creaked very loudly. I looked down at my waist and saw the knot begin to unravel. I sucked in my breath and gripped the rope with two hands just as the knot came loose and the rope dropped from my legs. I looked up to see the little heads of my companions looking down on me.

"Some knot," I muttered. I looked down at the river, its mist drenching my boots, then looked over at the cave. I was level with it now, and it was just there. Right in front of me. I could almost reach it. I swung a little, stuck out my legs, and just missed the ledge.

I swung again, reached it this time, and planted my legs firmly against the flat rock. I let go of the rope with one arm and grabbed hold of a shrub, then pulled myself forward and pressed my body against the rock. I smiled. I had scaled the cliff face. I looked back up at my friends and gave a wave, and they all waved back.

It was only around noon that I reached the bottom. The gushing current surged past me, and I sat in the cave entrance and meditated, waiting for sundown. Emrys told me to enter Wilere's realm at twilight, and so for twilight I waited. Evening seemed to arrive faster than my descent down the cliff face. I watched the horizon as it went from blue, to purple, to grey. It was time.

I entered the cave, my hand against the wall. There was little light, but I could still see a few inches ahead of me. I followed the dripping wall for a while, until I came to what appeared to be a dead end. I felt around me and discovered I was surrounded by rock. I had come to a space big enough for only a short man, and I had to bend over to fit.

Is this the end? I thought. *It can't be.* I turned around in circles, running my hands against the walls. I must have missed something. There must be an entrance to Wilere's realm somewhere. Was I too late?

I pressed my hand against the back wall once again, but this time stumbled forward. There was no longer any wall. The cold, black rock had given way to emptiness, and I fell into it. I climbed back to my feet and then took another step forward. Then another. Darkness engulfed me, and the dripping sound grew quieter.

I continued on. I felt a gentle warmth radiating from ahead of me. Then came the sounds, faint at first, but they soon became the unmistakable sounds of distant revelry. Music echoed up from the depths of the World, accompanied by cheery voices and the hammering of dancing feet.

I followed the noise, but then stopped dead. Another sound approached, a sound from behind. Roaring. Screaming. Like the thunder of a thousand hooves. The Aed, that torrent rushing past the cave outside, echoed through the crevice in the cliff. It grew louder and louder.

Then water began to pool at my feet. It was cold, like ice. It seeped through my boots. It was rising, soaking my ankles, then my calves. I panicked. I yelled and splashed, stumbling forward deeper into the cave away from the water and, perhaps, towards my own doom.

The river burst into the cave, in one mighty deluge. It rushed forth and embraced me. It swept me off my feet and flushed me deep into that cave. It filled my lungs and I felt a crushing pain in my chest. Then everything went black.

I woke, coughing and spluttering, gasping for air. I lay on my back, on cold, hard stone. I was still in the cave, but there was light. A warm glow. I turned my head to the side and could just make out a large hall. Braziers and fire pits decorated the room. The smell of sweet, floral incense filled my nostrils.

My vision was blurred, but I blinked and rubbed my eyes and it started to clear. Shapes materialised. Little grey blobs, moving and swaying. Slowly, those blobs took form, and I realised they were people. Men and women clothed in thin, revealing gowns and adorned with gold. What mesmerised me most about them was their seemingly perfect beauty, with flawless skin as black as pitch. Their hair was also black as night, yet their eyes glowed a striking yellow. They looked and moved like people, but they *felt* Otherworldly.

The people danced around the fires, or feasted at the tables spread throughout the vast hall while sweet, gentle music filled the room. There was an erotic mood in the air. Their dance was sensual, and occasionally pairs would kiss or embrace.

I sat up, my bones and muscles aching. One of the women approached me, gliding gracefully across the stone floor. She gave me a warm smile, gently took my hand, and sung my name. She pulled me to my feet with little effort, then led me to a cushioned, high-backed chair by one of the fire pits, where she left me to warm myself. Another woman came with a small plate of strange, puffy sweets, while yet another brought a thick fur cloak, which she draped over my shoulders. She began to massage my neck.

Then there was a bang, and the women all slid slowly away from me. The one massaging me softly kissed my cheek, then slinked away. The hall went silent, the carousing fell to a whisper, and the music stopped.

I turned to see where the bang had come from, and saw at the end of the hall a great stone door had been swung open. I had not noticed it before. It appeared to lead into a great, black void.

In that doorway stood a man. He wore long, flowing grey robes, and he had the same charcoal skin as the others. He had long, braided hair as white as fresh snow and a clean-shaved face with a hard jawline and a sharp nose. Unlike the others, his eyes were white like those of a blind man, yet he could certainly see.

An old, grey-coated hound walked at his feet, and he strode across the room to a high stone throne that stood by the wall opposite where I had been seated. He slumped down in the seat, ran his long painted nails through his hair, and then he smiled.

"It has been nigh on three centuries since I have had guests in my kingdom," he said. His voice was deep. Booming. It filled every corner of the hall. At the same time, it was warm and kind, and his strange accent soothed me.

I opened my mouth to speak, but no words came out. I only stared at the unusual man. He pointed to one of the women and clicked his fingers. "You. Bring our guest a drink."

The woman stood, and in her hands was a glass chalice. She passed me the cup, which was filled to the brim with an unusual purple wine. She then knelt beside me and started massaging my leg. The enthroned man nodded, and I took a sip of the wine.

It was more delicious than any drink I had ever tasted, a perfect mix of sweet and sour, like honey and lime. Even attempting to describe the flavour would do it an injustice. My body tingled as the warmth of the drink flowed through me, and I took another sip, only to be embraced by the same feeling.

Before I could think twice, I had drained the chalice. The dark man laughed, snapped his fingers, and in an instant my chalice was filled once again with the delicious wine.

"What is your name, friend from the World?" he asked.

"Edward, My Lord."

"Welcome to my kingdom, Edward of the World. My name is Wilere, Lord of the Cave."

It was in that moment I remembered why I was here. I touched the root around my neck and for a moment the woman's fingers kneading my thigh did not feel so warm after all.

"I thank you for your hospitality, Lord Wilere," I said.

Wilere nodded. "What brings you to my realm, Edward Worldling?"

I was going to lie. I remembered Emrys's warning to me, about how this dwarf was deceitful, and thought that only deception would put me on top of him. Yet when I opened my mouth, I could say nought but the truth. "I seek an end to Emrys's curse."

"Ah. I remember that name. Why has Emrys not visited my hall?"

Again, I found it impossible to lie. "He was locked away beneath a mountain for three hundred years, but has recently been freed."

Wilere laughed. "I was beginning to believe he had reclaimed his crown, but I assume that is untrue, considering your arrival here. You are in luck, Edward Worldling, for I can end that which ails Emrys. For I am he who cursed him."

"Forgive me, My Lord, but if I may ask, why did you curse Emrys?"

"An excellent question," Wilere said. He laughed again. "Emrys was arrogant. He was greedy. He was filled with an inflated pride in his own skill and his own wisdom. I invited the king into my hall one evening, and for three nights I gave him my hospitality. But for those three nights, he and his men spat on my gifts to them. They took them for granted and not once did they show the respect owed to a host by a guest. I cursed him as a lesson in humility."

"I see," I said.

The woman at my side stood, then made herself comfortable on my knee. She took one of the sweets from the little plate and placed it against my lips. I hesitated, but could I really refuse a gift from a gracious host? No. I let the woman slip the sweet between my teeth, I chewed, then swallowed. That same feeling from the wine rushed through me, and I washed it down with another sip.

The woman kissed me, and I put an arm around her waist and rested my hand on her thigh. She smirked.

"Why should I end Emrys's curse?" Wilere asked.

The woman pulled away from my face and gently kissed my neck. Wilere stared intently into my eyes — or at least, he seemed to — and he gave me a kind smile.

"He threatens my people and our country in his efforts to take his crown and break his curse," I said.

At that, Wilere laughed. He laughed loud and deep. He did not stop. He tipped his head back and laughed and laughed and laughed. The woman on my knee nibbled and pecked at my neck. The music resumed. Folk returned to their seductive dancing, their conversation, and their meals. The fire crackled and burned hotter. Wilere continued to laugh.

"Can you break the curse?" I yelled. Wilere's laughter died and he smiled at me yet again. He seemed to pity me.

"Why should I care about the fate of your world, Worldling? It has been long since Man has cared for ours. Besides, it will be easier for Emrys to break the curse than myself. When Emrys went on his way, I gave him a gift. Do you know what that gift was?" he said.

I thought for a while. Was Wilere testing me? It seemed so. I opened my mouth to answer, but then paused. At first I thought it was jewels, or wealth, or some other item valued by all. But that is not what Wilere meant. "You gave him a dog."

Wilere placed a hand on the hound at his side. "I gave him a little grey puppy. And I told Emrys, 'should the grey dog dismount, or should you wear your crown once more, this curse shall be broken.'"

"With respects, My Lord, I was already aware that those things would break the curse," I said.

"Emrys was a fool. He is a fool. He took my words literally, but the curse was in the form of—"

"A riddle."

"A riddle." Wilere wore a cruel smile. "You are much wiser than he, Edward Worldling. Indeed, the key to freeing Emrys lies not in wearing his crown or waiting for his puppy to jump from his saddle, but in solving that riddle. Can you solve it, I wonder?"

I did not answer. I could not answer, for the woman in my lap brought the chalice to my lips once more and poured its sweet contents down my throat. She tried to kiss me, but I pushed her face away.

"What is this drink?" I asked.

The woman giggled, and Wilere spoke. "It takes men to a place where they will find all they desire. Shall we see what Edward Worldling desires?"

I stared down into the cup and swirled the purple wine around. The woman bit my ear, I hesitated, then desire and curiosity overwhelmed me. I downed the rest of the cup and kissed the woman on my lap, letting all my worries wash away as her lips moved against mine.

Wilere laughed, clapping, and I turned to him. He seemed to fade away, dissolving into thin air, as did the rest of his guests. The woman on my lap vanished too. I was alone. Then the dwarf-lord's hall began to change. The walls swayed and the light died. The room shrank.

I found myself in another hall, darker, narrower, yet more elaborately decorated. The walls were carved with relief depicting battles and noble deeds. Alcoves lined the walls, and in each one stood a sculpture of some warrior or king. Heroes. I was in the Hall of Legends.

I stood and walked through the hall, admiring the heroes as I passed them. I saw mighty kings and queens of old, men and women whose names are still spoken with reverence; and legends known only from song who lived deep in the mists of the past, yet whose deeds still ripple through the fabric of our time.

I reached the end of the hall and came to another sculpture, larger than the rest, with his sword held triumphantly and his face bearing pride. I recognised the man standing above me, for he was me. I looked older, wiser, but still recognisable. My name was inscribed in gold at the base of the sculpture, along with a list of my deeds.

Edward Godspeaker, Heir of Godwin, Slayer of Oldford's Leech, Hero of Tillysburg, it read. The following deeds I did not recognise. Deeds I had not achieved. Was I shown my fate?

Or perhaps the vision merely showed me that which I desired. I admit, my heart swelled with pride upon reading that list. *Bane of the Immortal King, Champion of Ardonn, Child of the Sun, King of the Twin Kingdoms, and Conqueror of Vylan, God of Shadow*. My heart was racing. Was this what I would become?

I stared up at myself for a while until I heard a sound from behind me, echoing down the hall. The sound of a thousand voices, cheering in the distance. I turned and followed the noise, which grew louder and louder, until I reached a heavy double door.

I pushed it open and was momentarily blinded by the light streaming in, and deafened by the noise of shouting masses. They chanted my name. *Edward, Edward, Edward*. My eyes adjusted and I beheld a long, wide street lined with houses and thousands upon thousands of cheering people. I recognised that street, for I had been there once before. It was the final stretch of the Royal Way, cutting through the Capital from the city's gates to the palace.

I made my way down the street, smiling and waving at the

people tossing flowers and coins at me in adoration. They were ecstatic, their faces bright and gleeful. Men and women alike reached out to try and touch me. Some succeeded, but most were held back by a line of faceless warriors.

One woman broke through the line, tore open the bust of her dress, and fell on her knees before me. I gave her a smile before two of the guards swept her up and pushed her back into the crowd. My attention was caught by a man in tears, weeping with joy at the sight of me as he declared his love and loyalty. Young boys wore their hair like mine, and men trimmed their beards to resemble my sculpture.

I was overwhelmed with pride. I was the centre of the world. I continued down the street, greeting and thanking the folk I passed, and I could not help but feel above them. I was glorious — godly, even — and they were the slavish masses. I held my head up high.

I came to a hall greater than any I had seen — the royal palace — and ascended the steps to the two great doors. I turned and waved to the crowd one last time, then four warriors pushed the doors open and led me inside.

The hall was packed full with lords and ladies from Ardonn and beyond. They clapped and cheered as I entered the hall, and beamed at me as I walked along the rich red carpet towards the throne at the end of the hall, followed by the four warriors. I nodded to each of the nobles I passed, and even recognised some of them.

I climbed the steps to the throne, and as I took a seat the crowd let out a resounding roar. They called my name in reverence, followed by, "Lord King!" All kneeled, and then one by one, men and women stood and came to offer fealty before me. Beneath me. They bowed their heads but said nothing, and after a moment they each stood and left the hall in turn.

My friends and old oathmen came to me first. Dughlas was there, as was Philip. Those who had died — Osmund, Egil, Cubert, Alfred, and the rest — also knelt before me. They were followed by Matilda and her family, and then came William and his wife Eleni. After they left the hall, Lord Odo and his family knelt at my feet. Hakon was there too, and it felt good to see him humbled.

Then, to my shock, came Carol and Clodild, the last of the Eomundson line. They knelt for a long while, a look of misery on Carol's face. Eventually they stood and left the hall, solemn and defeated. My heart sank a little, but then I was approached by Lord Adalbert of Oldford and his daughter Ecwyn.

Adalbert left the hall after they knelt, but Ecwyn did not. Instead, she stood and smiled up at me, then climbed the steps to the throne. She took my hands in hers and I stood. Ecwyn led me back down from the dais and presented me to the crowd, who let out a cheer one last time before Ecwyn led me from the throne room.

She took me by the hand through the palace to the royal bedchamber, then led me over to the rich, wide bed where the king and his wife would sleep. She sat me down and began to undress, blushing as she did so, then leant forward to kiss me. I kissed her and helped with her dress, running my hands along her soft, cold skin as her hand found its way down my chest.

Ecwyn pulled back an inch away from my face and bit her lip. She looked into my eyes, then moved to my ear. She whispered to me. "Remember yourself, Edward of Winterhome. You are lost."

She pulled away again and winked, but this time it was not Ecwyn who looked into my eyes, but a beautiful woman with mismatched irises and skin like snow.

Aoife.

She was there for a moment, then transformed once more into the dark dwarven lady from before. I stared at her, confused, and she frowned. The bedchamber fell apart and the walls collapsed around me.

I found myself once more in Wilere's hall and returned to my senses. It was empty now, aside from the woman on my lap, the old grey hound, and Wilere, who sat up on his throne and glared at me. The woman stood, her smile no longer sweet. She glided over to the brazier before me.

I threw the cup aside and let it shatter on the stone floor. "You tried to fool me," I spat. I instinctively reached for the root that hung around my neck, but found nothing.

"No," Wilere laughed. "I know it takes more than a cup of wine to deceive a Godspeaker. And yet, you were swayed for long enough."

He glanced at the woman now facing the brazier. She raised her hand out above it, my heart dropped, and she let go of the rope she held. The little oak root fell and turned to ash.

I shot up in panic. Wilere simply laughed. "Where are you going, Edward Worldling?"

I composed myself and then bowed. "I thank you for your generous hospitality, Lord Wilere, but I fear I must depart. I pray we may meet again one day."

"As do I, Godspeaker, as do I."

I made for the large door through which Wilere had entered. The hound stood and barked, but Wilere grabbed its collar.

"I warn against that exit, Edward Worldling," he sneered. "Should you go that way you will be lost forever. There will be no hope of return."

I ignored him. I had had enough of his venomous words. He was likely right, but where else could I go? The cave through which I had entered was nowhere to be seen, replaced instead by a wall of cold, hard rock.

There was only one path. Through that door, and into the unknown.

While time in my own world raced ahead.

6

Dying

Wilere did not stop me leaving his hall through the great stone doors. Perhaps he felt he did not need to. I stumbled out from the warmth of his hall into a cold, dark night. There was a short step, and I tripped and fell to my hands and knees.

I found myself in a clearing facing an enormous boulder about the size of the temple in Oldford. Surrounding the clearing were trees. Dense forest, through which no light penetrated. Was I back in Ardonn? Back in the World? I could not tell, but something did feel off.

I looked up at the night and saw no moon. Only the stars lit up the sky. If I were in the Otherworld then the moon would be full over Ardonn, as everything is mirrored there, but would that mean only hours had passed, or months? Or perhaps years? Centuries? I could not tell. I needed to find my friends. I needed to find Matilda.

I stood, then turned when I heard singing. It was soft and high, and came from a distance, yet I could hear it clearly. Something told me I should follow that voice. Besides, I had no other option. I had no clue where I was or how far these trees went. I could not even tell which way was which, for I did not know if the North Star was in the north or, if I were in the Otherworld, the south.

Wilere's hall was nowhere to be seen. There was only myself, the boulder, and the endless forest around me. I had nowhere else to go, and so into the trees I went, hacking at vines and branches as I pushed through. I followed the soothing sound of that song as it grew louder and louder.

I was still tingling and dizzy from whatever poison Wilere had me drink. The scent of strawberries and wine lingered in my nostrils. As I moved deeper and deeper into the woods the smell lessened until finally, once it had completely dissipated and I could smell only pine, I came to yet another clearing.

A stone fountain sat in the middle of that clearing, and the woman who was singing sat in the fountain washing herself. She was a divine beauty, incomparable to any mortal woman, for this lady was of the Otherworld. She was an elf.

I came into the clearing, my footsteps heavy, and the song came to an abrupt halt. The woman in the fountain turned around and smiled.

I breathed a sigh of relief.

"It's you," I said. I fell to my knees and all my fear, rage, and pain washed away from me at once. I felt something I had not felt in a long time. I felt hope.

"It's you," the woman echoed. She climbed out of the fountain and picked up a thick cloak, only just whiter than her pale skin and snowy hair, and wrapped it around herself. The woman glowed in the darkness. She grinned at me with her perfect teeth and looked down upon me with her astounding eyes, one green, the other blue.

"I am lost, Aoife," I said.

"I know," she replied. "I sung for you so that you may find your way."

"I just want to go home."

"Where is your home, Edward?"

I thought about that question. My mother came to my mind. My sister. My father. My old childhood house near Winterhome. I thought of my burned-up hall near Oldford. I thought of Giant's Rest. Of Matilda. "Nowhere," I said. "I have no home."

Aoife laughed. "Come, Edward. I shall show you the way to your world."

The elf held her hand out for me and I took it. Her skin was icy cold, but soothing at the same time. She helped me up, smiled, then led me off into the woods. The trees seemed to part for her, and I did not need my sword to whack at the foliage anymore. An owl swooped above us as we walked, then hooted when it landed on a nearby branch.

It did not take long until we reached a river. It was loud. Gushing. A great torrent of water hurtling along beneath us. It was a violent, raging storm. Aoife stood at the river's bank staring down at the frenzy. "Only those who fear not the Otherworld may leave it. Yet all men shy at the crossing of the borders twixt worlds, for one cannot escape a fear of the unknown," Aoife said. She turned to me then gave a sad smile. "You must die, Edward Worldling, else the Otherworld shall claim you. But can you do this?"

"What are you talking about, Aoife?"

The elf took both my hands in hers. "The visions Wilere revealed to you were nothing more than the desires of Edward the Man, which he endeavoured to make you succumb to. That lust for life, which men cling to so jealously, binds you to this place. It is a lesson, I suppose, woven into the laws of our worlds by the Gods. Death comes for all but the fearless."

I looked down at the river. It was churning, roaring, tumbling over itself. No man could survive the embrace of its waters. "You want me to jump in there?" I said. I had to yell over the river's rage.

Aoife nodded. "Shed your fear. Embrace the fate that all men must endure."

I looked back at the river and gulped. "Is there truly no other way?"

"No."

"I think I understand."

Aoife grinned. "Of course you do. You are Gifted."

"How much time has passed in my world?"

"Any answer would be a mere guess."

"Will I ever see you again?"

"I am always with you, Edward. I am a part of you." She placed a hand over her heart, then over mine.

"Do you know how to break Emrys's curse?"

Aoife shook her head. "The places in your vision hold the answers you seek. Go to the hall where great men live eternal, carrying with you the sword of Godwin, and there all will become clear."

"I must go to the Capital?"

"Yes. But I will be there with you, guiding you, as I always am."

"Is all of this real?"

"What do you think?"

"It feels real."

"Whether something is experienced within the mind, or without it, is irrelevant. You are in the Otherworld, therefore the Otherworld is real. I am real, just as you are real. Whether it is your mind, your body, or your soul that is here is not for me to say."

I smiled. "Gods, you're confusing."

Aoife laughed. "Go, Edward. Die, and be reborn."

Before I could say another word Aoife kissed me, let go of my hands, then pushed me. I had no chance to grab hold of anything

and my heart leapt out of my chest. As I fell back from the edge
of the river bank and into the ferocity of the watery tempest, time
seemed to slow. I looked up at Aoife and she looked down at me.
Her face wore a sorrowful smile.

But I felt no fear.

I trusted Aoife. Her indescribable beauty, backed by the starry
sky, was the last thing I saw before I was engulfed by the frigid,
thundering torrent. I was crushed, ripped to pieces, in almost an
instant. My lungs filled with water and were wrenched from
within me. I died. Edward of Winterhome, the Godspeaker of
Oldford, the Witch-Slayer, the Corpse-Whisperer, the Hero of
Tillysburg, was dead.

My companions waited a month above the dwarf-lord's cave.
After a few days they built some shelters out of turf and
branches, and William and Dughlas made snares for rabbits and
set up a fish trap further upriver.

They waited, listening to the endless raging of the River Aed
as it poured from between two wooded cliffs and out into the
calm countryside below. One month. The full moon waned,
slowly dying until it went dark, then waxed again and went full
once more. My friends decided they could wait no longer.

"It's hopeless," Dughlas said on the night of the full moon.
"As much as it pains me to think of it, he's gone. He's not
coming back."

"I agree," William said.

"One more day," said Matilda. "One more day. He will return tomorrow, you will see."

"You've been saying that for the past fortnight, my lady," Dughlas said.

"Please, just give him one more day."

"Alright, we'll give him one more day. But trust me, Tilly, he's lost."

Matilda sobbed. "Thank you," she said. She sat by the fire staring out over the cliff, awaiting some sign. A light, or a call, just *something* from the cave below them.

"He lost the root," Philip said. He was in a grim mood — they all were. "He will be in there, and will not be back for hundreds or even thousands of years. Edward admitted to me the night before he went down the cliff that he was terrified that he would not be able to resist the flow of the Otherworld's time. Even Godspeakers cannot resist it fully. We should have stopped him."

Matilda turned to him, her face wet with tears. "Do not say that! He is not dead. He is not trapped. He will be back tomorrow."

"You loved him, didn't you?" Thorry asked.

Matilda turned to him and nodded. "I *do* love him. Oh Gods, oh Gods, I wish I had told him sooner."

"You could not know this would happen," William said.

"I should have. I failed him."

"Tilly," Dughlas said. "If anyone failed Edward, it was definitely not you. Gods, you were his light. Whenever he was afraid, or angry, or hopeless, he would always think of you. That would give him the strength to get him through whatever he needed to."

"He told you that?"

Dughlas nodded. "He doesn't sleep much, and so sometimes we'll sit together in the early hours of the morning with a cup of ale and just talk. Do you know what he told me once, in Giant's Rest?"

Matilda wiped her eyes. "What did he tell you?"

"I don't know how much he's told you about the Battle of Tillysburg, but he nearly died that day duelling Lord Odo. He told me that if you hadn't given him that kiss before the fight, he'd have given up beneath the weight of Odo's hands," said Dughlas.

Matilda said nothing, but began to weep again. Dughlas sighed and a tear fell down his cheek.

"I saw Edward fight that day," William said. He then laughed. "He nearly killed me! He fought like a true warrior then."

"I wish I could've seen it," said Dughlas.

The men chatted for a while longer but Matilda stayed sitting by the cliff's edge, sobbing to herself. Philip lay on his bedroll staring up at the quiet moon. They let the fire die down on its own, and when it did, they all tried to go to sleep.

Matilda took the watch that night and did not wake the others to change shifts. She had not slept in three nights. She could barely even shut her eyes.

When morning came, Matilda stayed by the edge of the cliff and stared down at the river. She refused to eat the food Dughlas had made for her and instead just pulled it apart into tiny little pieces. No one spoke much that day.

"I don't suppose anyone knows how far it is to the nearest town," Thorry said, breaking the silence. "We can't stay out here forever. Does anybody know where exactly we are?"

"I know this place," Matilda said. "I know these woods."

"You do?" said Thorry.

Matilda pointed to the west. "If we keep going along that way we will come to a little track. Edward…"

"Edward?" Dughlas said.

Matilda began to sob again. "Edward and I followed that track from Henton, when I first met him."

Dughlas glanced at William, who only shrugged. "Alright. Tomorrow we'll leave, and take that road to Henton. We'll take you home."

"No!"

"No?"

"You cannot take me home. I forbid it. I refuse. Edward would keep me by his side. I need to be by his side." Matilda clenched her jaw and glared at them. There was fury in her burning eyes.

"Okay, my lady. You can stay with us. You're a free woman, after all. But we should go through Henton for supplies, then head back to Carol and—" He sighed. "And tell him the news."

The five companions stayed another night above Wilere's cave, and once again, Matilda begged and begged for them to stay one more night. Just one more. But the others refused. They needed to leave. They could not stay on the edge of a cliff in the wilderness forever.

The next morning, Dughlas found Matilda sitting on the edge of the cliff, watching the meadows below turn to gold as the light of the morning sun shone upon them. He sat beside her, and for a time they said nothing to one another while the others made ready to leave.

"He lives still," Matilda said. "I can feel it."

"That may be true," said Dughlas. She looked at Dughlas with teary eyes, and he took her hands in his. "But we cannot linger here forever."

"Have I failed him?"

"No. Edward would tell us that Fate weaves the threads of our lives. There was nothing you could have done, and there's nothing more you can do but follow the path she has set for you."

"I feel that without Edward I do not know that path."

"Ah, none of us know our destiny, milady — not even Edward. But when walking through darkness the best we can do is take the next step." He put a gentle hand on her shoulder. "You're young, you're a free woman, a lady; you've got a whole future before you. Do you want to be the hero of your own story?"

Matilda took a deep breath, then sighed. "I know I cannot stay here, it is just hard to leave."

"I know. I loved him too."

Matilda nodded. "I think I am ready."

Dughlas smiled and stood before helping Matilda to her feet. "To Henton then, my lady, and our fates."

They abandoned their makeshift shelters and travelled along the edge of the cliff for a few days, though conversation was minimal. William, as usual, tried to cheer up the group as they went, telling the occasional joke or singing the odd song, but none of this succeeded in lifting the others' spirits.

The cliff grew lower as they travelled westwards, or perhaps the ground beneath it rose. Eventually it disappeared altogether and they travelled level with the countryside to the south. Around noon they reached the path Matilda had spoken about. They had to stop the horses when they arrived, for Matilda was weeping.

She mumbled about the last time she had taken that path, and how she could not bear to travel along it, but Dughlas told her they would leave her if she did not follow. William reassured her that she was strong and that the courage she needed to continue on resided in her heart. After a while, Matilda clicked and urged her horse on.

They travelled north through the woods for the rest of the day, camped at night, then at dawn continued their journey. Dughlas was eager to reach Henton because deep down he hoped to part with Matilda there. He cared for her, and would be sorry to leave her behind, but he felt that with them the path before her would be filled with nought but misery and death. The best place for her was at home.

They arrived in Henton at nightfall.

"I will take you to my father's hall," Matilda said. Her voice was choked.

"Lead the way, then," William said.

Matilda brought the others through the village to Earl Harold's hall. It was a poor place and the buildings were all in disrepair in one way or another. At night it seemed an eerie little town surrounded by the vast woodland.

The group came to a misshapen palisade. The man standing guard was surprised to see Lady Matilda had returned. He bid her welcome and the five of them carried on into Harold's courtyard. They dismounted and stood before the hall. It was two storeys, old, and a dim light emanated from an upstairs window. The rest of the house was dark, and it seemed everyone was asleep.

The gate guard took the horses to the stable to rest and have some food, and Matilda slowly made her way to the door. The others stood back, thinking it best that Matilda met her family first. She knocked lightly on the door and waited. When there seemed to be no response she knocked again, harder this time.

"Hello?" she called. They all looked up at the window to see the light move, grow fainter, then disappear. A few moments later the big oak door creaked open and the face of a young woman appeared. She was the spitting image of Matilda. Her eyes went wide, and the woman ran out and embraced Matilda. She was her sister, after all.

"Alia," Matilda said. Her voice cracked.

"Matilda, by the Gods, I did not know you were coming," Alia said. "We have missed you."

Matilda pulled away from the hug then gestured to the others. "These are my friends. We have come a long way and have not seen a bed in weeks."

"Of course you can stay here, I will let Ma and Da know," Alia said. She pulled the door open wider and smiled at the others. "Gunn is in Oldford, but never mind that. Is the Godspeaker with you? Edward?"

Tears formed in Matilda's eyes and she shook her head. Alia frowned. "He—" Matilda began.

"He's with the elves, My Lady," Dughlas said. "Edward was too good for this world, so now he's in the Other."

Alia's jaw dropped and for a second seemed struck by a sudden cold, but then she retained her composure and stood firm. She looked a lot like Matilda in that moment, with the same fortitude. She took her sister in her arms, and Matilda wept. A few tears fell down Alia's face as well, but she stayed strong for her sister so she could grieve.

For me, a man who had died.

And in dying had been reborn.

All that I did not learn until much later, when Dughlas told me the tale. In the meantime, however, I was on my own little adventure.

I remember waking up on a pile of hay in some peasant's shack, by a warm oven, to the sound of children chattering and the scent of stew brewing. My clothes, weapons, and other gear were sitting beside me, and I was wrapped in hides and dressed in some holey burlap tunic and ragged trousers. I sat up and groaned. Pain shot through my body and throbbed in my chest.

"Just bruised a bit, lord; it'll heal," said a man. I turned to see sitting across from me a bearded, middle-aged man on a stool drinking a mug of ale. "Drink this. You'll need it, I imagine."

I propped myself up against the wall behind me, grimaced, then took the man's mug. I took a big swig of his drink and downed the whole thing, then coughed. The man laughed. "Tastes like dog's piss," he said. "Not that I'd know, mind."

I managed to force a chuckle and handed the man his now empty mug. "Where am I?"

"Willosted. I'm Red, and this is me house. Ain't much, but it keeps the wife and sons warm."

"How did I...?"

"You washed up on the bank earlier this evening. Me and Wyn thumped the water out've you and I brought you back here to dry you off and ask: where in the Heavens have you come from?"

I groaned and tried to remember. It was all coming back to me now. Emrys, Carol, Matilda, Wilere. My journey through the Otherworld. My death. *I died.* "My boat was wrecked on the rapids up the Aed," I lied.

Red's eyes widened. "Gods, you must've been chewed up and spat out by the cliffs. Not many survive that, but we get one or two every few years. You kept mumbling 'eefa' when we fished you out the river. What does that mean?"

"Aoife," I said. I looked around the room. It was a truly pitiful place, but it was cosy. "How far is it to the falls?"

"Must be about a half-day or so if you follow the bank."

I nodded. Red offered to bring me more drink if I promised to tell him who I was. He brought more of his disgusting, sour ale — of which I downed several mugs — and served me some of the stew his wife had cooked while I told him lies about how I ended up in his river. I did not tell him I was a Godspeaker, for many superstitious peasant folk feared people like me, but he could tell by my sword that I was no ordinary man.

I lied, saying I was one of Lord Edric of Beglen's housecarls and had travelled downriver with a message and gifts for Lord Adalbert. I told him that I needed to get back to the falls to see if I could find the items I was meant to deliver, but if not I would simply return home.

He seemed to believe the story well enough. He began telling me of his life and how he and his friend Wyn worked tilling the soil for the local thane, but made a little money on the side scavenging things that floated downriver from the boats that wrecked at the rapids. He talked about his four sons, of whom he was most proud, and his lovely wife.

I admit, I was not very interested. Instead I was lost deep in thought, wondering about what had happened, and why. I was confused, bewildered, and somewhat awed. I knew I could ask those questions another time, however. All that mattered then was returning to my friends and to Emrys with the hope that we could break his curse.

Wilere had told me the curse came in the form of a riddle, but to that riddle I had no answer. *Should the grey dog dismount, or should you wear your crown once more, this curse shall be broken.* I knew that the answer to that riddle would be what broke the spell.

I would not find my friends on the cliff above the cave, however. I spent the night in Red's little house, and the next day he gave me some porridge for breakfast and a few coppers for the road, which I refused, as well as a loaf of bread his wife had baked.

"Thank you, Red. Good deeds are always rewarded by good fortune, one way or another. I won't forget this kindness. You saved my life," I said.

"Bah, it's nothing. Stay safe, lord, and remember: you'll always have a friend in Willosted."

I headed off north, following the bank of the Aed as Red had instructed. I could see the high cliffs and the woods atop them in the distance, so I marched as fast as my aching legs would take me. I still had not recovered fully from my experience and had to stop several times to vomit. There was a funny taste in my mouth too that I could not seem to wash out.

I wondered how much time had truly passed in this world. I was too afraid to ask Red, but the fact he understood who Lord Edric and Adalbert were meant there was some hope. It was not much, but it kept me going.

I reached the cliff face by nightfall and decided it would be best to climb the next day. A rope hung over the cliff above the falls where I had climbed down, which filled me with even more hope. I fell asleep under a little outcrop that night, staring at the now waning moon illuminating the sky.

The next day I followed the little path along the cliff face up to the ledge outside Wilere's cave. A shiver ran down my spine as I stared into the darkness. Something was calling me back inside, I felt. I did not enter. I called up to my friends, shouting their names, but received no answer.

I took hold of the rope that dangled down in front of the cave, gave it a few hard tugs to make sure it would still hold fast, and began the climb up the rock face. It was much, much harder than the climb down, but by afternoon I made it. I found the remnants of a fire, but my friends were nowhere to be found. My heart sank. They had abandoned me. Or had I abandoned them?

I lit a fire in the remains of what I assumed was one built by my friends and made myself comfortable in one of the turf shelters. It was then, in the light of that fire, that I noticed something odd about a nearby pine. Something was carved into it. I took a closer look and saw one word.

Henton.

Below it, an arrow pointed west. I had not been abandoned after all.

And so, I travelled westwards along the cliff as my friends had done only a day beforehand, though I did not know that yet. My journey was slow and it took me longer than it usually would.

It took me eight days to reach the path Matilda and I had taken on our way to Oldford all those months ago. Once I reached that path, it took me a further six days to travel north through the woods. I ate berries, mushrooms, and roots, as well as bits of Red's wife's bread that I had rationed for myself. Eventually, however, I made it to Henton.

I was in a sorry state by that point. I was hungry, tired, and weak. I felt like death, but at the same time felt like a new man. I knew I could not die out in the wilderness around Henton. The desire to see my friends once more drove me on. I only hoped I had not been in the Otherworld for too long.

Fortunately, my Gift was more powerful than I realised. A whole century should have passed for someone subject to the full force of the Otherworld's time differences, but after I lost my root I only missed a month in Ardonn. Only a month. I thanked the Gods for bestowing that blessing upon me.

I found that out once I arrived in Henton, along with the tale of my companions' journey there. I limped through the village the evening I arrived, came to the palisade, and argued with the gate guard. I did not reveal my identity, and despite the laws of hospitality he did not want to let in such a disgraceful-looking vagabond.

Soon enough, though, the door to the earl's hall swung open and William emerged.

"What's going on out here?" he demanded.

The guard turned to face him, and pointed at me. "This wanderer here wants a roof," he said.

William looked back inside. "Lady Eloise, there is a beggar here in need of shelter." He looked back to the guard. "The lady says to let him—by all the Gods in all the Heavens, Edward!"

At that Dughlas appeared in the doorway. He paused, then charged and tackled me to the ground, his arms wrapped tight around me. He was grinning, and tears fell down his face. "We thought you were dead." He kissed me, then fell back and laughed at the sky.

Dughlas helped me to my feet and we embraced once more. "So did I," I said.

"What happened?" William asked. "You have to tell us. Did you find the dwarf?"

"I found the dwarf." I frowned. "I am afraid he was of little help."

Dughlas shook his head. "Doesn't matter. Don't care. Emrys and his curse can go to the Pits. Gods, I'm just happy you're alive."

I smiled and felt a happiness I had not felt in what seemed like forever. It had been a hard journey, and relief finally washed over me. I was safe.

Or so I thought. For then, in the doorway, appeared Earl Harold. He stormed out, flanked by four armed warriors, and the five of them made their way towards me. They drew their swords and I drew mine. William stepped back, his hands raised, while Dughlas pulled his sword from its scabbard and stepped in front of me.

Harold stood before him, a head taller, and the two glared at each other. Then Harold looked to me. "Will you surrender peacefully, Godspeaker, and face justice? Or must I cut down this man of yours?"

"You can try," said Dughlas.

I hesitated, then threw my blade to the ground. "Stand down, Dughlas. This is not your fight."

Dughlas glanced over his shoulder. He nodded, sheathed his sword, and stood aside. Two of Harold's men came and took me by the arms, while another picked up my sword. The earl glared into my eyes.

"You are under arrest, Edward of Oldford, for kidnapping and horse-theft. You went against my word, and here in Henton, my word is law."

So it was. There was no fight left in me, and I did not want my friends to die here. It was time for me to face justice in Henton at last.

7

Race

"I should have you killed," Harold barked.

He glared down at me from his high chair. I knelt before him, my wrists bound, with two housecarls standing behind me. News had swiftly reached Matilda of my arrival, and she had come to kneel beside me. She was in nowhere near as much trouble as I was, and had already had her scolding long before I arrived.

I feared I would receive more than stern words, however.

"You spat on the hospitality I so generously offered to you, ignored my wishes, and stole my daughter." Harold looked up at the priest who stood at his side. "What is the punishment for such a crime?"

"Certainly death, Earl Harold," said the priest. Although he was blind, he appeared to be staring straight at me.

"Death," Harold repeated. "If my daughter — *daughters* —

were not so fond of you, Corpse-Whisperer, you would be dangling from a tree this very moment."

"Father, please—" Matilda began.

"You be quiet." Harold stood and marched over to me. He glared down at my face, a wild fury in his eyes. I could tell he had been long awaiting this moment.

Present were me, Matilda, Harold, the priest, and the two guards. The others had been treated well and granted hospitality on account of them being Matilda's companions, though William had to conceal his identity.

I said nothing to Harold. I was starving, thirsty, tired, and weak. I was also proud and could not bear this humiliation.

"I see you have nothing to say for yourself. Tell me why I should not hang you?"

I stared down at the floor.

"Because he is a far greater man than you could ever hope to be," Matilda snapped.

Harold frowned at her. "How dare you speak to me that way?"

"How dare you treat your own daughter in this way? You speak to me as though I am a *thing* with no will of my own. I wanted to go with Edward, and every day I thank Hefenstea that I did. If you want to hang Edward, go ahead, but hang me too."

Harold's mouth hung open. He did not know what to say, and I suspected Matilda had never spoken back to him like that. When I first met her she was a shy and obedient young lady, but her time away from home had made her bold.

"Earl Harold," I said. I looked up at him. "There is far more at stake here than this. The warlord Emrys from legend has returned, and if I do not return to him he threatens to destroy Ardonn."

"Emrys has already marched," he said.

"What?"

Harold went to sit back in his chair and sighed. "I have had men watching his camp not far to the north of here. This morning my scout returned with news that Emrys was preparing to march. He has likely already left."

My heart dropped. I was too late. "Then let me go — I can stop him."

"How?"

"He had me seek a cure to his curse. If I could do that, he would cease his war effort."

"And have you? Found a cure?"

"I have my suspicions, but I am not certain."

Harold closed his eyes and rubbed his temple. I glanced at Matilda, and she half smiled at me. "I sense you love him, Matilda," said Harold.

Matilda nodded. "I do, and thus I shall go where Edward goes. If that is to the grave then so be it."

Harold sighed. "Very well. You and your friends may stay this night, but I expect you gone tomorrow. And I want your oath, Edward Godspeaker. Swear to me that no harm shall come to my daughter so long as she is by your side."

"I swear it, Earl Harold, by all the Gods in all the Heavens. Matilda will be safe with me."

"Good. Cut his binds."

At that, Harold stood and headed for the door. One of the guards took my wrists and cut the ropes around them. I rubbed the marks where the ropes had burned my skin. Harold left the hall, followed by the priest and his warriors.

Once we were alone, Matilda threw her arms around me and sobbed into my shoulder. I hugged her back and the two of us sat there for a while in silence.

"You need a wash," she said at last. She pulled away and grinned.

"I also need to trim my beard."

Matilda ran her fingers through it. "I like it."

"I don't."

Matilda laughed. Her eyes were wet and puffy, and her cheeks red, but she was happy and I could not help but smile.

She was right; I did need a wash. But more than that I needed food. I had not eaten properly in days. Matilda and I went to the kitchen, where she cooked me a delicious rabbit stew with a side of bread and cheese, and poured us both a cup of warm wine. It was then that the others came to see me, and we greeted each other properly. Even Thorry had a tear in his eye.

Dughlas caught me up with everything that had happened. Emrys had indeed marched, and Everlynn was still besieged by Stephan, though rumours told that Odo's supplies were running dangerously low. Emrys would definitely be going there to relieve his ally, which meant we had two options: find Emrys and hope I could figure out a solution to Wilere's riddle, or race to warn Stephan of the coming threat. True, Stephan was a false king, but it was better he win the war than Emrys or Odo.

After I had eaten, Matilda prepared me a bath, then left me alone to wash. The water was steaming hot and seemed to burn away all the tension and pain within me. I just sat there for a time, engulfed by the scalding water, and let my mind drift away.

My rest was interrupted, however, by the Earl of Henton's eldest daughter.

"It is good to see you again, Edward," she said.

I opened my eyes and looked up to find her standing in the doorway. Her black hair fell loose over her shoulders and she stared at me with those deep blue eyes, so much like Matilda's.

"And you, Alia," I said.

She closed the door behind her, pulled up a chair, and sat beside the bath. "I wanted to thank you."

"For what?"

"For what you have done for Matilda. She has told me all about your adventure together, and I can see how much she has changed. She is becoming a brave young woman."

"I cannot take too much credit. Matilda has saved my life a few times."

Alia smiled. "I know. Do you want to know a secret?"

I nodded.

"When Gunn was sent to hunt you down, there were times when he would deliberately stall Merewald and his men, or lead them astray. He wanted to give you two time to get away, because deep down he knew you were simply giving Matilda what she always desired."

I grinned, but then that grin became a frown. "Where is Gunn?"

Alia sighed. "Oldford, with a dozen of my father's finest warriors. Lord Adalbert is assembling an army."

"Gods, why?"

"Security, he says. He refuses to take a side in this damned war, but whether he likes it or not war will come south. Soon enough, Henton's boys will be chopping more than lumber." Alia leaned forward, fear in her eyes. "Edward, what do the Gods tell you? Will war reach us here?"

I took Alia's cold, thin hand in mine. "Forgive me, my lady. I do not know."

She sighed. Before another word could be said, the door swung open and standing there, a pile of folded clothes under her arm, was Matilda. She clenched her jaw and her eyes went wide. Alia pulled her hand away from mine and bowed her head.

Matilda cleared her throat. "Edward, I thought you would like some fresh clothes."

"Thank you, Matilda," I said. I gave her a smile. "Just put them down on the table there."

She did as I asked and then stared blankly at her sister. "Why are you here?"

"Edward and I were merely talking, that is all. Custom dictates an earl's daughter should greet his guests," Alia said. She stood, curtsied to me, then headed for the door.

"I do hope you were not greeting him as you did the last time he was here."

Alia said nothing and left the room.

"We were just talking," I said. "Your sister was telling me about Gunn."

"I hoped I would get to see him," Matilda said. She came over to the bath and knelt behind me, picked up a rag and dipped it into the water. She wrung it and began rubbing it slowly along my arms.

"I'm sure you will see him again someday soon," I said.

Matilda nodded. "What is our next move?"

I admit, I did not know. At first I thought I would return to Emrys's camp and hopefully prevent the warlord from devastating Ardonn, yet now that Emrys was on the march things were a lot more uncertain.

Even if Emrys regained his mortality and abandoned the war for Ardonn's throne, would that stop Lord Edric and the rest of Emrys's horde? Would it stop Odo? The struggle was no longer merely about Emrys. He was simply the spark, but the blaze was already raging.

"We will go to Stephan," I said.

"Stephan?"

"He needs to be warned. His men will be tired and weak from the siege, and will not be able to stand against Emrys and Edric's combined forces, especially if they catch him off guard."

Matilda ran the rag across my collarbone. I could feel her breath against the back of my neck. "So we are on Stephan's side now?"

"Stephan may be a usurper's bastard, but he fights for Ardonn. As do I."

"I understand. I will tell the others we leave at first light, but you need to rest and regain your strength," she said. She let the cloth fall into the water and began massaging my shoulders. "You have grown thin."

"I know."

"I will prepare us plenty of food for the road."

I sighed. "Thank you, Matilda. I owe you a great deal."

She shook her head, then gestured for me to sit back. I did so, and she continued to massage my neck and arms. "I knew you would come back. The others did not listen, but I knew. I knew."

"I did say I would return, did I not?"

Matilda nodded. "You did. I believed you. I love you, Edward."

I said nothing. She kissed the back of my head and I let her continue in silence as I slumped against the edge of the bath and let my mind wander.

She was right. I needed to rest, so rest I did.

And at dawn, we began our race against the Immortal Horde.

It would be just over a week-long journey to Everlynn, if we were lucky. We would follow the track through the woods westward, then north-west across country to Everlynn forest. Once there, the plan was to follow the edge of the forest till we arrived at Everlynn. Emrys and Edric had a day ahead of us, and to make things worse for us their journey would cover less woodland. We had to hurry.

We did have one advantage, however. We were few in number and travelled light, whereas Emrys and Edric's horde would be moving slowly, weighed down by all their supplies. There was a chance we could outpace them, but even if we did Stephan would have little time to withdraw from his siege. Would he even listen to our warning?

The dirt road we followed through the woods was the same that had led me to Henton the winter past, where I first met Matilda and her family. It looked different now that the skies were clear and the snows were gone, though we had little time to admire the surrounding forest.

We loaded the horses and headed off just as the first rays of light peered over the treetops. We rode as fast as the trees would let us, which was nowhere near as fast as I would have liked. Since we only had five horses Matilda and Philip shared a saddle, which also slowed us somewhat.

"If we keep this pace we will make it," I told them. "But only just." I could see that Matilda suffered worst of all, but she wore a hard face and did not falter. I was proud of her.

We reached the edge of the woods on the evening of the third day and made camp within a grove of beautiful oaks. The ground beneath the trees in this part of the wood had been cleared of all trees and shrubbery, so that only the oaks and the grass remained. It was likely local folk used this place for lumber, but left the oaks standing, for those sacred trees are revered in Ardonn and the peasants have a superstition about felling them.

As the others set up camp in the fading light, I sat with my back against a tree looking out over the countryside to the west. Rich meadows and fields of wheat and barley stretched for miles across the gentle landscape where cattle and sheep grazed and a handful of peasants made use of the last few moments of the day.

Smoke was rising up behind a hill from the chimneys of a village a few miles away, but I did not want to stop there that night lest someone bring news of our passing to our enemies. The folk here were likely loyal to Lord Edric and I was wary of encountering a spy. We would be safer camped beneath the trees.

"The land here seems peaceful," Dughlas said. He came to sit down beside me. "Perhaps that's a good sign."

I nodded. "Perhaps. We cannot know what lies beneath the surface, however."

"Indeed. I've been praying we don't bump into Emrys and his horde."

"We wouldn't this far south, but as we head north that is a possibility."

Dughlas said nothing for a moment, then let out a chuckle. "I just realised; if we head north-west we'll reach the edge of the Mirelands. You remember Mudhill? What a bitch of a fight that was."

I smiled. "If only we could have gone with Cubert, to a better place than this."

Dughlas nodded, then frowned. "Did Ward ever tell you what was in that box?"

"No, but I think about it often. He said it would change my life — but how?"

"Maybe it's got something to do with your father. Ward did say he knew him, after all," Dughlas said. He shrugged. "After this war, we should—"

"I am not going back."

"Not even for Edith?"

I looked at him, and he looked back at me. "Edith doesn't need me," I said.

He nodded and stared back out over the fields. We sat there for a while in silence until the last bit of light was consumed by darkness. We joined the others around the small fire, but we spoke little. We were tired, and worried for what we might face in the coming days.

I feared I was bringing my friends to their doom, but most of all feared the one prophecy that had not yet come to pass — the dream I received during Winterlow in which Matilda's face and hands were dripping with blood.

We set off before dawn the next day. We left the road behind and headed north-west across the fields and paddocks. There was no doubt that folk saw us, but as long as we did not speak with them they would not know who we were or where we went. As far as they knew, we were merely warriors going to war.

We encountered no trouble on the first day out of the woods. The land was peaceful, the sky clear, and the air warm. We rode with some haste, but I did not want the locals to notice we were in a hurry in case we raised suspicions.

The second day, however, was when we first saw them. It began with a glimpse of a lone horseman who appeared for a moment atop a hill to the east, before swiftly disappearing behind it. William noticed him again an hour or so later, but I told the others to keep riding as normal and pretend we had not seen them.

Then, late that afternoon, we spied two of them. They were partly concealed by the trees of a small patch of woodland, but Dughlas's keen eye spotted them. I was certain now that we were being followed.

"See those trees over there?" I pointed westwards to a copse standing in the middle of a wide meadow. "We will camp there tonight. No fires."

"Will that help us lose them?" Thorry asked.

"Probably not," Dughlas said.

I shook my head. "They'll find us again tomorrow, but at least the trees might conceal us for the night. They won't go searching for us in the dark if they cannot see us from afar."

"They are Emrys's men," William said. "I remember the way they looked at Tillysburg."

"They are," I admitted. I did not want to say so for fear it would make it true, but there could be no denying it.

"That is a good sign, then," Philip said.

"Good?"

"Yes. If they are following us from the east, would that not mean Emrys's horde is behind us?"

I smiled. "Clever boy. But how far behind, I wonder?" A hawk circled overhead a few times, then flew towards the copse. An omen. "Let's go."

We rode for the trees, making certain we were not seen. There was still plenty of light in the day, but I did not want to waste the opportunity to make that copse our hiding place. It was perfect, and we may not have had a better chance had we kept going.

We tied the horses deep among the oaks when we arrived and set up camp. This place had been left to grow wild and untamed, so we were well concealed by the shrubbery and low branches of the trees. The hawk I saw earlier was perched on a branch above us, watching with curiosity at the people who had come to its home. I waved up at the bird.

"Have you seen the men who tail us?" I asked. The bird only stared back.

"Who are you talking to?" Thorry asked.

"Edward can speak the language of birds," Matilda said as she lay out her bedroll. "Leave them be."

Thorry's jaw just dropped and the hawk tilted its head to look at him. I asked again if it had seen the men, and she told me she had. There were six of them in total, and were indeed scouting for the army that followed about a day behind them. The hawk thought we were another scouting party at first, but when I assured her we were not, she was willing to tell me what she knew.

The bird had seen Emrys and Edric's army. It was moving fast. It did not stop to pillage or raid, or even to demand tribute from local settlements, and as it moved westwards it was joined by earls I supposed were loyal to Edric. The hawk guessed the horde numbered a total of around four thousand men, with half of those being on horseback. A truly formidable force.

I also asked if she had news of the siege at Everlynn, but she had only heard whispers. There were rumours that Odo's people were starving, and despite the numerous offers for peace by Stephan, Odo would not give up his city. A wave of dysentery had supposedly washed through both the city's defenders and Stephan's army, and both sides were tired of the affair.

Some birds the hawk had spoken to, however, believed King Stephan was only days away from victory.

I had us take turns keeping watch throughout the night, and fortunately we had no trouble. Matilda thought she heard hoofbeats in the distance during her shift, but also said she could have been imagining it. We were all on edge that night.

We departed the next morning while it was still dark with the hopes that we could put some distance between us and the men following before they awoke, but I should have known that would be futile. I held on to the hope that we were followed by mortal men, for Emrys's men did not need sleep, but as the first rays of light crept over the hills the men were once again on our tail.

"We keep moving as normal," I told the others. "Scouts are like wild dogs. If they sense fear or weakness, it will ignite a bloodlust within them."

"How many did you say there were?" Dughlas asked. "Six? I say we turn and fight them."

"Or we could talk with them, convince them we are not their enemy," William said.

I shook my head. "I fear the only reason they have not attacked is because of our number. If we talk with them they will know we have a woman and child. Thorry could pass as a warrior, but those two cannot."

"I am not a child!" Philip retorted.

I grinned. "You want to do mounted combat with ancient immortal horsemen?"

He said nothing to that.

"They will already suspect that Philip is a child," said William. "Lurians are a small people even when grown."

Philip only glared.

"A suspicion is not a certainty," I said. I glanced behind us and caught a flash of sunlight reflecting off a helmet behind a low ridge in the distance, which disappeared almost as soon as I saw it. I then gazed off westward, seeing far in the distance the vast stretch of woodland that was Everlynn forest.

My heart dropped. "I know why they have not attacked us."

"Why?" Dughlas asked.

I pointed to the distant treeline. "They're waiting for us to reach the forest. It will be much easier to ambush us there than in open country."

Dughlas sighed, and Matilda's face went pale beneath her helmet. "No honour," she mumbled.

"I imagine you would lose all sense of honour if you were trapped within a tomb for three centuries," I replied. I pulled my horse to a stop. "I will go speak to them."

"Alone?"

"No. Dughlas, you'll come with me. The rest of you ride on. We will catch up."

Matilda moved her horse over to mine and reached for my hand. "Gods be with you, Edward. Come back to us."

"We'll be back, Tilly," Dughlas said. "The two of us can handle a few dusty old men."

I smiled, then Dughlas and I turned eastward. The others carried on while we kicked our horses and rode for the ridge in the east. We reached the ridge and stood atop it, scanning the surrounding countryside. I wore my helmet's faceplate closed in case our enemy recognised me, but Dughlas wore no helmet and his vision was keener than mine, despite his single eye.

"There," he said, pointing to a patch of oaks in the field below.

I saw a lone horseman there watching us from beneath the trees. I removed my glove and waved it above my head as a show of peace, then the man disappeared deeper into the copse.

A few moments later he emerged with six others. They rode out into the field, then stood side by side atop their horses. Dughlas and I rode down to meet them. I was nervous, but their acceptance of our offer to talk was a hopeful sign.

We stopped several yards away from them, out of the reach of their spears. I could see them in their full glory now — shining coats of mail and polished steel helmets, with rich woollen cloaks draped over their shoulders. They wore gold and silver around their necks and arms, and sat atop the finest warhorses, while the sharp iron tips of their spears glinted in the sunlight. One of the horsemen, I noticed, wore a cloak of deep red.

"Greetings," I said in the ancient tongue. I bowed my head, and one of the horsemen bowed his. His horse took a step forward. "Why do you follow us?" I asked.

The man removed his helmet to reveal his fearsome face. His loose, red hair fell down his back and his long beard was tied into a single thick braid. His piercing blue eyes observed both Dughlas and me in turn. Then he smiled, showing a menacing set of teeth sharpened into points. "We are curious as to where you wander," he said. His voice was deep and hoarse.

"Why does Lord King Emrys wish to know where we wander?" I replied.

There was a flicker of amusement in his eye. "All armies need scouts. We are merely working to ensure we are not ambushed."

"You do not look like scouts."

"You are a clever one. No, we are among our lord's finest warriors, sent to find any who would report our horde's movement to the enemy."

"And what do you do with those you find?"

The man drew his sword and held it in front of his face. The cold steel blade was stained with blood. The horseman grinned.

"What is he saying?" Dughlas whispered.

I held up a hand to him, then turned back to the horseman. "May we know your names?"

"My name is Idris, and I was once lord of the mighty Eiradin. Even today your poets sing songs of my renown. These are my men," said the horseman.

My heart skipped a beat. *Idris of Eiradin.* There is not a child of Winterhome who has not heard of Idris and his ancient deeds, for Eiradin is what that city once was called. I had known him only as a legend lost to time and never imagined I would one day face him. He was there, living and breathing no more than a spear's distance away from me. He was not a man one would wish to anger.

"I have heard of your glory, Lord Idris," I said. Dughlas raised his eyebrows when he heard that name. I gestured to the man with the red cloak. "This is one of Edric's men, is he not?"

Idris nodded, and gestured for him to come forward. He did, and like Idris removed his helmet. "I am Godwald of Beglen, youngest son of Lord Edric," he said in our own tongue.

The man was young — almost a boy, in fact — perhaps no older than sixteen. He wore a wispy attempt at a moustache, had a thin face, and wide, nervous eyes.

"Edric insisted he come with us so he could have a taste for killing before the real fight," said Idris. "He does not speak our tongue, nor do we speak yours, so he has not been much use. Now tell me, warrior, where do you and your companions ride to?"

"We seek your king," I lied.

"You are travelling the wrong way."

"I thought so, but the others would not listen. Point us in the right direction and we shall leave you be."

Idris let out a friendly chuckle and shook his head. "You can be honest with me. You need not fear, for I do not feel you are enemies."

"What's going on?" Dughlas hissed.

Godwald drew his sword and kicked his horse forward. He glared at me, but his eyes revealed fear. "He is going to kill you no matter what," Godwald said in Ardish. "Act like I am threatening you, and flee."

I did not need to think twice, and nor did Dughlas. He snarled, while I drew my sword and pointed it at Godwald. Idris looked amused. "You stupid, ugly bastard!" I yelled at the boy, baring my teeth. "Your mother was a whore and your sister lay with dogs. Thank you for your warning."

We turned our horses and rode for our lives. I kicked mine so hard it almost stumbled. Idris yelled something in his own tongue, and almost as soon as we sped off we heard the thunder of hoofbeats behind us. They shouted and jeered, barking like hungry dogs.

We made for the ridge. Dughlas turned in his saddle and loosed an arrow, but I did not need to turn to see if it found its mark. Almost as soon as the bowstring snapped I heard a man cry out in shock before tumbling from his horse. "By all the Gods, I'll never make a shot like that again in my life," laughed Dughlas.

"Please do!" I shouted.

We did not stop when we reached the top of the ridge. Our companions were in the distance, but when they heard shouts they stopped and turned. Thorry and Matilda kicked their horses and raced off westwards. William, however, drew his sword and tore in our direction. Dughlas turned and loosed another arrow, but missed.

"Spare the boy in red!" I shouted as William drew near. "Slay the rest!"

The hoofbeats were so close their rumbling was deafening. I reared my horse and turned just in time to deflect the thrust of a spear with my blade. Its wielder raced past me, the air almost blowing me from my saddle.

"For Everlynn, and all Ardonn!" William cried. He rushed past a horseman whose spear only just scraped William's arm, but who in seconds had his head cut clean off. William laughed and reared his horse, then charged to face another while the man he killed slid from his saddle and crumbled into dust. His spear buried itself in the earth.

I turned my horse to the sound of a high-pitched yell, and parried the blade that came at me. Godwald. He swung again, and I blocked. "I am going to lunge!" he shouted.

As promised, Godwald thrust his sword at my gut. I parried that, knocking his blade aside and raising my fist to his face. His head snapped back and his horse reared, throwing him from the saddle.

I pointed my blade down at him as he spat blood. "Stay down!" I yelled. He nodded, then lay groaning with his hand over his bloodied nose.

I took pause to assess the situation. Three horsemen were left. William was engaged in a fierce clash of steel with Idris, while Dughlas was being chased by the other two. I caught a glimpse of Thorry, Philip, and Matilda disappear behind a hill far away and held on to a small sliver of hope that even if the three of us were to die there, the others might escape.

But I was not ready to die. I kicked my horse and raced for the spear in the ground, sheathed my sword, then reached down and pulled it from the soil. I gripped the haft tight and tucked it under my arm.

"Dughlas!" I yelled. "Bring them to me."

He heard me, then drew his pursuers back to where we were. I kicked my horse and sped towards him, the spear cutting through the air. The horsemen came closer. Closer. One of them turned away when he noticed me, but the other was too late.

"Die!" I cried.

The next few moments rushed by in a blur. Dughlas sped past me, and not a second later a mighty shock pulsed through my arm and shoulder as the spear ripped through mail and flesh. There was an ungodly scream as the spear scraped bone and the force of the blow tore the spear from my hand. The horseman landed on his back with a thud and a brief, helpless yelp before time caught up with him.

I turned the horse and drew my sword, and then watched as another of Dughlas's arrows found its mark in the throat of the other man who had been pursuing him. He slumped forward in his saddle while the horse galloped away and over the ridge. Dughlas gave a cheer, then raced to aid William in his struggle against Idris. I went too, and soon the three of us had the warlord surrounded.

He turned his horse sharply to the right, then to the left, and snarled. I pointed my sword at him and Dughlas drew his bow. William, panting, gave me a nod.

"Sheath your blade," I ordered.

Idris glared at me, and for a moment I thought he was going to fight us to the death, but fortunately he saw sense. It would have been pitiful to die here after waiting centuries for life. He sheathed his sword and raised a hand.

"Victory favours you," he sighed. "Show me your face and reveal your name. I wish to know who it is that bested the mighty Lord of Eiradin."

I did as he asked and removed my helmet, tossing it to Dughlas.

Idris frowned, a look of familiarity in his eye. "Have we met before?"

"I am Edward Godspeaker, Heir of Godwin."

Idris raised his eyebrows and grinned. "Had I known that, I would not have fought you."

"Why?"

He leant forward. "Do you wish to know a secret? Our King Emrys fears you, Godspeaker. He does not admit it, but we all know it was you that had him fleeing the battle beneath the mountains. And if the legendary Emrys fears you, the rest of us would be fools if we did not also. I can see now that his fear is justified. But tell me, have you found a cure for our curse?"

I have," I lied. In truth I had no idea.

"What is it?"

"You would not believe me if I told you."

Idris laughed. "Very well. Will you kill me?"

I thought for a moment and glanced at my companions. They had not understood what was being said, but they seemed to understand the choice I was now making. I looked over at Godwald, who stumbled to his feet. "No, you can live. I do not wish to make an enemy out of Emrys. I only wish to make peace."

Idris put his hand to his heart and bowed his head. "I must admit I am grateful to you, Edward. I pray we do not meet on future battlefields."

"Your sword, Idris." I sheathed my blade and held out my hand. He hesitated, a flash of shame in his eye, but then did as I asked and unbuckled his belt. He handed his sword to me, sheath and all.

"Treat her well," he said. "That blade has never failed me. Until today."

I nodded and moved aside. We watched as he made his way over to Godwald and spat down at him, then continued on his way eastward without the boy. Godwald and I glanced at one another and I gave a slight nod. He picked up his sword and mounted his horse, then turned to follow Idris.

"Lord Idris!" I yelled. The horseman stopped and turned. "Tell your king that I ride to settle the siege at Everlynn. If he halts his army, I promise I shall cure him as soon as I am finished with Stephan."

Idris laughed. "I shall not be returning to Emrys, Godspeaker, for should he hear you bested me it would mean my death. Besides, I feel that with you as his enemy my lord is doomed. I go my own way now."

"Where will you go?"

He shrugged. "North, perhaps. I feel my beloved Eiradin calling to me."

I nodded and waved. He waved back, then carried on to disappear behind the ridge. Somehow I knew that was not the last I would see of Idris.

But before then, I had a task to complete. Everlynn awaited. The three of us galloped westward with a renewed fire in our hearts, our blood pumping with the rush of our victory.

We met the others that evening hiding among the trees at the edge of Everlynn forest. Matilda and I dismounted and ran to embrace each other, and she stood on her toes to kiss me. Her lips tasted like salt, of sweat and tears, but the kiss calmed my heart and soothed my mind. Even if only for a few moments, I had respite from the troubles of the world.

I wished we could stay out there in the woods, just the two of us, beneath the great ash we camped under, away from the chaos engulfing our land. I recalled the tale of King Edmund and Melisende, who spent their youth in those woods and there became lovers. I thought of the two young women I had met as a boy, who now dwell forever among the trees near my master's home. How I longed for a life like theirs.

But it was not to be. The following morning, we carried on westwards.

To Everlynn. To war.

8

Defeat

"Gods, that looks grim," said Dughlas.

We sat on our horses atop the hill overlooking Stephan's siege camp. Dughlas was right. The smell of smoke, faeces, and rotting corpses wafted on the air, and the earth was brown and muddied. There was not a sign of cheer in the camp. Men wandered around tired and slouched, wearing dirty, bloody armour and hopeless frowns.

The space between the camp and Everlynn's walls, where the soil had been churned up, was like a graveyard. Bodies lay strewn about, some half-buried, with their lifeless eyes staring up at the sky or their faces pressed into the mud. Arrows stuck out their bodies like pins or littered the ground around them. The ravens feasted, while a mangy dog was tugging at a corpse's leg.

Beneath the city wall was a wide trench that had been filled with wooden stakes, some of which had mangled, broken corpses impaled upon them. Above them, peering down at the camp with watchful eyes atop the city's ramparts, stood a few dozen warriors and bowmen. I spotted one keel over and vomit.

We had little time to take in the scene, though I hardly wanted it. Soon after we arrived at the hill behind the camp, a patrol intercepted us and demanded to know our names and business. I told them we needed to speak to Stephan, for I came with both a warning and the key to Everlynn's gates.

"I'm in no mood for joking," their leader growled.

"Nor am I. Who do you think this is?" I nodded at William, who sat on his horse beside me, emotionless.

"How the fuck should I know?"

"He is William of Everlynn, only son of Lord Odo."

The man raised his eyebrows, then glared at William. "I lost a brother to your men at Tillysburg."

"Believe me, I wish it could have been otherwise," said William. "I had no knowledge of my father's treason."

"Yet you're a traitor all the same. Fine. We'll take you to the king."

The patrol led us down the hill and through the camp. It was even more miserable up close, and we received a cold welcome. Men, weak and demoralised, stared at us with both pity and longing as we rode past. They must have been wondering who we were, and what news or hopes we would bring.

"Why are the men so broken?" I asked our escort.

He sighed. "They're sick of this siege. No man knows if he'll be among those to die in the next assault. Gods, I'm tired of the assaults. The king thinks we should just wait and starve them out, and I agree, but his advisors put a lot of pressure on him. 'One more assault,' they say. 'That should do it!' It never does it. King Stephan delays them for as long as he can, but he can't deny his advisors."

"When is the next assault?"

"Tomorrow. If we lose this one I doubt we'll have enough men to continue this siege. It'll all be in vain." The man shook his head.

"Can Stephan not bring more men?"

"He'd bring his son's men if Tidegate didn't need defending against those savages from the Almond Isles." He spat. "You hear that, William? Your whore's kinsmen have brought their little boats to Ardonn."

William clenched his jaw, but remained silent. So, Lord Odo was making use of *all* his allies. That was the first I had heard of the Maricari assaulting Ardonn's shores — at least, as more than mere raiders. If Odo could only hold out against Stephan for a few more days, his victory would be certain. No wonder he had not yet surrendered his city.

Soon enough we reached Stephan's tent, as far from the city walls as possible at the back of the camp. It was much larger than the others, made from the finest cloth. The patrol had us wait outside while he went in and spoke to Stephan. Two men of the Royal Guard stood at the door to the tent, their spears not quite vertical and their shoulders slumped.

After a few moments our escort emerged from the tent and informed us that Stephan was willing to see us, but to be aware that he was in a sour mood. The soldier took our weapons and led me and William inside, while the others waited outside.

Stephan sat hunched by a fire in a chair with a bearskin draped over it to give it the appearance of a throne. The man was only in his forties, but he appeared a lot older than he had when I saw him just over two years prior. His hair and beard, which had once been vibrantly brown, were now dull and bore streaks of grey. He was much thinner, too, and the lines on his forehead and around his eyes were deep. He wore a simple grey tunic and had wrapped himself in a thick woollen blanket.

"My man tells me you have something to say that I may wish to hear. This had better be worth my time," he grumbled, his eyes fixed on the fire. "I have little opportunity for rest these days."

"Lord King," I bowed. William bowed too. "I have both good news and terrible news."

"Tell it to me plainly." Stephan sighed, then sat up straight and stretched. He then looked up from the fire and his jaw dropped. "By the Gods, it is you."

"I am Edward of Oldford, yes, but that does not matter right now—"

"By rights I should arrange for you a date with the executioner, but indeed, I can deal with you later. And who is this?"

Before I could answer, William went down on one knee and bowed his head. "William of Everlynn, Lord King," he said.

That was enough to make Stephan stand. "The traitor's whelp. I trust you both have an excellent reason for being here."

"As we waste time here introducing ourselves, Emrys marches with Lord Edric and some thousands of men," I snapped. "Now unless you plan on taking Everlynn *tonight*, sit back down and listen."

There was an awkward silence in the tent at that, but I heard Dughlas chuckle outside. Stephan stared at me agape, then slowly slumped back down in his chair. He waved his hand.

"Should I summon your advisors, My King?" asked our escort.

Stephan shook his head. "No. Gods, no. I do not want them hearing of this conversation."

"Emrys was about a day's ride behind us several days ago, but whether that distance has shortened or lengthened since I cannot say," I said. "Of their number, around half are cavalry. They do not stop to plunder or demand tribute, and lords have been joining them along the way through fear, loyalty, or ambition."

"If this were true, why have my scouts not reported it?"

"How many of your scouts have returned?"

"None. They were instructed only to return with news."

"You must trust me. None of your scouts have returned because they have been slain by Idris, one of Emrys's dogs. A legend. We encountered him on the way here, along with Edric's son Godwald. If you want proof of that, I took his sword." I pointed to one of the blades our escort held and he pulled it from its sheath. The leaf-shaped blade was still stained with dry blood.

Stephan scratched his beard. "I admit, it does look like the weapons the horsemen used near Tillysburg. And this Idris told you that information?"

"No, it was revealed to me by a hawk."

The soldier stifled a laugh, and Stephan grinned. "You really expect me to believe that?"

"Come to your senses, you fool!" William barked. He stood, a menacing frown on his face. "The Gifted have abilities you could not even imagine. I would not believe it too had I not seen for myself the things Edward can do. If you scoff at this man, you scoff at the Gods."

Stephan rubbed his temple. "Do not speak to me that way again, William, especially in the position you are now. There are many in this camp who would take great pleasure in parting your head from your shoulders, and much more."

"I grow tired of this," I said. "Lord King, I have told you what I know. Do with that information what you will." I turned to leave, but Stephan stood.

"Wait, Edward, wait," he said. "Even if what you say is true, what am I to do? If I abandon Everlynn now, I will lose my kingdom."

"Abandon Everlynn? No. Occupy it," I said. "I have come here with a gift: Lord Odo's beloved and only son, and the key to your victory. *That* is why I have brought William here."

Stephan looked back and forth between us. "You wish to help me? Both of you?"

"If my father knows I am in your custody I have no doubt he will yield to you. There is nothing he cares for more than his lineage," William said.

"And should he refuse?"

"Then you can cut off William's head and toss it over the city's walls," I said.

William looked at me agape.

"Neither of you support my reign. What is your purpose for doing this?"

William regained his composure and looked back to Stephan. "We do it for Ardonn, Lord King, not for you."

Stephan sighed and stared into his fire. "As do we all. Very well, but if what you say is true, Edward, we must hurry. I want my men behind those walls before the wolves arrive."

"When will you parlay with Odo?" I asked.

"Now," Stephan stood and picked up his sword. "Alfhelm, bring the horn. Edward, William, come with me."

"My King, should I inform your advi—" the soldier began.

"To the Pits with the damned advisors! I will have Everlynn's gates opening for us before they can even squeak."

"They'll hear the horn, lord," said Alfhelm.

"Good."

Stephan marched from the tent with Alfhelm close behind,

and our weapons were returned to us. William gave me an uncertain glance, which I returned with a smile. I put my hand on his shoulder. "I would not do this if I thought it meant your death, my friend," I assured him.

He nodded, and we followed Stephan from the tent. The false king seemed to be filled with a renewed fire, a hope for victory, and his men seemed to feel that. As we marched through the camp towards Everlynn's walls, many of his warriors followed. Matilda, Dughlas, Thorry, and Philip all waited at Stephan's tent. I wanted them out of harm's way if things went downhill.

Stephan stopped at the edge of the camp before that cursed ground where his fallen warriors rotted. His man, Alfhelm, stood to his left, while William and I stood to his right. A mass of soldiers had gathered behind us. We stared at the men on Everlynn's tall, dark walls, and they stared back. Some of them drew their bows.

Then, Alfhelm sounded his horn. Three long, low groans carried by the light breeze over the city's walls.

We waited. One of the spearmen above the gate disappeared from the ramparts while the others glared down at us. The air was deathly still. All we could hear was the quiet flapping of banners in the wind and the flies buzzing around the corpses. It felt like time had simply stopped and we would stand in anticipation forever. I silently prayed we were not too late.

After an eternity, the spearman appeared once more on the ramparts above the gate, and with him was Lord Odo. He wore his full war gear, and I recognised his helmet from the battle near Tillysburg. The battle in which he had almost killed me.

Stephan strode forward alone. The archers on the walls readied their bows. One arrow was all it would have taken to end this, but none of them loosed.

Then Stephan stopped about a dozen yards before the trench, drew his sword, and thrust it into the soil.

"Have you come to surrender, Stephan the Bastard?" Odo yelled. A few of the defenders chuckled.

"No!" shouted Stephan. "But I have come to accept yours."

Odo laughed. "Now why would I do such a thing? I could hold this city for years."

"Because you do not wish to see your son's head on a pike."

Odo said nothing, and Stephan gestured for William to step forward. The young nobleman went to stand beside the king.

"He is alive…" Odo said.

"He is alive," said Stephan. "And I am willing to return him to you, for a price."

"And what price would that be?"

"Your city, in exchange for your heir. I think that is a fair trade."

Odo spat down from the wall. "What use is an heir with nothing to pass on to him."

Stephan and William spoke to one another for a moment, but I could not hear what they said. Then, Stephan yelled back up at Odo. "True, I cannot let you remain lord of anything, but I promise I shall spare your life and honour, and once this war is over I will grant Everlynn to your son. You have my word."

Odo was silent for a very long while, and I feared he may have rejected the offer. But the Gods favoured us, for the drawbridge was lowered and Odo descended from the ramparts.

Then, a trumpet was blown and the great gates opened up. Odo rode out atop a mighty black stallion, with two dozen spearmen marching behind, and a young woman on a bay beside him. She wore a plain brown cloak and a scarf was pulled up over her mouth and nose, but I recognised her as Eleni.

Odo stopped a few yards before Stephan, dismounted, and marched over to him. Odo was nearly a foot taller than the king, and towered over him, looking menacing with his shining mail and helmet, his fur cloak, and his fearsome axe. Eleni climbed down from her mare, threw back her hood, and sprinted over to William. The two embraced, and I caught William smile.

Odo then knelt before the king and removed his helmet, and then placed his axe at Stephan's feet. "I surrender my city to you, Lord King."

"Good. I accept your surrender," said Stephan. "Now swear fealty and you may have your son."

And so Odo swore his oath to Stephan once more, and Stephan's men cheered. Odo's warriors looked humiliated, but I sensed an air of relief about them. It was over, at least for now.

Then, as Stephan gestured for Odo to stand, we heard the horns. An echoing, foreboding drone that filled the air and chilled us to our core. Many of the men outside Everlynn that day were all too familiar with that harrowing sound.

Then came the drums. The deep, terrible rumble that heralded the coming of battle.

I froze. I did not want to look, but I forced myself to turn my head and saw, there on the hill to the east, a long line of horses forming. They carried swords and spears, and like a pack of wild dogs possessed a lust for blood that could be sensed by my very bones.

Emrys had come.

Panic followed. The Royal Guard amassed around Stephan while he barked orders to his soldiers and horns were sounded, but half of them seemed to ignore their king. Many fled, others scrambled for weapons and struggled to pull on their coats of mail, while those ready for battle were hurried to the eastern edge of the camp. Odo's men rushed back over the drawbridge and through the gates.

"Edward, come to the city with us!" William shouted. Eleni held tight to his arm, while in his other hand he held his sword.

"No, I need to find the others," I said.

William looked back to his father, who was mounting his horse, then looked back to me. "William!" Odo yelled.

William glanced back again, then turned and nodded at me. "We are with you, Edward."

I smiled, but it was not time to chat. Instead I raced back through the camp with William and Eleni close behind. I almost tripped and fell a few times, and was shoved back and forth by panicked warriors. One man tried to hurry me to the front, but I kicked him in the gut and carried on.

Everlynn's horn then trumpeted three times and I looked over my shoulder to see Odo waving up at the men on the ramparts. He stormed towards the city gates as the drawbridge was slowly raised. Would he make it? I did not have time to find out.

Nor did it matter. We thought only for our own survival in those moments. We pushed through the crowd and, to my relief, we found Dughlas. He was looking for us. "Eleni?" he said. "What are these two still doing here? What happened with Odo?"

"I'll tell you later," I said. "Where are the others?"

"I sent them north; we can catch up with them. Although I'll be surprised if Tilly doesn't wait instead."

Sure enough, she did, with Philip and Thorry too. They were with the horses at the northern edge of the camp, and Matilda was gnawing at her nails before she saw us.

"Get moving, go!" I shouted.

The three of us mounted our horses, and that was when the screaming started. Gods, I will never forget it.

Emrys's horde charged down the hill, cheering with excitement for the coming slaughter. The feeble shield wall Stephan had tried to assemble was swamped in an instant by that mighty wave. One moment they were there, standing shield by shield, and the next they were gone. All that remained was their haunting screams echoing on the wind.

Then the horde made for the camp, and that was when the true horror began. There was neither mercy nor remorse. The horsemen slaughtered without discrimination. It mattered not to them the difference between veteran warriors and camp followers.

We fled, of course. There was no sense in staying to fight. We rode with the wind, pushing our poor beasts as fast as they could go, and some more.

We were not the only ones to escape. Those lucky enough to find horses before they were butchered hurried north or west. Some tried to escape on foot, but many of those were ridden down by Emrys's warriors. I felt, in those moments, a sense of despair like never before.

Dughlas spun around in his saddle and loosed an arrow. "Two on our tail!" he yelled. I looked over my shoulder and saw a horseman close behind me, a ruthless snarl on his face and his sword held high above his head.

I pulled my horse's reins and turned, then drew my sword just in time to parry the downward slash of the rider's blade and slice down into the man's neck. There was a sickening crunch as steel met bone, the man gasped, and in one swift motion I pulled the sword across his throat. Blood poured over his mail and he slumped forward, his horse carried on, and he fell lifeless from the saddle.

I cracked the reins and rode onward, and heard the scream of a horse as Dughlas's arrow buried itself in its chest and it tumbled forward, sending its rider rolling across the ground. I did not look to see his body shrivel up and decay.

"How did the bastards catch up to us?" Dughlas shouted.

"Emrys's horde must've rode ahead through the night," I replied. "Perhaps Godwald told them about us."

I glanced over my shoulder and caught a glimpse of the slaughter we had left behind. The screams of man and beast still echoed from the camp, and great pillars of smoke rose up from the blazing tents. Some men were still trying to fight, making a final stand and earning themselves a place at the Table of the Slain. Most others, however, ran for their lives, but many of those were not fast enough. A great welcome feast would be held in the halls of the dead tonight.

I felt like a coward, as though I should have done more. But what could one man do against such bloodlust? What could I do but flee? In the panic my instincts had taken over and my only will was to survive. There was no honour in such a pitiful, merciless death. No songs would be sung about the glory of the men who died that day, ravaged like sheep by packs of ravenous wolves. The halls would be filled with their widows' mournful wails.

We reached the Royal Way and carried on along it northwards, following the others who had fled. We rode hard until evening, and when it was clear that Emrys and his horde were not following us, we finally allowed our poor horses to rest.

The first of those to flee Everlynn had already set up camp in the old, ruined fort along the road to the Capital. I recognised this place — it was where Odo's army made camp the night I did battle with William's mara. This time, however, there were no tents or men excited for war. Instead, men and even some women were huddling around small fires among the crumbling towers and walls, a weighty sense of misery hanging in the air.

Once we finally stopped, Thorry leaned forward in his saddle and vomited onto the grass. Eleni leaped from William's horse, fell to her knees, and began to cry. Her husband climbed down from the horse and knelt down with her, holding her in his arms.

I dismounted, while Matilda raced over and threw her arms around me. She brought a wave of relief and the pain from that hard ride lessened. I felt safe. I held her for a few moments, then she pulled away and looked up into my eyes. Hers were red and wet, but she did not weep. "It was just like Tillysburg," she said. "The killing, the screams, the—"

"We are safe now," I said.

She clenched her jaw and nodded.

I looked around at my friends and the people camped among the ruins. Thorry was on his knees, still emptying his stomach, while Philip was rubbing his back and talking to him. He was no more than twelve winters old, but the boy was strong. He had witnessed the brutality of the Immortal Horde before, after all.

Dughlas was sitting with his eye shut, whispering to the little axe-shaped amulet he wore about his neck.

It was all my fault. All that death and suffering had been caused by my own foolishness that past winter. Yet Fate had made me a fool, so that was what I had to deal with. I had to live in the world I had created, and all I could do was try to fix it.

I went over to William and put a hand on his shoulder. His wife was still wrapped in his arms, but she had finished crying. Now she just stared, emotionless. "Forgive me," I said.

"It is not your fault," said William. He sighed. "I will need to hide my identity among these men, but I fear for Eleni. It will be a lot more difficult for her to pass as a nobody."

"William," she mumbled. "William. I want to go home."

"We will, My Lady," he said. "Once all this is over, I promise that we will board a ship and sail to Maricar. But now we must be strong. Think of those beautiful, white shores of your islands you often tell me about. The gentle seas shimmering in the warm sun, and the call of gulls in the dawn. And trust in the Highest."

She closed her eyes and nodded, then looked up at me. "Thank you, Edward, for bringing my husband to me. There were rumours he had fallen at Tillysburg."

I smiled. "William has the Gods on his side, My Lady. I only wish I could have done more."

"You did much. We are indebted to you a second time."

Matilda came to stand beside me, and I turned to her. She was a mess. Her hair was tangled and knotted, her face dirty, and her eyes wet with tears, but she looked stronger than ever. I unbuckled Idris's sword from my belt and held it in both hands. "I want you to have this," I said. "You have been training to use a sword, so hopefully this can keep you safe."

She stared down at it, then took the weapon and unsheathed it. She clenched her jaw and admired the blade. "It is heavy. I am not used to the balance."

"Yes, the shape is a little different to what we use now, but you will come to know it soon enough."

Matilda sheathed it, then looked into my eyes and nodded. "Thank you, Edward."

"You're welcome. I wish we lived in better times, when women need not use such things, but this is the life Fate has given to us."

Matilda opened her mouth to speak, but was interrupted by shouts and the drone of a horn. Hooves beat against the Royal Way and I turned to see about two dozen horsemen riding by, carrying torches and the banners of King Stephan. He had survived.

"Make way for the king!" a man yelled.

The horses rode through the camp and stopped before the ruins of what was once the fort's keep. I watched as the king dismounted and headed inside with his men.

"Shall we go see him?" William asked.

I shook my head. "No. We owe Stephan nothing."

"But my sisters. My parents. I need to know their fate."

"Very well," I sighed. "Thorry, compose yourself, man. I need your help."

"Yes, lord. Sorry, lord," he said. He climbed to his feet and wiped his face with his sleeve.

"Go with Dughlas and ask the folk around here if they know anything of Lord Odo and his family. Did anyone see him die, or make it into the city? Does Everlynn remain unconquered?"

Dughlas finished his prayers and stood, and Thorry nodded. "Yes, lord," he said. "I'll see what I can learn."

The two men went off, wandering from fire to fire to see if they could learn any news from the refugees. As the night went on, more survivors would certainly arrive and they would bring rumours and tales of what they had seen. I only hoped, for William's sake, that his family was unharmed. I did not wish for any to learn of our presence here, because Stephan's men would be aching for vengeance and blood.

Carol the Pretender's champion would be an excellent scapegoat.

"William," said Eleni. "Your uncle was in Everlynn."

My blood ran cold and William gave me a fearful glance.

"Hakon?" I asked.

Eleni nodded. "He arrived ahead of Stephan's army with another warrior. They were not allowed into the keep."

"Then if my father is dead…" William began.

"Hakon will control Everlynn," I said.

"Gods help us all."

"Eleni, who was this other warrior with Hakon?"

She shrugged. "He was a big man, middle-aged, with a beard. His name started with a 'B.' I am sorry, that is all I remember."

"Baldric?"

"Yes, I believe that was it."

"Bastard. Thank you, Eleni. The best we can do now is wait. And pray."

"And make camp," said Matilda.

I nodded. We were exhausted, and the air was getting cool, so a fire was a good idea. I doubted any of us would get much sleep that night, however. As we sat huddled around the fire I noticed some glances and glares from a few of the men that wandered by. Did they know who we were, or was I just paranoid? I kept my blade close in any case.

Late that night, Dughlas and Thorry returned and took a seat by our small fire, then told us what they had learned. Some said they had seen Odo charge into battle, and among those there were some who claimed to see him die.

Others, however, swore they saw Odo retreat into the city before the gate was closed. That is what I thought. One thing was certain, though — all of the later arrivals declared that Everlynn remained an island of safety in a sea of death.

For now.

Edric's men arrived outside the city that night and began making camp, and Everlynn was besieged once again. But was it Odo that resisted, keeping his oath to Stephan? Or Hakon, desiring revenge against the Immortal King for his humiliation?

Whatever the case, it mattered little. All knew Everlynn's gates would open for Emrys soon, one way or another. The feeling of hopelessness hung heavy over the ruins where the survivors had made camp, and it seemed that night that Ardonn had reached its final days.

Then at dawn the next day, as the survivors were making ready to head further north, we received the news we all feared. Everlynn had surrendered to Emrys.

And that dreaded news was brought to us by none other than Lord Odo himself.

9

Besieged

It was Hakon.

Of course it was Hakon. Lord Odo had managed to escape into the city after all, remaining loyal to Stephan for the sake of his son, but almost as soon as the slaughter below Everlynn's walls ended and Edric set up his siege camp Odo's treacherous half-brother began stirring up the cityfolk. By nightfall a revolt had broken out within Everlynn's walls and the exhausted, demoralised defenders joined Hakon in mutiny.

Hakon's promise was peace. Everlynn was starving and ravaged by illness, and Odo's soldiers were tired of staring over the walls at the doom that awaited them. To them, there was no longer any difference between King Emrys and King Stephan. Hakon was the only man who offered the peace they desired.

Just after sundown, the doors to Everlynn's keep were broken down by the statue of Richard the Foreign-Lord, one of Odo's ancestors, and Hakon had his city. His first deed as Lord of Everlynn was, as he promised, to make peace with Emrys.

Of course, Odo and his family did not stay to see the ancient cavalry march through their beloved city's gates. As Richard's head pounded against the keep's doors, Odo fled through an underground passage with his wife Eadswith, his daughters, a priest, and several loyal servants and housecarls. They rode through the night with as much speed as their horses would give, bringing news of what had happened.

It was then that William revealed that he lived. I urged him to remain incognito, but he was a free man now and I could not stop him from seeing his family. Eleni and I went with him, because if plans were to be discussed, I wanted to hear what was being said. Matilda insisted on coming too, and tried her best to look imposing with her mail, helmet, and sword.

I felt glad at seeing William reunite with his family, but also a pang of guilt for having kept him from them for so long. True, it was his wish to stay with me regardless, but he was still technically my prisoner until I handed him over to Stephan.

William first embraced one of his sisters, and they held each other for a long while. He then hugged his mother, until at last he stood before his father. They stared at each other for a few moments, but soon clasped hands and nodded.

Then Odo glanced at me and did a double take before glaring. He gestured for me to approach, and Matilda gripped my arm, but I pulled free and strode over to the lord.

"I cannot piss properly because of you, Corpse-Whisperer," Odo said.

"Perhaps you shouldn't have tried to kill me, My Lord," I said.

"We were in the midst of battle."

"Indeed we were. And I won."

Odo clenched his fists and took a step forward, but his daughter — the one whom William first greeted, and whose name I learned was Arlette — grabbed his arm and held him back. "Father, not now. Do not let your lust for vengeance ruin this happy moment," she said.

"Thank you, My Lady," I said.

"I will humour my daughter, Edward, but do not take it as forgiveness. A day will come when I take what I am owed," said Odo.

"Speaking of what is owed," I said. "I believe you promised gold. Ten pounds, was it?"

"Not now, Edward," William snapped.

I bowed and went back to Matilda, leaving William to his reunion. She squeezed my hand and flashed me a small smile.

Soon after, Stephan emerged from his makeshift camp in the ruined keep and called those of us nearby to gather round. Odo went to kneel before his king, and everyone else stood in a circle around them. Matilda and I pushed into the circle beside William and watched.

Odo bowed his head and begged forgiveness from Stephan —

not just for his betrayal at Tillysburg, but for his loss of Everlynn and, most importantly, for plotting allegiance with the Immortal King and unleashing his horde on Ardonn. The men watching called for justice to be done.

Yet justice for Odo would be light. Stephan asked instead how Odo would make amends. He admitted he had little to offer since the loss of his city and men, but what he did have was a daughter. The hand of his eldest daughter, Anora, was promised in marriage to Stephan's son Wim, the Lord of Tidegate. Anora swore the oath then and there, and Stephan accepted it as sufficient. For now, at least.

Once Odo had suffered his humiliation, Stephan declared it was time to discuss the next move, but before he could continue he noticed me. He sighed. "You are alive," he said. All present turned to me, and some whispered to one another.

I nodded. "I am, Lord King."

Stephan gestured to me and looked around at his men. "For those who are not aware, this man is Edward Godspeaker, whose name I am sure you have all heard by now!" he shouted. "And let it be known that Edward is not our enemy. True, he serves the Pretender. But it is also true that Edward held the line at Tillysburg against the foul horde of Emrys, and even drove the warlord away. It was Edward who defeated Lord Odo in battle, and broke his shield wall. Are we not fortunate, then, to have such a warrior with us? Some say the Gods favour the Gifted above all men."

Many of the men nodded and murmured in agreement, and William gave me a nudge. I was not blind to what Stephan was doing. He could have punished me, but instead he was using me. I sensed the warning behind his words — that should I abandon them now, my life would be forfeit. Fate had bound me to that ragged group of survivors and I had no choice but to play as Stephan's pawn.

"What they say about us is true," I replied. "And the Gods have shown me victory in the future. I am with you, as are they."

Stephan nodded, and his men cheered. I admit, I loved the feeling those cheers evoked. To have renown and be loved and respected by good men is a fine thing. Stephan may not have thought highly of me, but after my deeds at Tillysburg his warriors certainly did.

Stephan's plan was straightforward. We would march with as much speed as we could muster and head straight for the Capital along the Royal Way. We would barricade the gates, destroy the bridges crossing the River Ard, and fortify the city. If Stephan could not defeat his enemies in open battle then he would break them against his walls.

Nobody had any argument, so wasting no more time we made for the Capital. Emrys would likely have wished to catch us before we could reach the Capital because his horsemen would be almost useless in a siege, but he would be slowed by Edric's men and their mortal needs. Though shattered, we were low in number and desperate to survive, so speed was on our side.

It was a two-day journey along the Royal Way to the Capital. Two days, because we moved with haste and stopped little. We stopped once at a farmstead for a few hours during the night to give the men and horses time to rest. The churl who owned the land let us camp in his fields. The barn was also lent to us, and that is where Stephan and his most important men were allowed to sleep, including myself and my companions as well as Odo's family. Odo himself, however, was forced to sleep outside as further humiliation for his treason.

I let my companions sleep, but I could not. The anticipation for the coming battles gnawed at me. The Gifted are always far more sensitive to such things than most, for we can sense the unseen omens around us. The warnings of the Gods. I left the barn to get some fresh air instead, and take in the quiet peace of the night.

"May I join you?" a woman said. It was Eleni, and she came to stand beside me and looked up at the stars. We smiled at one another.

"How are you, My Lady?" I asked.

She sighed. "I am not well, but I must not show weakness in times like this."

"Are you having trouble sleeping?"

"When I close my eyes I see the slaughter outside Everlynn. When I am left alone with my thoughts I can hear the screams. Will this haunt me forever?"

"No," I reassured her. "You are experiencing the shock that befalls those who are not meant for war, but it will pass."

"Men often talk of the glory and honour in war, but I have not seen it. I see only misery."

"There is glory in the art of warfare, My Lady, and deeds in battle bring great reputation and honour to the heroes who overcome the struggle and conquer fear — but what Emrys brought to Everlynn was not war. It was bloodshed."

Eleni nodded slowly, but I felt she did not believe me. "What will happen to those men? The ones who died?"

"They will be in the Hall of Ancestors now, feasting with fallen warriors at the Table of the Slain beside the god Alcyn himself."

"A better life than this, I suppose."

"It is," I said. "My Lady, where is your husband? He's not inside the barn."

"He is with his sister somewhere. Lady Arlette. They are quite close and have not seen each other in some time. I admit, I do wish he would spend more time with me, but I cannot take a man away from his family. William loves his sisters, and I suppose as their only brother he feels he has a duty to protect them."

We said nothing for a moment, and just listened to the sound of snoring and the hoot of an owl. "Forgive me for troubling you with this memory, My Lady," I said, breaking the silence. "But is Lady Arlette the sister whose form William's mara sometimes took?"

Eleni frowned and nodded, then looked up at me. "What does that mean?"

I shrugged. "Nothing, really. I just remembered that detail and was curious."

"Do you have family, Edward?"

The owl hooted again, and I hesitated. "Yes," I said at last. "I have a father and an older sister who live on a small steading in the Shires of Winterhome."

"What about your mother?"

"My mother died bringing me into the World."

Eleni bit her lip and took my hand in hers. "I am sorry. I should not have asked."

"It's fine," I said, pulling my hands away. "In truth, Edith and my father could be dead already. I have not seen them since my master took me away from home as a boy, and I have not written to them."

"Why not?"

I did not answer that question. Eleni shuffled her feet and we stood in silence again for a while. The skies were clear that night, and there was not a breath of wind. It was peaceful. The calm before the storm. One might be fooled into thinking the war was but a distant memory.

"Tell me we will have peace, Edward," Eleni said. She looked up at me and I looked down into her big, sad eyes. I did not want to lie. I was not certain what the future would hold, and whether Eleni would live to see it, but I could not tell her that.

"We will have peace, someday. The Gods have promised it."

Eleni forced a smile and then yawned. "Thank you. I think I

should at least try to sleep before we ride again tomorrow, so I will bid you good night. I am glad to have met you, Edward."

"As am I, My Lady," I said.

She curtsied and then headed back inside the barn. I remained outside, staring up at the stars and wondering why Fate had put me on such a path. Why was *I* given the Gift, and not another? I feared I would never have the ordinary life I so desired. Perhaps I should have stayed in the woods with Aoife, but it was far too late for that now. My Fate was bound to the World.

I spent the rest of the night in meditation. Several hours before dawn, a horn was blown and the men and women made ready to leave. We were off again. Stephan hoped to reach the Capital by nightfall, so he hurried us on that day without stopping once to rest.

"William and I have no choice but to go with Stephan to the Capital, and wait out the siege," I said to my companions sometime that day. "But none of you have that obligation. You are all free to go where you wish."

Dughlas laughed. "I've sworn an oath to you, boss. You really think I'm running away now, after everything?"

"As have I, lord," said Thorry. "I do wish for safer lands, but an oath is an oath."

"I do not wish to leave your side again, even unto death," said Matilda.

"And what of you, Philip?"

He said nothing for a moment, but then looked over at me and grinned. "One Lurian is worth one thousand of you Ardish men. It would be cruel to abandon you all now."

We all laughed, but it was nervous laughter. We did not know how much longer we had left in this world, and how much more time we would get to spend with one another. But, I was pleased to know that if I were to die, my friends would be there with me. I would have liked them to be safe, but I could not hide the warmth in my heart inspired by their loyalty.

We rode on, and a few hours after nightfall we arrived at the Capital.

The Capital was a glorious city, and the largest in all Ardonn. We could not see it in its full majesty due to the darkness of the night, but I had seen it in the past, and back then it had filled me with awe. It was still a sight to see at night, as thousands of lights floating in a sea of shadow.

The Capital, the proper name of which was Ardonn, sat on a hill by the River Ard, where it seemed to bulge outwards away from its straighter course, then curve back the other way, almost running in a complete circle.

The city's hill was nearly made into an island by the shape of the river, with only a narrow strip of land connecting the hill to the rest of the country. There had been times when the river had flooded and the city completely surrounded by water as a result. It acted as a natural moat for most of the city.

The city was divided into three parts. There was the Old City, which was located at the highest point on the hill at the western side of the island. The Old City has existed for as long as men can remember, since times recorded only in legend. As with many of Ardonn's ancient cities, some say it was built by giants. It had heavy walls built from enormous granite blocks, and was home to the city's wealthiest and most powerful individuals. The king had his residence there too, in the immense stone keep.

At the other end of the island, on the northern edge of that narrow strip of land leading to the hill, was the Old Fort. Much like the Old City, the fort was an ancient stone fortress guarding the way to the main part of the city. It housed the city's main garrison and its commander, but was also large enough to fit clusters of homes for the city folk to live, protected by the high stone walls. A large wooden palisade built of thick logs stretched from the Old Fort to the southern edge of the strip and protected the city from invasion.

Between the Old City and the Old Fort lay the New City. This was built in more recent times as the importance and population of the Capital grew, and was the poorest and largest of the city's districts. Much like the city of Oldford, this district was dense, with homes stacked upon homes and an intricate webwork of narrow streets and alleys winding between the wooden, jettied buildings. This district was also divided into quarters.

A horn was blown and Stephan hailed the men guarding the wooden gate to the city, and it was pulled open. Illuminated by the light of the torches, the party of survivors surged into the New City, and then the gates were quickly shut. I looked up at the fort to the north and saw the shadows of men watching us, the firelight glinting off their spears and helmets.

Some of the soldiers with us rode off the main street and up the road to the Old Fort, while others dispersed as we moved past the cosy, crowded homes of the New City. The Royal Guard remained with us. Folk watched from the windows or their doorsteps as we passed, eager to see if their loved ones had returned and hear what news we brought of the siege in Everlynn. Most would spend the night in mourning.

My companions and I rode with Stephan and Odo's family to the Old City, and the royal keep. We were to be housed there as royal guests, but Lord Odo had a place reserved for him in the Old Fort. It seemed Stephan wished to continue his humiliation, or perhaps he merely wished to avoid the resentment of his men for forgiving the man.

We passed through the Old City's wall under the great archway, and Stephan ordered the gates to be closed. Only those with authority were now allowed to pass between the districts through the little door beside the gate.

The buildings in this part of the city were much finer, made with higher-quality wood and some even of brick, and the folk who watched us pass were cleaner and better-dressed. Men in mail came down the street to meet us and escorted us to the palace.

"Gods, I have never seen a building like this before," Matilda gasped.

It was indeed magnificent. An intimidating building it was, with many floors, stretching high into the sky and overlooking the entirety of the kingdom. Stephan's banners, a white dragon emblazoned on a dark green field, flew from the towers, but in the faint moonlight I noticed they were torn.

The two tall, wooden doors were pushed open with a loud groan, we dismounted, and Stephan invited us in to a vast hall — the royal chamber. I had been there before, when I refused to swear an oath to Stephan, and had seen it in the dream I received the Winterlow past. The memory of that dream came back to me then, in that dimly lit, cavernous hall, and sent a bitter chill down my spine. I glanced at Matilda, who was looking around the hall in awe.

"It is impressive, isn't it?" I said to Matilda. "It is nothing like what it would have been when it was first built, though."

"Why not?"

"By the time our ancestors came to these lands, the palace was in ruin and disrepair. Up until the reign of Carol the Great, kings resided within the Old Fort in a wooden hall."

"Why did they move back here?"

"I suppose Carol wanted to enhance his glory by moving his home to the legendary keep. It was rebuilt with wood and brick, but it still falls short of the glory the Edan gave it."

"The Edan?"

"An ancient race, preceding mankind. Folk call them giants now."

Matilda did not respond, only stared with wonder at the tapestries hung up on the walls in recent years, which were lit up by the massive braziers, and the scenes carved into the old stone columns at the hall's sides, with their intricate detail and strange letters telling the stories of forgotten deeds.

"What do they say, Edward?" Matilda asked, nodding to the reliefs.

"Nobody knows. The letters feel familiar to me, like I *should* know them, but I can neither read nor understand them. These carvings were old even to those who spoke the ancient tongue."

A door at the side of the hall swung open and a dozen men in mail came through, followed by a young, handsome man with messy brown hair, a plain tunic, and a cloak lazily thrown over his shoulders. He grinned when he saw Stephan and strode over to him.

"Father," he said. "Thank the Gods you are safe."

"Wim? What are you doing here?" Stephan asked.

He sighed and bowed his head. "We lost Tidegate, father. I brought my men here after those savages from the sea stormed the city."

There was silence in the hall. A long, awkward silence. No one, not even Stephan, knew what to say.

Eventually, Stephan broke the silence. "It matters not. We can retake Tidegate, but we must hold the Capital. I am glad you are here."

"Lord King," Eleni said. Stephan turned and frowned at her,

and his son glared. Eleni curtsied. "Lord King, forgive me, but I believe I may be able to help."

"Your father has been leading the assault on our shores, has he not?" said Stephan.

"Yes, My King, but I may be able to convince him to withdraw."

"Why would your foul people leave?" Wim interrupted. "They have a city, wealth, and slaves. They would give that up? Ha."

"Wim!" Stephan barked. "Let the lady make her case."

Wim scowled, then nodded. "Forgive me, my lady. I am merely sour from the horrors I witnessed in my home."

"I understand, My Prince," Eleni said. "But my people value loyalty and family above all else. My father would have taken Tidegate on the assumption he was aiding my husband's family. If Odo is now loyal to you, Lord King, then my father will be also."

Stephan grumbled, looking from Wim to Eleni. "I suppose Lady Eleni is right. We have Odo to blame for inviting the Almond Islanders here. Can you leave for Tidegate tomorrow?"

"Yes, Lord King."

"The council will need to approve of this," Wim said.

Stephan nodded. "I will summon them at dawn, while the lady is having her breakfast. Once they have approved, Eleni can leave as soon as possible."

Eleni curtsied, and William whispered something to her. Stephan waited to see if anyone had anything else to say. When nobody did, he turned and went from the hall with his son, leaving the rest of us standing there.

Soon after Stephan left the hall some servants escorted us to our quarters. They led William and his family somewhere else, while my companions and I were taken down a wide, dark corridor and up a flight of wooden stairs.

Tapestries and other artworks decorated the walls wherever we went, but I suspected they were to hide the cracks and holes in the masonry. We passed many wooden posts and beams that were likely set to support the ancient stone. They bore carvings in the Ardish style, perhaps to distract one from the fact they held up a crumbling ruin.

Matilda and I each had our own rooms, while Thorry, Dughlas, and Philip shared. The three rooms were all close to one another, and although not the finest ones Stephan could have offered, they were comfortable and had all we needed. The beds had feather pillows and mattresses, with quality linen sheets and fur blankets. A welcome luxury after the past few days.

We bid each other goodnight and retired to our rooms as soon as we arrived. There was an air of uncertainty, but we did our best to warm each other's spirits and not succumb to despair. I was glad they had decided to join me in the Capital.

A lukewarm bath had been prepared for me and I was left alone to bathe. Once I was finished, one of the servants came into my room with a tray of food and some wood, then started lighting a fire in the small hearth beside the bed.

"I'm sorry this was not burning sooner, lord. We had no time to prepare for your arrival," she said.

I said nothing and just lay down on the mattress, watching her ignite the wood and then stoke the flames. She was pretty, with beautiful brown hair, pale skin, and a sharp face. I admit, after all I had been through since leaving Giant's Rest, I longed for the closeness of a woman.

"What is your name?" I asked.

She glanced up from the fire, then looked back to what she was doing. "Wynflaed, lord."

"Are you married?"

"No, lord."

"Why not? I am sure someone like you has many suitors."

Wynflaed grinned. "I like my work here in the king's palace."

"You like being a servant?"

"Yes, lord. It makes me feel important, bringing smiles to the faces of Ardonn's most renowned men and women, and hearing their words of gratitude. We've all got our purpose in this world, haven't we?"

The fire cracked and sparked, then Wynflaed stood. I sat up on the bed. "Does King Stephan treat you well?"

Wynflaed smiled and nodded. "He does, lord. He knows us all by name and wishes us well whenever he sees us. He even gives us nameday and Winterlow gifts — personally. My mother told me Edwin was never like that."

"You were servants to King Edwin?"

"Slaves, lord, but I don't remember much of it. I was only nine when the king's father took the throne."

"I see. Come, sit down beside me. There's no need to stand there," I said, and shuffled over. "And call me Edward. I'm not a lord."

Wynflaed raised her eyebrows and took a seat on the bed. "I've heard of you. You're the Pretender's Elfman."

I nodded, and Wynflaed frowned.

"What is Carol's position on slavery?" she asked.

"He would see it remain outlawed, but some of his more influential supporters disagree with him. They only make noise, though, and it is my hope that they fall in line with Carol's wishes once he sits on Ardonn's throne."

"I pray he and the king can make peace soon and unite against Ardonn's real enemy. You have come from Everlynn, haven't you? Is the news true?"

I sighed. "It is, but have faith that the Gods will grant us victory in the end. Stephan prepares his defences as we speak."

"And this Emrys, from the legends — has he really returned?"

"I have spoken to him, and even wounded his horse. He is back, and all that they say about him is true."

"I heard of that deed. They call you the Hero of Tillysburg."

I chuckled. "They exaggerate. In truth, I was shitting myself."

Wynflaed laughed and shuffled her feet. I felt a strong desire in that moment, an urge for something I had missed. Thoughts of Matilda crept into my mind but I shoved them aside. It would not mean anything, would it? There would be no betrayal, no wrongdoing?

I told myself it would just be a little something to keep my mind off the coming siege, nothing more, and put a hand gently on Wynflaed's leg. She looked into my eyes and blushed, but did not stop me.

"I am allowed to deny you," she said, her voice hushed.

"Will you?"

She smirked, and shuffled closer, but in that moment the door to my quarters eased open and in came the Lady of Henton herself. Her eyes went wide, her jaw dropped, and she stood there frozen. She had changed out of her mail and into a fresh nightgown, and her hair was washed and combed.

Wynflaed looked back and forth between us, but neither of us spoke. After a few moments of awkward silence Matilda clenched her jaw and bowed her head. "I hope you enjoy your night, sir," she said.

"Matilda—" I stood, but before I could say anything more she closed the door and left.

I sighed. I did not follow her, but perhaps I should have. I wish I did. Instead, I returned to Wynflaed. I was angry with myself and the Gods, furious for what they and myself had allowed to happen since winter. I tried to let all that frustration out with Wynflaed, but although she seemed to enjoy herself, I did not.

I lay awake for the rest of that night staring up at the cold stone ceiling while Wynflaed slept peacefully beside me, yet my troubles were no less than they had been before.

At dawn the next day a council was summoned, plans were made, and an army arrived at the city's gates.

10

Treason

We stared down at them from the ramparts of the wooden wall guarding the New City, and they stared up at us. Horsemen, thousands of them, standing in one long line just out of reach of our arrows.

Behind them were the soldiers of Beglen and her allies, accompanied by what was left of Everlynn's forces. The army was immense, and we all knew then that the coming siege would be long and hard. If we were to win, we needed the favour of the Gods.

Dughlas stood beside me and chuckled. "We're so done."

I could not help but laugh. "Done indeed."

"What's so funny?" Matilda hissed. She scowled at me, then shook her head.

"What did you do?" Dughlas muttered.

I ignored him. Stephan stood not far from me, wearing a grim look. He was deathly pale. The king turned on his heel and marched back down to the street with his housecarls. His son, Wim, stayed for a few moments before he too followed.

"They're trying to frighten us!" I shouted. "Intimidate us into submission. But remember, men, we are the sons of Ardonn. We will not fall so easily, and certainly not before they have broken themselves on our walls!"

There were some murmurs from the men on the ramparts, and a few uncertain cheers, but I felt I could do little to boost their morale when faced with such an imposing foe. They would try to assault the walls in the coming days, and they would certainly fail the first time. That failure might give the city's defenders the glimmer of hope they needed to hold out for a time, at least. Yet hope was not enough to win wars.

"I am going to see William off," I said. Our enemy did not seem to be preparing for an assault; they were merely showing their force and setting up camp outside the city's walls. The fighting would come, but not then.

William was with Eleni in the Old City, making ready for their journey westward to Tidegate. The council had approved of the motion. We could have supplies or even men sent upriver from the sea to grant us relief and allow us to hold out for longer — but not until Eleni's people released their grip on Tidegate.

I met them by the Old City's western gate, where they prepared their horses. William greeted me and the others with a smile. "You have come to see us off?" he said.

I nodded, and we clasped hands. "Of course. You two will need all the good wishes you can get."

William laughed. "Then I am grateful for you, my friend."

Eleni gave me a smile, and I bowed back. She, like her husband, wore a coat of mail. They had a dangerous journey ahead of them.

"Make sure you come back," Dughlas said. "I would hate for you to miss my glorious death."

"If he does miss it, Dughlas, I'll be certain to tell him all the details I observe from a position of safety," said Thorry.

We all laughed, aside from Matilda. She was miserable. "William, Eleni, goodbye and good luck," she said. "I shall pray each day for your safety and success."

"Thank you, My Lady," William said. He bowed, and Matilda curtsied.

"We should hurry, my love," Eleni said.

William nodded and tightened his jaw. "Yes, we should. Goodbye, my friends, and may the Gods favour you in the coming days."

"And you," I said. "Both of you."

I felt uneasy. A tingle in my bones. A tightness of the chest. Something was wrong, and my Gift was warning me.

I said nothing. William bid farewell to his mother and sister, who had also come to see him off. His mother wept for him but wished him well. Arlette showed no emotion. The two embraced, then William helped Eleni onto her horse and he mounted his. Stephan had given them steeds he promised were his fastest. I could only hope he was right.

The gates were opened. William and Eleni trotted out while my friends and I went up onto the ramparts to watch them leave from high up on the stone wall. During the night Stephan's men had destroyed the bridges crossing the river, so William and Eleni were transported across by a barge. It moved far too slowly for my liking, but they reached the other side soon enough, and William looked back and gave a wave.

I waved back and once more that dread crept up my spine.

It was too late, however. William and Eleni kicked their horses and rode westward along the road. I bit my knuckle as they rode past fields and paddocks towards the hills in the distance.

Then Matilda gasped. I turned to see four riders emerge from the trees to the south. They rode with speed, their swords held high, and once they reached the westward road they charged along it. I shouted into the wind, but I doubted William or Eleni could hear me.

The horsemen gained on them, and William turned his head before cracking the reins of his horse. Eleni did the same. An arrow was loosed by a man on the wall, and then another, but they both fell far too short.

My friends and their pursuers raced off to the west, then they disappeared behind the hills. My heart was thumping. Only the Gods knew then what their fate would be.

"Gods, I hope Stephan was right about those horses," Dughlas muttered.

I said nothing and descended the stairs from the ramparts. Standing before me was William's mother and sister. Arlette wiped a tear from her eye, and both of them stared at me. "My Ladies," I said.

"Something is wrong, Godspeaker," Eadswith said. "What is it?"

I sighed. "William and Eleni are being chased by four men on horseback. They disappeared behind the hills before we could see if they had escaped."

Arlette gasped, while her mother merely closed her eyes and walked away.

"You are lying," said Arlette.

"My Lady, I—"

Tears formed in her eyes, and she stared down at the ground, shaking her head. Her hands were trembling. "It cannot be true. You must be lying," she mumbled. "I told him not to go, I tried to tell him, but he would not listen. He would not listen. He said the Gods were with him."

"My Lady, do not despair. William is an adept rider; he will escape them."

Arlette's breathing grew frantic and short. I instinctively reached out to comfort her but she slapped my hand away and stared up into my eyes. "Do not touch me! Gods, oh Gods, oh Gods, why is this happening to us?"

Arlette fell to her hands and knees and then curled up into a ball, hugging her legs close to her chest. She rocked back and forth, sucking in air but letting none out. A crowd had gathered, and Arlette and I were encircled by a mass of onlookers. I looked around at them and held out my arms. "Do you people have nothing better to do? Scurry off!" I yelled.

Some listened, while others stayed. I ignored them and knelt down before Arlette, and she looked into my eyes. She resembled William, with the same wavy, dark blonde hair and thin face, but appeared much more fragile. This was neither the time nor the place for someone like Arlette.

I smiled at her. "Focus on your breathing, Arlette. Let in as much air as you can, then hold it, before letting it out again slowly. Breathe with me."

I inhaled deeply, then exhaled again. Arlette tried to follow me, but was off rhythm.

"With me, Arlette. Just breathe."

She nodded. Gradually, her breath slowed. Soon, she was matching mine.

I smiled. "Well done, My Lady. William will return, I promise you. The Gods have shown me."

"Truly?" she asked.

I nodded. It was a lie, of course, but I did not know what else to say to her. I helped her back to her feet, and Matilda came running over to us. She glanced at me, then smiled at Arlette and took her hand. "Come, My Lady. Let us go to the temple and pray for your brother's safety," she said.

Arlette looked to me, then back to Matilda, and nodded. The two linked arms and made their way through the crowd. I breathed a sigh of relief, and Dughlas put a hand on my shoulder. "No one else would've done that," he said.

"What do you mean?" I asked.

"You showed great kindness just then, a kindness that few would have in them. Your master would've been proud."

"I suppose."

"We need more men like you here," said Thorry. "I've never been in a siege before, but something tells me that was only the beginning."

I nodded. "We also need warriors. Dughlas, starting today I want you training Philip and Thorry. Philip is still rusty, and Thorry just knows how to whack things."

"Aye, Boss," Dughlas said. "And what of Tilly?"

I grumbled. "If Matilda asks to practice, give her practice, but don't go easy on her. Edric's men won't."

"Will you train with us, lord?" Thorry asked.

"I'll do whatever the king tells me to. Hopefully I will have time to join you, though. Philip!"

"Yes, Edward?" Philip said.

"After Dughlas has given you a sufficient beating today, come find me. There is something in this city I wish to show you."

Philip grinned, then he went off with Thorry and Dughlas to the training square. I hoped Dughlas could teach them what they needed to know soon enough if they were to survive the coming days.

I went back up onto the ramparts and looked out over the fields and hills, hoping for a sign that William was safe. I feared for him, but he was in the Gods' hands now. I saw nothing. I told myself that perhaps, because Emrys's riders had not yet returned with bloodied blades and severed heads, my friends were still alive.

Another group of about two dozen horsemen soon approached from the south and rode along the riverbank. They stopped across from the north gate and stared up at us.

"What do you want?" I mumbled to nobody in particular.

"They're assessing our defences," said the soldier next to me.

I stared back at them. "May I throw your spear?" I asked.

"What?"

"Your spear. Do you need it?"

"I can get another one," he said.

I took it, held it over my shoulder, and launched it as hard as I could towards the horsemen. It hissed through the air. Emrys's warriors watched it unflinching as it curved down and disappeared beneath the surface of the river.

"Let that be a warning to you!" I shouted down at the riders. "And a curse on you and your people! Let it be known that Edward Godspeaker, Heir of Godwin, defends these walls. Your master failed to defeat me once, and he will fail again and again before the Gods grant him death. Tell him. Tell him that within this city waits his doom.”

The riders did not respond. They merely turned their horses and carried on northwards. Some of the archers on the walls loosed arrows at them, and a few nearly found their mark, but the riders were soon out of range.

I needed a distraction so I went to find Wynflaed. I could do nothing more than hope that William and Eleni would make it.

I sat up on the Old City’s stone walls that afternoon overlooking the wooden homes crammed together in the New City. The city folk seemed to be going about their daily lives as if a horde of immortal horsemen and the armies of Beglen and Everlynn were not camped outside.

Philip said nothing as he came to stand beside me. He looked out over the city. Although he tried to appear strong, I could sense his fear.

“I am glad you found me,” I said. “Come, I learned of a place that might make you feel a little better about all this.”

“What is it?” Philip asked.

I smiled at him. “You’ll see.”

I stood, then led him down from the wall and through the little door into the New City. We made our way down the main street, passing by merchant stalls and shops, a band of street performers, and a wandering monk shouting about the Gods. Soldiers patrolled the street in twos or threes, but aside from them life appeared to be normal.

We turned down a side street, this one just as lively as the main street, though a little more cramped. An old man gave us a nod as he walked past with a herd of goats, and I tossed a piece of silver to a young beggar-girl who had come scurrying over to us.

We then entered a narrow alley, shielded from daylight by the high, stacked homes. A man sat on a doorstep huddled under a blanket with a young woman, while a cat rubbed against their legs. The pair and their cat stared up at us as we passed.

Soon Philip and I came to a small, open square with a little stunted tree growing in the middle beside a modest fountain. Houses two to three storeys high surrounded the square — except for on one side, where there was a low, single-storeyed, wooden building. It was built in a style unlike most buildings in Ardonn, but it was familiar to Philip.

"That looks like the temples in Luria," he said.

I nodded. "The Capital has a small Lurian community living in this quarter of the New City, and years ago they built this temple to three of your gods. It is not the most exquisite temple in this city, but it is the only Lurian one."

Philip raised his eyebrows and made his way over to the building. It was indeed crude, and had moss and fungi growing up the columns and sprouting from the planks at the threshold, but it was one of the few places where Lurians in Ardonn could properly worship their gods.

"There is a lone priest who tends it," I said. "It survives mostly on the donations made by Lurian traders from the south, but I fear in the coming years their numbers may dwindle. Go ahead, make yourself at home. I will wait for you out here."

I did not expect Philip to run over and hug me, but that is what he did. I chuckled and tousled his hair.

"Thank you, Edward," he said. He turned and went back to the temple, hesitated at the threshold, then went inside.

I took a seat at one of the benches surrounding the tree and the fountain, and sat in meditation. I could hear Philip and the priest conversing inside, in their own tongue, and felt glad that this place existed despite its apparent neglect. We all needed to stay close to our gods in those days.

While I waited, a few others I assumed were Lurians, mostly older individuals, came to the temple. They nodded to me as they passed, but otherwise said nothing. They must have wondered why an Ardishman sat outside their temple.

A younger woman came past with an olive complexion and curly dark hair like Philip. She approached me. A young boy, who must have seen no more than five winters, hid behind her skirts and stared at me. The woman smiled at me.

"You are welcome to enter our temple," she said, her accent strong.

I smiled back and shook my head. "Thank you, but I am merely awaiting my friend."

The woman looked down at my mail and the sword at my hip. "Are you a soldier?"

"No, but I am here to fight for the Capital alongside them."

"My husband is a soldier. He is Ardish, like you." The woman sighed. "I have not seen him since the king left for Everlynn, and he did not return with the men last night."

"I was at Everlynn. What is his name?"

"Cuthric. They say he is likely dead, but my heart tells me otherwise."

I stood and put my hands on the woman's shoulders. "Then trust your heart. It may be that he fell behind, or escaped in another direction."

She smiled and nodded. "I will do that. Thank you."

The ringing of a bell echoed from inside the temple, sounding the start of the evening rites, and the boy pulled at his mother's skirts. She laughed and patted him on the head.

"I must go now, but what is your name?" she said.

"Oh, I'm just one of the many Edwards in Ardonn," I replied.

She bowed her head. "Then you will be in my prayers today, Edward of Ardonn."

She hurried into the temple, and I sat back down at the bench. I waited for a little while longer while the rites and prayers were performed inside. As the light faded and day turned to night, the worshippers emerged from the temple with Philip grinning.

"Thank you for this, Edward. The priest has told me I am welcome there anytime," he said.

"I'm glad. Just let me know if you would like to come back."

"I would. I met a Lurian girl about my age…"

I laughed. "Go for the Gods, not the girls."

The two of us made our way back down the alley, then through the torchlit streets to the Old City. Even as night approached the streets were still alive, but soldiers were soon coming past on horseback ordering people back into their homes. A curfew had been put in place so that only those authorised by the king and his council were allowed to roam the streets at night.

"Philip," I said as we walked. "You know our Gift grants us many abilities, but there is something I have not yet taught you."

"What is it?" he asked.

"You may have noticed it is easy to get folk to like you. People are drawn to you, as if you have a hidden charm."

Philip said nothing, then nodded. "I have noticed that."

"It's our Otherworldly nature. The Gifted are not of this world like most men, and that makes others see us as greater than we are. An incredibly powerful Godspeaker who has mastered his Gift after many decades would be perceived as a king, or perhaps even a god. It drives men to love us, women to desire us, and the powerful to fear us."

Philip smiled. "That's great!"

"Is it?" I frowned down at him. "It can be a blessing, yes, but it can also be a curse."

"It doesn't sound like a curse to me."

"Take an ambitious man like Odo, for example. Who is he more likely to resent? A man he sees as little more than a wandering peasant, or a man he feels has the potential to rule the world?"

Philip said nothing.

"Or perhaps imagine a girl you are fond of. Oh yes, she will certainly be fond of you too, but is it love that inspires her affection, or is it merely your Gift drawing her to you?" I let him think on that, then continued. "Ordinary folk will either love or hate you, Philip, but it will not be for you as a man. It is why my master never married. It is not Edward of Oldford or Edward of Winterhome that Stephan's men love and respect, but Edward the Gifted."

"Is that why—" He paused, and thought better of asking that question. "I think I understand."

"Good. Meditate on it. It can be incredibly useful, make no mistake, but it does sometimes make it difficult for us to live among ordinary people."

"Is there any way people can overcome this effect of our Gift?"

I nodded. "A lesson for another time."

We passed through the door beside the gate to the Old City, greeting the guard, and headed back to the keep. It was dark by now, the sun far behind the hills, and I thought again of William and Eleni. I could not sense their deaths, but I was not certain. If they were still being tailed, the night may have concealed them enough to lose their pursuers. I could only hope.

The streets were far less lively now that the soldiers were enforcing curfew, but some folk still wandered about on royal business or were returning home. There were more guards in this part of the Capital, but despite the situation an eerie calm hung over the city.

"I admit, I expected panic," Philip said.

"Aye, me too," I said. "Especially as the memory of the siege a decade ago would be fresh in many people's minds. It is strange indeed."

"Do you think Emrys will win?"

"I cannot say. Wim broke into both the Old and New Cities after a year-long siege, although the Old City's gates were opened by a traitor."

We reached the keep and hailed the guard, who opened the courtyard's gate for us after a series of questions. The gate was quickly closed behind us. I took Philip around to one of the keep's side doors, which opened into the hallway leading to our rooms, and bid him goodnight.

"Where are you going?" he asked.

"Oh, I am not ready to retire just yet. I have special permission from the king to wander at night."

He did not question me further. I watched him make his way down the hall, and felt a touch of pride in my heart. In the short time I had known him, he had learned a lot. I was glad I had taken him in as my apprentice.

I found a torch and headed across the vast courtyard to the building beside the palace's temple. It was as old as the palace itself, but much smaller, and time had been kinder to it. The ancient bronze door was still there, with its relief depicting the mighty deeds of heroes and gods, though it had tarnished significantly. Two guards stood at either side of the door, and I bowed to them.

"Is the hall open?" I asked.

"Who's asking?"

"Edward of Oldford."

The guards looked at one another, then one of them grimaced. "We're not supposed to let anyone in at night without the king's permission."

"The king told me I could go where I pleased."

The guard shrugged. "I'll take that as permission, but if we get in trouble I'm naming you."

I stood back as they both pulled at the heavy handles of the door. It scraped along the stone, the sound echoing around the palace courtyard. The men sighed and puffed when it was open just enough for me to enter.

I gave them a nod of thanks, then slipped through the doorway and into the darkness. I held my torch in front of me to illuminate the long hall ahead. The Hall of Legends, where heroes have their names immortalised. Two black stone walls stretched seemingly endlessly into the darkness, each bearing a row of little alcoves where shrines to Ardonn's legends were held.

It was exactly as I had seen it in Wilere's cave.

Some of the alcoves had statues, but most had only names, with their deeds carved in stone plaques beneath the altars. Some of the words of those closest to the entrance had faded with time, and their shrines showed no sign of use. The immortality this hall was said to give men was not truly eternal, it seemed.

I made my way down the hall all the way to the end. There, standing before me, were two twin statues carved in stone, flanking a doorway that opened up to a staircase spiralling downwards.

The sculptures were as tall as two men, carved with far greater skill than any could match now, and they seemed to glare down at me. These men wore mail and bore shields and swords, though their heads were helmetless and their hair wild and free.

Candles had recently been lit at the base of these statues, and incense burned. Their names were carved in gold at their feet. *Eomund*, one read. *Eored*, said the other. These were the shrines to the leaders of the Exiles, our ancestors who had come down from the north and conquered the lands between the Alps and the River Cris. The founders of the Twin Kingdoms, Ardonn and Aedonn, now united.

I bowed and left a piece of silver at each of the shrines before heading down the stone stairs. I came to another hall just like the one above, with rows of shrines cut into the black stone walls, but these were much newer. The writing on the plaques was less worn, and some names I even recognised.

The first I passed were those of the renowned Exiles —
legends like Cedwin the Tidebringer, Uring Bullhorn, Hadric of Eiradin, Merewulf Thrice-Drowned, Bladswith Firemaiden —

and after those came the greatest of the Twin Kingdoms' rulers and lords.

I did not know what I sought here. I only followed Aoife's guidance, but then at last I found myself before a pair of shrines and knew I was in the right place. They were only a few centuries old, and someone had even placed fresh flowers at one of them no more than a few days past. These ones had sculptures, a warrior and a priest, with gold plaques bearing their names.

Carol the Great, Unifier of the River Thrones, and *Godwin Godspeaker, All-Knowing and Wise*.

I stood before them and bowed long and low, then lit the candles on each of their altars. I placed two lumps of silver at each one, then stood back and stared. Their lists of deeds were long, and to stand there in front of their shrines filled me with awe and pride.

Something drew my attention to the base of Godwin's shrine, just beneath the plaque bearing his deeds. A thin crack, almost unnoticeable. I knelt down and peered at it. It had hundreds of small scratches and chips around it, as if someone had tried to push something through or hack away at it.

I frowned and ran my finger along the slit. It was definitely not natural, and had been placed there on purpose. It was straight, perfectly centred, and in line with the rest of the shrine. Odd, I thought. I checked the other shrines nearby, but none of them had the same feature.

An idea came to me, from something Aoife had said. I drew my sword — Godwin's sword — and carefully slid it into the opening. It scraped against the stone, sending an awful shiver through my bones, but it seemed to be a perfect fit.

I pushed it inside a few inches, then the blade stopped, and a loud click echoed through the hall. I froze, then looked around before slowly pulling the blade back out.

The plaque listing Godwin's deeds had shifted slightly, and was now tilted to the side. "Godwin, what are you hiding?" I whispered.

I pushed the plaque further to the side with great effort, cringing as rusty metal scraped against stone. A spider scurried past my hand from inside a small opening behind the plaque. I lifted the torch close to it and saw a few items lying within.

I shuffled closer and pushed the plaque open a little more, then took the items from inside the shrine. They had been left there for some reason; perhaps not for me, but evidently for whoever carried Godwin's blade. I wondered if I should have just put the plaque back in its place and forgotten about it, but curiosity got the better of me.

Whoever had opened the secret compartment before me had left three things inside: a piece of heart-shaped amber the size of my palm, a piece of rolled parchment, and an old iron key. Were they Godwin's possessions? I did not know.

I turned the amber over in my hands and pocketed it before unrolling the parchment. I squinted in the torchlight at the scrawled handwriting, and thought it was nonsense before realising it was written in the ancient tongue.

From the ashes,
The remnants of the ruin of war,
Once the Wolf has returned to scourge the land,
And return he will,
Only then will the true king rise.

One cannot hide from the Wolf,
Nor flee his snarling jaws.
One can only face him,
Fight him,
Hunt him,
And make the Wolf a dog.

The Dog must dismount.
The Dog must dismount.
The Dog must dismount.
Only then can the king be free.
And yet dismount the Dog will not.

Make him.

A cryptic puzzle, perhaps, or merely the ravings of an old madman? It had no signature and no telling who it was meant for, or why it was hidden away within Godwin's shrine, but I sensed it was important. Was the wolf Emrys? It certainly seemed so.

Then it hit me. The answer. The cure for Wilere's curse. Aoife had led me to Godwin's shrine, I knew, and there I had found our salvation.

I heard a scraping noise echo down the hall. The bronze door. I quickly heaved the plaque back into place, heard a click, then sheathed my sword and stood. I slipped the parchment and key into my pocket with the amber.

"Edward of Oldford?" I heard someone call.

A torchlight came down the hall towards me. I said nothing, and saw a man approach me from the darkness. No, two men, their mail shimmering in the light of the fire.

"Edward?"

"Who is it?" I asked.

The two men approached. I had not seen them before, but they wore the colours of the Royal Guard. "What are you doing?" one of them asked.

"Paying my respects."

He nodded, then the other one stepped forward. "Edward, you've been summoned to the council chamber."

"You're lucky we found you first," the other man said. "And not the First Minister's men."

"At this hour? Why?" I asked.

"They've been debating it all evening, but the king eventually had to give in. The Kingmoot wants you to stand trial immediately."

"Stand trial for what?"

"Treason. Sorry, Edward, but they insisted."

Treason.

I never should have come to the Capital.

11

Justice

The council hall was not an old building, at least not when compared to the ancient palace. It was built by Carol the Great's successor, Francis, and had become the centre of justice and administration in Ardonn. It was where the Kingmoot, the king's council, came to conduct trials, debate on laws and edicts, and choose a successor.

I was brought into the wooden building through the back entrance by two of Stephan's housecarls. They were supposed to bind my wrists, but I refused, and they made no attempt at forcing it. I was led through a narrow, windowless corridor, had my weapons confiscated, and then was taken into the council chamber.

Fortunately, the men did not take the items I had found in the Hall of Legends, though they were curious about the amber. I simply told them they were all Godspeaker trinkets and they did not question it further, perhaps fearful of what magic they might be imbued with.

The chamber was wide and spacious, and resembled those in other parts of the kingdom, such as that in Tillysburg. Tiered seating lined the room, with space for hundreds of people surrounding a small space in the centre where speakers would stand and face the king and those gathered.

I squinted as my eyes adjusted to the sudden light. The warriors, who held my arms at my side, walked me to the centre of the chamber. The many people sitting in the rows whispered and mumbled to each other. One man shouted, "The Hero of Tillysburg!" and was immediately escorted from the hall.

I looked around at the faces in the seats. There were perhaps one hundred people gathered, with a few more coming in. Word must have spread that Edward Godspeaker was facing trial for treason, and the Old City's citizens wanted to see the outcome.

At the end of the hall opposite the door I had entered were three high-backed chairs in their own box separate from the rest of the seats. In the middle seat slouched Stephan, a golden crown on his brow and an exquisite cloak draped lazily over his shoulders.

To his right, in the seat traditionally reserved for the king's High Priest, sat Prince Wim. The High Priest was supposed to preside over all the Kingmoot's trials, so his absence was highly improper. Perhaps in his great age he no longer had the strength to oversee such things.

To Stephan's left sat a man whom I recognised as the king's First Minister. His long, grey hair was combed back behind his ears, and he had a long moustache hanging down below his chin. His sharp eyes fell on me, and his lip twitched.

"We now begin the trial of Edward of Oldford!" the First Minister called. "Who has been accused of treason against our glorious king and for breaking the peace of our beloved Ardonn."

Gods, that man made my blood boil. He was a vile creature. His wealth and his scheming had earned him a place at the king's side, and now he was the most powerful man in Ardonn. The king ruled Ardonn, yes, but it was the First Minister who told him how. He was insidiously clever, and although he had never in his life held a blade he was by no means a coward. The man loved to take risks, caring little for the consequences, and those risks had paid him well. Crawmaer, his name was.

"Who made the accusation?" I said.

Stephan closed his eyes, and Crawmaer ignored me. "Edward believes he is special, that he is somehow an exception to the law, above other men," he continued. "He has used the mystique surrounding his supposed 'gift' to seduce men and women across the kingdom into granting him forgiveness for his crimes. But, Edward, your deception has come to an end, for the good and wise men in this chamber will not be fooled as easily as the whores and desperate men you enjoy bending to your whims."

Stephan sighed, and put his head in his hand. "Present his crimes, Crawmaer," he said.

"As you say, Lord King." Crawmaer peered down at the parchment on the stand in front of him. "His first crime was the unauthorised execution of Katla, daughter of the mayor of Oldford, who was not given fair trial before her death three winters past."

I scoffed, and there were some disapproving murmurs from the crowd.

"Nevertheless, we can overlook this as being a matter concerned with Lord Adalbert, as the crime was committed within his domain. Is this acceptable, Lord King?"

"Yes, yes," said Stephan, waving his hand.

"Very well. Then we defer the sentencing of this crime to Lord Adalbert, should Edward be cleared of all other charges here," Crawmaer said.

There were some nods among the people gathered. As he continued, I noticed Lady Arlette enter with her mother and older sister, followed by Matilda. The latter glanced at me and our eyes met briefly, then she turned to watch Crawmaer speak.

"When the noble King Wim departed this world and the throne passed to Lord Stephan, Edward was summoned to the Capital to swear an oath of fealty to his new king, as were all free lords, earls, and churls holding tenants with no less than two hundred acres of farmed and unfarmed land. Edward, however, refused," Crawmaer said.

"Since when has it been law in Ardonn for the king to require the oaths of all freemen?" I demanded. "What next, shall we ask King Miron of Luria for an oath? How about every grown man and woman among the Salmon-Folk?"

I heard whispers from among the crowd, someone stifled a laugh, and the warrior beside me gently squeezed my arm.

"Edward will remain silent until he is invited to speak, will he not, Lord King?" Crawmaer said.

"He will," said Stephan, nodding at me.

"Excellent. Fortunately for Edward, the king was gracious enough to grant him forgiveness, despite his disloyalty, and until last winter that forgiveness has proved well-founded. Edward had largely kept to himself since his departure from the Capital, but in winter he decided to commit further crimes — these unforgiveable.

"Shortly after the month of Winterlow, Edward is known to have ridden north and met with Odo of Everlynn, whom we all know to have committed treason against the king. It is reasonable to believe that Edward and Odo made an agreement involving payment, and the latter has attested to this.

"Following his meeting with Odo, Edward rode to Tillysburg, where he swore an oath of fealty to the rebel pretender Carol, and proceeded to work alongside Carol and the traitor Roger in a plot to throw our kingdom into chaos. Edward is also known to have fought for the pretender at the battle of Tillysburg, slaying many of Ardonn's loyal warriors. Do you deny this, Edward?"

"No, I did fight for Carol, but—"

"Then we may continue."

Stephan's eyes were closed again and he was rubbing his temple, while his son stared at me with excitement in his eyes. The men and women bearing witness were muttering to each other, some making gestures to me. Matilda stared blankly at nothing while Arlette whispered in her ear.

"Now hear, good people of the chamber," said Crawmaer. "Edward's crimes are far more sinister than what you have just heard. We have received word from trusted sources that it was Edward who conspired to release the scourge Emrys from his tomb and unleash him upon the land."

At that the people in the chamber collectively gasped, and the room fell silent.

"We all know the tales. The legendary Godwin, may he be blessed, sealed Emrys away centuries ago. So, who else would know how to release the warlord but the Heir of Godwin himself?"

"I object!" yelled the woman. I looked up to see Lady Anora standing, her hand raised. "It was my father who conspired to release Emrys. He has admitted this. Who are *your* sources, First Minister?"

"Trusted persons, My Lady," said Crawmaer. "In any case, it is unlikely to be a coincidence that Edward was seen by our contacts in Beglen on two occasions a little over a month before Emrys marched. And is it not strange that mere hours after

Edward arrived in our good king's camp outside Everlynn, Emrys and his horde began their slaughter?"

"Edward did bring us William, Minister," Stephan said. "Without him, Odo would not have surrendered to us."

"That is true."

"Where is Odo?" I asked, earning a glare from Crawmaer. "You admitted he committed treason, so when is his trial?"

"Yes, Odo has committed treason, and faced trial earlier this afternoon," Crawmaer said. "He was punished in accordance with the deal struck between him and Stephan at Everlynn. His titles and lands were stripped of him and have been passed on to his only son."

"May I speak, First Minister?" Anora asked. He nodded. "Edward may be guilty of the other crimes, but any involvement he has in the release of Emrys is mere accident. The agreement made between my father and Edward concerned a mara that tormented my brother. Both William and Lady Eleni can attest to this."

"The Lord and Lady of Everlynn are not present, so cannot in fact attest to anything," Crawmaer said.

"As the new heir of Everlynn I act in my brother's place, in his absence, according to the laws of this land. Or have those laws changed, First Minister?"

"They have not."

"Then I swear to Edward's innocence on this particular charge. Lady Matilda of Henton can also attest to this, as she has travelled with Edward up until now."

Everyone turned to Matilda, and I stared up at her. She glanced down at me, squinted, then nodded. "Lady Anora speaks the truth," she said.

Crawmaer sighed. "Are there any objections to this?"

There were more murmurs among the attendees. Wim said something to his father, while Crawmaer and I stared at each other with intense hatred. I do not know why he despised me so much, but he had looked at me the same way years earlier when I visited the Capital to refuse the oath-swearing.

As the hall fell silent, and none objected, Crawmaer raised his hand. "Then by the intercession of Lady Anora, on behalf of Lord William of Everlynn, I absolve Edward of the charge of conspiring with the traitor Odo to free Emrys," he said.

I breathed a sigh of relief, and many others did too.

"However," Crawmaer continued. "There are still the matters concerning Edward's alliance with Carol the Pretender, coupled with his refusal to swear fealty to our king."

Crawmaer had caught me there, and in that moment I realised his cunning. I had been foolish enough to believe that Anora's grace had saved me from this trial, but now I suspected Crawmaer had intentionally used the ridiculous and weak charges of conspiring with Emrys in order to strengthen his case on this issue.

If two of the charges had been dropped, it would make it easier to sentence me for the others. He had revealed what he truly wanted me to suffer for. The chamber was silent. He had almost won.

"Are you *really* going to charge me with treason? Now, while the enemy knocks on your doors?" I asked.

Crawmaer opened his mouth to respond, but Stephan raised a hand. "It is time Edward made his case," he barked.

"Men and women of the chamber, please raise your hand if you had sons or brothers who fought at Tillysburg!" I shouted.

There were about three dozen hands raised. Less than I had hoped, but it would do.

"I thought as much. I am sure you have heard the accounts of that battle, and how it was Carol's men that formed a shield wall in front of Stephan's. The two armies fought side by side with one another in that brutal struggle — not for Stephan, not for Carol, but for Ardonn."

A few men muttered and there were some nods. Crawmaer glared at me, while Stephan appeared to stare down at his feet. Wim only frowned.

"We fought against a common enemy that day, and we fight against a common enemy now. I ask you, Lord King, who would you rather have at your side these coming days? Myself, or Crawmaer? Perhaps we should be placing charges of treason not on me, but on the man who conspired against his own king, Edwin Eomundson, not two decades ago!"

I received some grumbles for that, and Stephan now frowned at me. We all knew the rumours. We all knew who men accused, in their whispers over ale, of opening the Old City's gates to the usurper and unleashing butchery on the people within.

"But I will not demand a trial for Crawmaer because now, while Edric prepares to batter down this city's walls and unleash Emrys's impatient horde upon us, the actions of one man done for this or that claimant matter little. The real enemy is the Immortal King, who has numerous times in the past plagued our lands with death and destruction, and threatens to do so again. I saw what he did to Tillysburg, and if you men had too, you would not be in this chamber now but on the walls of your city, spears in hand, ready to defend it against a similar fate."

Crawmaer gave a small smile and bowed his head. "Fine words, Edward, but I fear they do not excuse you from the law. A traitor must be punished. If we do not uphold this sacred law passed down to us by our ancestors and our mighty kings of old, then we commit a sacrilege and risk incurring the wrath of the Gods. All know this. This is not a time to take such a risk."

Judging by the nods and murmurs, the audience seemed convinced by that, save for a few. No matter how much they respected me and wished for my absolution, all sensible men feared the Gods' ire, especially when an army threatened to destroy them and all they held dear. Or perhaps they feared the wrath of Crawmaer. Both were just as likely, and just as terrible.

"It seems there are no objections," said Crawmaer. "I understand we all love our famous Godspeaker, I truly do, but the Gods demand retribution for such crimes as severe as treason. And since Edward is without significant wealth or noble title, the fine must be paid in blood."

There were some shouts of objection from the crowd, but it was too late for such things. The chamber could object to charges, but not the sentences for charges they had approved. The power to sentence was the right of the king, which meant it was held by the First Minister.

I looked up at Matilda, who watched me with her hand over her mouth. Arlette had her hands on Matilda's shoulders and was speaking into her ear, while Anora sat forward biting her nails. Prince Wim grinned, and Stephan yawned.

Crawmaer, however, sat cold and emotionless. The First Minister raised his hand, and within seconds there was silence.

Then I made my move. I did not know what I was thinking, but I had to act, or die before the night was over. Crawmaer wanted my head, but I would not give him that satisfaction.

I writhed free of the warriors holding me, and they did not try to resist. In one move I pushed one of them to the side and pulled the knife from his belt, kicked the other man in the gut, then held both my hands above my head. "You want blood, Crawmaer?" I shouted.

Stephan shot up from his chair and Crawmaer raised his eyebrows. I placed my index finger against the blade, gave a yell, and sliced.

The pain was immense, and worse than anything I had felt in battle. Almost everyone in the hall gasped, Stephan's jaw dropped, and Matilda screamed. Another cry, much more pitiful this time, escaped me.

I dropped the knife and pulled my hands to my chest, pressing the wound hard. The two warriors grabbed me by the arms and held me there, and with gritted teeth and blurred vision I scowled up at Crawmaer. The hall was in uproar now.

"There's your retribution," I snarled. "Put it in a jar and keep it by your bed if you desire a trophy. The scales are balanced, and the Gods have their justice."

"Guards, take him away," Crawmaer ordered.

"No!" Stephan shouted. "It is done. Edward has faced justice and paid his blood-price."

"As you say, Lord King." He bowed his head, and sat back in his seat.

I had beaten Crawmaer, but only just. I would need to take care. A similar stunt would not work again, I would wager.

So, the petty battle in the council chamber had ended, but soon the real battle would begin. A battle in which the sacrifices would be far greater.

I lay on my bed, stretching out my left arm and staring up at my hand. Shortly after the trial I had been taken to a healer, who heated an iron rod and pressed it against the wound.

The pain of creating the wound was great, but it was little more than a tickle when compared to the pain of healing it. What had once been my finger was now an ugly stump. A throbbing pain still radiated up and down my arm, but it was dull and bearable now, and the bleeding had stopped.

It had been a long night. I heard a knock at my door and thought about ignoring it, but it was only Dughlas, Philip, and Thorry.

"Let's see it, then," Dughlas said, a wicked grin on his face. I frowned and held up my hand. Philip and Thorry grimaced, but Dughlas laughed. "Welcome to the missing-parts band, Edward Nine-Fingers."

I smirked. "It isn't funny."

"It is funny, no need to be so sour about it," said Dughlas. "I only wish I could've seen you do it. Gods, I would've been proud."

"They wouldn't let us into the chamber," said Thorry. "Nobles and Old City citizens only."

"Tilly told us what happened. She's not happy," said Dughlas.

"Not happy with me?" I asked.

"Oh, she thinks it was clever of you, she just wishes she didn't have to see it. Have you not spoken to her?"

I sighed, and lay back down. "I don't think Matilda wants to speak to me."

The men glanced at each other. "Right, I won't ask."

They stayed for a while longer, and we talked about things of little importance to keep our minds off the fact that thousands of men were camped outside the city eager to kill us. After all that had happened, I was glad I had their company.

As the hour grew late, the three of them retired to their rooms and left me alone. Except I was not alone for very long, as Wynflaed came to see me. I had asked for her and she had come, but that night we just lay beside each other and talked.

I hated myself for it. I hated that I wanted her, and that she brought me comfort, but even more I hated the emptiness and longing in my heart that Wynflaed could only momentarily satisfy. Those days were hard, and the coming days would be harder, and since it seemed as though the Gods had abandoned me, I needed Wynflaed's soft presence.

For the next few days we lived with a grave uncertainty hanging over us. Emrys's horsemen patrolled the city on all sides, staring up at us from the river and counting our numbers, while Edric and Hakon's men were camped outside the New City's wooden wall.

A few trading boats made their way upriver toward the city, but Edric had archers shoot at them from the bank, sending them fleeing back downstream. At night, we could see thousands of campfires dotting the landscape, and every so often catch a faint orange glow in the distance. In the morning, pillars of smoke would rise up from where the light had emanated.

There was no assault on the walls; at least not yet. We saw Edric's men building ladders and knew fighting would come soon enough. Until then, we trained.

I spent most of my days in the training yard with Dughlas,

Philip, and Thorry, working on our sword-skill. It took some time for me to get used to gripping a shield with four fingers. When I was not training I spent my time with the Gods in the palace temple, and at night with Wynflaed in my room.

Days went by, yet we heard no news of William or Eleni, nor did we hear about the situation in Tidegate. How could we? Nobody was allowed into the city, so anything we did hear about was shouted to us from our enemies below the walls.

They told us of death and destruction as Emrys scourged the land, plundering settlements and slaughtering any in his path. Each morning, one of Edric's men would ride up to the gate, just out of range of our archers, and tell us all about Emrys's latest atrocity.

One morning, however, Emrys himself strode forward atop his imposing grey stallion. He sat there, unmoving and alone, staring up at the defenders. Soon enough, a man came running to the palace to alert the king. I met him at the gates and went with him to Stephan's hall.

"What does he want?" the king grumbled.

"He doesn't speak, My King. He just…stares," said the soldier.

"I will go and ask him then."

Stephan stood and strode from the hall. Two dozen housecarls followed him, along with a few councillors. He was already dressed in mail, and a soldier handed him a shield as he left the hall. I followed. I needed to see what Emrys wanted, and if he would be willing to strike a deal.

Stephan and his guard marched through the Old City, then the New, and climbed the steps to the ramparts above the city's eastern gate. He stopped and leaned forward over the wall, glaring down at Emrys.

The Immortal King stared up and raised a hand. He was dressed in his war-gear, but I recognised him by his wolf-faced helmet and the grey puppy in his saddle. The warlord removed his helmet and let his long, grey hair fall loosely down his back.

"Stephan!" he yelled. His voice, deep and hollow, echoed up to us. The very land itself had fallen silent. He spoke in Ardish. "I come to you with an offer."

"You wish to surrender?" Stephan shouted back.

I caught Emrys grin. "I wish to offer *you* the chance to surrender."

With those words Stephan began to turn away, but then some soldiers dressed in black came forward, led by a man I recognised — Baldric, Carol's treasonous oathman. I knew well which lord these men served.

Each man at Baldric's side pulled a rope, and at the other ends of those ropes, their hands bound and their mouths gagged, were people. Women, all of them.

They stumbled, yanked forward by Hakon's men, and were pushed to their knees in a line in front of Emrys. Their hair was messy and tangled, their faces dirty and bloodied, and their clothes torn. They looked up at us, eyes pleading for aid.

"These are your people, village-folk from the surrounding

land!" Emrys yelled. "Hakon's warriors have grown bored of them, so we thought we would give them back to you."

Stephan clenched his jaws and his fists, but said nothing.

"I hand these women to you freely, Stephan. They are a gift, a display of my good will to you and your countrymen. I do not wish to see more of these good folk suffer so that I may reclaim what is mine by right."

Hakon's warriors released the ropes and kicked the women forward. They scrambled to their feet and raced towards the city.

"All you must do, Stephan, is open this gate and let them enter," said Emrys.

Stephan raised his hand, ready to give the order.

"Don't," I hissed. "Don't."

"These are my people," Stephan snarled, turning to me. "I cannot abandon those I have sworn to protect."

The women threw themselves against the great wooden gate, screaming and beating against it, begging for it to open. Stephan looked down at them, then at Emrys's army, and growled.

One of Hakon's men drew a bow, loosed, and an arrow went hissing through the air before burying itself in one of the women's backs. She let out a shriek and fell to her knees, then moaned and writhed in the dirt.

"Open the gates!" Stephan yelled.

"No!" I shouted. "Do *not* open the gates."

Stephan grabbed me by the shoulder. "Do not presume you can override my orders, Corpse-Whisperer."

Another arrow struck its mark, ripping through the ribs of another woman. She howled briefly before her swift death.

"These women died days ago, Stephan," I said. "If you open these gates, the New City will be burning by nightfall."

There was a scream from down below, and one of Hakon's men laughed. Stephan squinted at me for a few moments, staring into my eyes. "Keep the gates barred!" he yelled.

Another of Hakon's men drew his bow, and it was then I raised my hands. "Wait!" I cried. "Stand down."

Emrys raised his hand and the bowman lowered his bow.

"Lord Emrys," I shouted. "Perhaps we can make a deal?"

"Ah, Edward," he said. "I believed you were dead. Or worse."

"I know how to break your curse."

Emrys began to laugh. It was an empty laugh, and several of the men at my side shivered. "So, you met the dwarf?"

"Yes. Withdraw your forces and I will meet you, then we can discuss your cure."

The warlord said nothing, and appeared to consider my offer. "And if you lie?"

"I do not lie. I give you my word."

Emrys shook his head. "It is too late for such things, Edward. The cure to our curse is behind those walls. I am sorry, I truly am."

"Please, Emrys. All you must do is—"

I was interrupted by another volley of arrows hissing before they buried themselves in flesh or wood. Emrys put his helmet back on, turned his horse away, and slowly strode towards the camp. Hakon's men grinned, they all raised their bows, drew, and then loosed. Again and again they rained iron upon those poor souls, and I could not bear to watch.

At least Stephan stayed up on the wall until the slaughter had ended — the slaughter that he had been forced to allow. He was a good man, and if his council did not have so much power over him I believe he would have made a fine king. I could see that then.

While Stephan and his men stayed on the ramparts, I headed elsewhere. A rage was boiling up within me. A lust for vengeance. Sure, it was Emrys who had ordered the savagery outside the gates, but I could not harm him. Not yet, at least. No, I needed to find justice *within* the Capital's walls.

There was one man I knew who could be blamed for unleashing the horror that Emrys had brought. One man who started all this.

Odo.

It was me who insisted on the branches. Odo wished to make things fast and get it over with, but I wanted to do it the proper, traditional way.

"Hurry it up," Odo barked. The servants hurried to place the hazel sticks in a circle around us, nervously bowing their heads. Odo glared at me through his helmet's visor, fury in his eyes, as he stroked the haft of his terrible axe.

I swung my blade from left to right and squeezed the handle of my shield. My grip was still weaker than it had been before the trial, but it would have to do. A shield would probably do little good against Odo's fearsome weapon anyway.

The men and women who occupied the Old Fort stood around us in a circle a good distance away from the hazeling ground. The few oathmen Odo had brought with him from Everlynn stood by and watched, expressionless.

Some of Stephan's men had closed the fort's gate on my orders, which I made with the king's authority. I did not have such authority, of course, but I suppose my tone made them hesitant to argue.

They only needed to keep the gate shut until the king heard of what went on there. He would undoubtedly come to put a stop to it, but I hoped to have finished with my enemy before then. I said a prayer to make sure.

"I am glad you chose to meet your death so willingly," Odo said. "Though I will gladly carve that willingness out of you and have you beg for mercy." He paced back and forth, and I did the same, matching his steps. The circle was complete, and the servants backed away.

"The Gods will decide who begs for mercy today, Lord Odo of Nothing," I said.

He grinned and stopped in place. I stood too, glaring at him, waiting for any sign he would attack. I could hear my heavy breath echoing behind my faceplate.

"It is a shame your Whore of Henton is not here to watch you die," Odo snarled. "I have heard she is quite fond of you — or rather, that thing between your legs."

I let out a growl and charged forward. We had no time for taunts. Word would quickly spread to the palace of our hazeling, and it was likely Stephan was already hurrying to prevent the duel.

I lunged at Odo, but he merely sidestepped and swung the bottom end of his axe towards my head. I ducked and thrust my shield at his gut, and he jumped back. We paced around each other, daring the other to make another strike.

Odo moved this time, and I blocked the thrust of his axe, which he then — with inhuman speed — brought up over his head and back down at me. I ducked to the side and the axe smashed against the ground, splitting the stone at our feet.

He swung again, a great sideways slash, and I could do nothing but hold up my shield and brace. The force of the blow thundered through my arm, the shield almost slipped from my grip, and to my shock it did not split. I made a mental note to thank the god Eocyn later for giving us shields.

I used the chance to lunge my sword forward, and I felt it scrape against Odo's mail, though it did not pierce the links. Odo stepped back, snarled, and made another overhead swing. I jumped to the side, and before he could slice at me I swung my blade. The blow was uselessly absorbed by Odo's mail.

We paced backwards from each other, both panting. Odo's mail was incredibly tough and was of far greater quality than most coats I had seen. It would take a strong, well-placed lunge to pierce that — a lunge I feared I could not make.

"What are you thinking, boy?" Odo said. "Going to cuddle my leg again?"

"Maybe," I puffed. "Perhaps I'll cut off your manhood, too. Or did I already do that at Tillysburg?"

He felt that. Odo gave a vengeful shout and charged, and I charged too. We smashed against each other, my shield crashing against his chest. I fell back, he fell forward, and we piled on top of one another. My sword went skating along the stone, as did Odo's axe, and Odo's big hands went for my neck.

I grasped his hands and pushed back. He pinned me down, snarling as he tried to force my hands to yield, but the fire of combat raced through me, awakening within me a strength I never knew I had. We both grunted and groaned in a contest of raw strength.

"Where is your fucking finger?" Odo growled.

"I was bored," I snarled. "So I chopped it off."

Odo almost laughed, then he grimaced and heaved against my hands. I gritted my teeth and fought back, but my strength was giving way. I glanced down at his waist but, unlike the last time I fought Odo, there was no knife there. I pushed and I pushed, but the pain was beginning to overwhelm me and my arms were giving in.

Then a horn was blown, a trumpeting groan piercing the sky. Odo looked away for a second and his force eased, so I took the chance to push him back and scramble away. He gave a yell and grabbed my ankle just as I got my sword. I slashed back at him, and he leapt out of reach.

The horn blew again, twice this time. Many of those who had been watching our duel now raced up to the Old Fort's ramparts. Odo and I glanced at each other and he scowled.

"It seems the Gods want neither of us to die," Odo said. "This day, at least."

I nodded. We both knew what those horns meant. My vengeance against Odo would have to wait.

For approaching the Capital, sailing up the River Ard, was a fleet of dark, fearsome ships. Their sails were black as night, and strange, ferocious beasts adorned their prows. Their oars cut through the river like blades, and their drums rumbled like thunder on the wind.

The horn was blown again. The Sea-Serpents had come.

12

Serpents

The men gathered along the southern wall hooted and cheered at the approaching ships. They moved painstakingly slowly against the current, with little wind in their triangular sails, pulled through the water by the oars.

We knew they had come to our aid, for they all flew the dragon of Ardonn alongside their own serpent banners — except for one, a ship larger than the rest, which flew a crudely made flag bearing a white hare.

Then the arrows fell. Edric's men raced to the riverbank and began pelting the ships with arrows and javelins, some of them blazing with fire. The men on board fought back, launching all manner of projectiles at the enemy, including flaming pots and enormous burning arrows from springalds — a weapon I had only heard talk of until then.

The first of the ships slid alongside one of the docks, and men leapt out to tie it. A few arrows made it across the river and buried themselves uselessly in the planks. Another ship came to dock, followed by another. There were perhaps two dozen— a substantial number — and while several of them stayed near the riverbank to keep Edric's men busy, the rest docked one by one. Soon the New City's docks were swarming with strange men. They made their way over to the dock-gate and waited for it to open.

Would Stephan let them in? That was the question on everyone's minds.

The larger ship docked at last, and then the few near the bank followed. Edric's men no longer saw any sense in wasting arrows and instead shouted curses across the river. When the last ship arrived, the men on the ramparts all cheered.

Yet still the gate remained shut.

The Maricari were gathering outside while Edric's men rushed back to their camp. A group of warriors hopped off the larger ship and onto the dock, carrying two serpent banners, and were followed by two imposing figures in the most exquisite mail and cloth.

One of them helped a woman onto the dock, and I recognised her as Eleni. She was followed by a man who could only have been William. He was handed the banner of the hare and then went with the group towards the gate. I waved down at him, but he did not notice.

They went to join the crowd that was swelling outside the dock-gate. They pushed past the men, and the two who I assumed were their leaders looked up at us. Their men parted, and William, Eleni, and the two Maricari leaders stood in the open space in front of the gate.

"We wish to speak to King Stephan!" called William. "My wife's people have come to our aid."

There was a resounding cheer from among the defenders, and the captain in charge of the dock-gate waved down. "The king is on his way. We are glad to have you back, Lord William!" he shouted.

"Lord?"

"Your father renounced his titles while you were gone. They were passed on to you."

William muttered something, but I could not hear what. There was a commotion further along the ramparts and men stood to the side as two of the Royal Guard with the king's dragon on their shields marched towards the space above the gate.

I stood aside and watched as they passed, followed not by Stephan, but Prince Wim, in very regal attire. He stopped directly above the arrivals and waved down at them.

"Greetings," he called, a broad smile on his face.

"Blessings to you, My Prince," William shouted. "May we enter?"

"Of course you may, Lord William." Wim gestured to one of his men, who pulled a rope from over his shoulder and tossed one end over the wall. "Hold on tight; we shall pull you up."

William frowned, looked at his wife and the two Maricari leaders, then back up at Wim. He squinted in the sunlight. "Will you not open the gate?"

"The gate must remain closed, My Lord," said Wim.

"What of my wife and her family? Their men?"

"The Maricari?"

"Yes, they have come to their ally's aid."

Wim rubbed his chin. I felt a man push into the gap beside me, and glanced to see Odo. He frowned. "Is that my son? What is happening?"

I nodded. "They've asked to be let in."

"And will they be?"

Wim leaned over the wall and peered down at the men below, pretending to think. "Are these the animals that stole my city?"

"They are the Sea-Serpents, my wife's father's fleet." William hesitated. "Yes, they captured Tidegate, but have agreed to return it in exchange for Eleni's safety."

"Excellent," Wim exclaimed. "Then your wife may climb up the rope as well. She will be safe behind these walls."

Eleni turned and said something to the two men accompanying them. One of them spat, while the other strode forward, drew his sword, and held it above his head with both hands. "We come aid," he said. "I Tripho of Cavoucara. Our swords for you."

Wim burst into a fit of laughter. "Did you hear that, men? They are giving us their swords."

There were some chuckles from among the defenders, but with little enthusiasm. Wim looked back down at the Maricari. "Almond Islanders, you may reside aboard your ships in the docks, and should our enemy cross the river here you will defend this gate."

Eleni spoke to Tripho, who glared back up at Wim and sheathed his sword. He yelled something in his own tongue, turned back to his men, and made some gestures. The man who stood at his side followed, while Eleni grabbed William by the wrist and pulled him away from the gate.

He yelled up at Wim, but nobody could hear him, for the Maricari started shouting in unison. They beat their swords, spears, and axes against their shields. Odo tried shouting down to his son, but in vain.

Across the river, hundreds of Edric's men were amassing, pulling behind them makeshift wooden rafts. They began pushing them into the water and piling onto them. The first of the rafts pushed off from the bank and began inching across.

I had to act. I pushed past the defenders along the ramparts and made my way to Wim, calling his name. He barked orders to the men, commanding them to ready their bows and spears. I grabbed the prince's sleeve, and he spun around and scowled at me.

"Godspeaker," he snapped. "What are you doing?"

"Let them in," I said. "They are not our enemy."

Wim chuckled. "They made themselves our enemy when they

stormed Tidegate's docks." He pulled his arm free and turned back to look over the wall. His housecarl shoved me away.

Then came the sound of a mighty crash, thundering from below. The Maricari had brought forth their ram and were now beating against the gate.

"Slaughter them!" Wim screamed. "Show them what we do to unwelcome guests. Give them a taste of Ardish steel!"

The arrows were loosed and spears began piercing the air. The Maricari held their shields over their heads, but there were some gaps, and a few of them fell as they hammered the ram against the dock-gate. Many of the Maricari archers stood back, shooting up at the defenders.

I pushed back along the ramparts as fast as I could, and Odo was making his way towards me. He grabbed me by the arms. "We have to stop this," he growled.

"Where is the king?" I asked.

He shrugged.

"I'm going to find him."

"Good!" Odo yelled. "I am tempted to throw the little prick of a prince from this wall."

I half-smiled, then fell to a knee and grimaced as a surge of pain shot through my arm. I let out a yell and cursed at the Maricari arrow buried in the flesh below my shoulder. My mail had taken most of the blow, but blood was trickling through the tear.

Odo chopped the shaft with his fist, snapping it near the wound and sending another ripple of pain through me.

"That will come out easily. For now, find the king," he barked.

I nodded and climbed to my feet. The city's bells were ringing now while horns and drums signalled the assault. More of Edric's rafts were pushing from the southern bank, and a few had made it to the city side. They climbed up onto the docks and formed a shield wall while the others floated across the river.

I made my way down from the ramparts and pushed through the panic that had erupted in the streets. Soldiers were rushing to the dock-gate while common folk fled to their homes, the temples, or somewhere else they might find safety. My arm was throbbing, but I pushed through the pain and ran as fast as I could.

I raced along the New City's main street and did a double-take when I spotted Dughlas and Thorry running the other way. I called out to them, they noticed me, and pushed through the masses to my direction.

"Gods, your arm," Thorry gasped.

"Where's the king?" I said.

"He's on his way. What happened?" said Dughlas.

"The Almond Islanders are here, but the prince wouldn't let them in."

"Why not?"

"He still bears a grudge from Tidegate."

"Gods, the bastards are trying to break through, aren't they?"

I nodded. "And Edric's men are crossing the river on rafts."

Thorry and Dughlas glanced at each other, then back to me. "Come on then," Dughlas said. "Let's go hurry the king."

We raced through the New City, deafened by the panic. I feared for William and Eleni, for most of Edric's men would have crossed the river by now. I could only hope that the Maricari were able to hold out until Stephan reached the gate.

The king was riding down the New City's main street on horseback, with three dozen mounted housecarls. They moved as fast as the crowds would allow, but no matter how much his men blew horns and shouted to make way, the panicked mob did not part fast enough.

"Stephan," I shouted. "Lord King!"

He noticed me waving above the crowd, and I pushed through to him. He pulled his horse to a stop and yelled back at me. "Edward, what is happening?"

I skidded to a stop before his horse and bent over, panting. My arm still ached from the arrowhead buried in the flesh. "The Maricari are trying to break through the dock-gate."

"The Maricari fight for Emrys?"

I shook my head. "They fight for their lives. Edric's men are crossing the river, but the prince won't open the gates for them. They offered aid but he refused."

"Gods damn that boy," Stephan spat. "Go fix that wound, Godspeaker. I will deal with this."

He needed no further explanation. The king kicked his horse and charged through the crowd, forcing people to jump out of the way or risk being trampled. His housecarls followed him, blowing their horns.

I watched the king push his way through the crowd, then Thorry pulled at my arm. "Let's go, lord. There's nothing more you can do."

I nodded, then winced at the sudden pain rippling down my arm. We made our way through the city, back to my room at the palace, where Dughlas went to find a healer. Thorry helped me remove my mail and shirt without bumping the arrow too much. The pain was much worse now that the rush of battle had worn off, and I grimaced with every move.

Soon Dughlas returned with a healer — the same man who had sealed the stump of my finger. He laughed when he saw me.

"Good Gods, Edward Godspeaker," he said. "Can you go a day without hurting yourself?" He hurried over to me, took a cloth from his bag, and soaked it in a jug of water. He washed my blood-stained arm and tutted at the broken arrow stuck in the flesh.

"Is it bad?"

"Barely a scratch." Without hesitating, he yanked at the arrow and ripped it from my arm. I let out a cry and swore, cursing the man, but within a few moments I felt a sense of relief. Painful relief, but relief nonetheless. The healer held the arrow up in front of my face and grinned. "You're lucky Almond Islanders don't barb their arrows."

"I wouldn't call this luck."

He laughed, then handed me the arrow. Gods only know why he thought I would want it. I turned to Dughlas.

"Where is Matilda? Is she okay?"

"The foolish little thing wanted to fight, so I locked her in her room," he said. He pulled a key from his pocket and winked.

"I want to see her," I said.

"In a moment," said the healer. He began bandaging my arm, binding it tight to stop the bleeding. I gritted my teeth, but the pain had lessened now that the arrowhead was gone.

"What about Philip?" I asked.

"He's fine," said Dughlas. "He'll be somewhere around the palace."

I sighed. "Good."

The healer patted my shoulder and smiled. "I will leave some bandages with you. Just wash the wound and replace the dressing regularly. You should be whole again in no time."

"Thank you," I said. "I will try to avoid being wounded again."

He smiled and bowed, then headed out of the room. Dughlas handed me the key to Matilda's, then he and Thorry left me in peace. I pulled on a tunic, made my way to Matilda's room, and tapped on the door.

"Who is it?" she called.

"Edward."

"Do you have the key?"

"Yes."

"Come in then."

I unlocked the door and slowly pushed it open. Matilda was leaning against the window, staring out at the city, wearing pants and a loose shirt. A coat of mail was crumpled on the floor beside her bed, on which lay her helmet and Idris's sword. A collection of dead bugs sat neatly in a tray on a table by the hearth. She turned when I entered, and forced a smile.

"Dughlas locked me in," she said.

"Good," I said. "He told me you wanted to fight."

Matilda's smile turned into a frown, and she paced over to me. I closed the door behind me. "And why should I not? I bet I have had more practice with a blade than half the men on those walls," she said.

"Because you are a woman, and women don't fight."

She shook her head. "What about you, then? I heard your screaming only moments ago."

"I was hit by an arrow."

At that she scowled and sucked air through her teeth. "So you expect me to just sit in here praying while those I care about are struck by our enemy's arrows?"

"Yes. We need prayers as much as we need steel."

Matilda marched forward to stand not an inch from me, then glared up into my eyes. "Whose duty is it to fight for Ardonn, Edward?"

I frowned at the question. "Ardonn's warriors. Her nobles and their oathmen."

"I thought so. And what are you?"

"What do you mean?"

She prodded my chest, her eyes watering. "I am a noblewoman. The blood of warriors flows through my veins. *I* should be fighting for Ardonn, not you. You are a farmer, a peasant. Nothing."

"Matilda, I—" I put a hand on her shoulder, but she shoved me off. A tear ran down her cheek.

"My father and grandfather fought as warriors for Edwin in the Usurper's rebellion. My grandfather died in that war, and went to meet his forefathers, who fought in many wars before him. My ancestors were oathmen to the Exile twins, and for their deeds became earls. Who was your father, Godspeaker? A drunkard, I bet. Too wretched to even raise his own son."

I struck her hard across the face, the sound of the smack echoing around the room. Matilda stumbled back, her mouth wide open, and I caught a flash of fear in her eyes. She held a hand to her reddening cheek and stared at me.

I immediately regretted it. I moved forward, but she stepped back. "Matilda, forgive me. I do not know what came over me. I have been quite tense lately, and—"

"I understand," she said. She clenched her jaw and folded her arms. "I am sorry I forced myself into your life."

"I want you in my life," I said.

"What about that servant girl? Do you want her?"

"She comforts me."

Tears formed in her eyes again and she walked back to the

window. I took a step to follow her, but then thought better of it. "What is wrong with me, Edward? What can she do that I cannot?"

"Wynflaed means nothing to me."

Matilda turned and looked at me with wet, pitiful eyes. She turned back to the window. "You make no sense. Go, find your whore. If we ever leave the Capital, know that I will still be by your side when you and Wynflaed part."

I said nothing. I just bowed for some reason, tossed the key onto her bed, and turned towards the door.

"Edward," Matilda said just as I was leaving. I turned, and she gave me a sad smile. "I do love you."

I nodded, and closed the door behind me. I sighed and then headed for the king's main hall to await news of what happened at the docks. The hall was full when I arrived, and before I had time to make sense of everything, Eleni ran to embrace me, followed by William. They were both a mess, but grinning.

"Thank the Gods," William breathed, his voice hushed. "We did not see you at the gate, and were not sure you had survived. My father said you were hit by an arrow."

"William, what happened?" I asked.

"Edric's men formed a shield wall at the docks, but my wife's folk gave up on the gate and drove them back into the river! Stephan arrived soon after and ordered the gates be opened for us. Lord Tripho is here now."

William turned and pointed to the scene in the centre of the hall. A large crowd of courtiers had gathered to watch what occurred. Tripho stood behind Stephan, with the other Maricari leader I later learned was Tripho's brother. In front of Stephan, on his knees and whimpering like a child, was Prince Wim.

A resounding clap filled the hall as Stephan slapped Wim across the face. Then again. And again. Over and over again Wim was beaten till his nose was bloodied and his eyes were red. Tripho and his brother stood there emotionless, but the rest of those gathered seemed ashamed to be watching the display.

"Tripho is my father," Eleni whispered. "He demanded retribution for the men he lost at the gate."

"He is certainly getting it," William chuckled.

"Your father, is he alive?" I asked. William nodded. "Where is he?"

"After the skirmish he returned to the fort. Why?"

"I want to make peace with him. We fought a hazeling, but your arrival interrupted us. I feel the Gods want us to make peace."

William raised his eyebrows, while Eleni appeared confused. "Hazeling? What is this?" she asked.

"A duel," said William. He winked at me. "I would have bet on you."

I smiled. "Have you seen your sister yet?"

"Arlette? Not yet."

"You should. She was distraught when you left."

William nodded. "Gods, that is my fault. Thank you, Edward, I will go and see her."

He gave a short bow and pushed past me, jogging off to the door at the edge of the hall. I turned back to Eleni, who smiled at me. "I want you to meet my father," she said. "We told him about you, and he is interested in talking to one of the Gifted."

"That might be hard, for I do not speak your tongue," I said.

She shrugged. "I can translate for you both."

Wim let out a yelp, and Eleni turned. We watched as Wim continued to receive discipline. Once it was done, Stephan and the two Maricari made their way to a more private room to discuss the next steps while everyone else slowly dispersed. Dughlas, Thorry, and Philip found us, then we went somewhere quiet so Eleni could tell us everything that had happened since she and William left the Capital.

I tried to listen to Eleni, but my mind was not quite with me. I could not push aside the thoughts of Matilda, and the guilt I felt at what I had done to her. It was not just the slap I regretted, but the way I had treated her since we first met. I had been a terrible friend.

Eleni told us of how she and William managed to outride Emrys's horsemen, though only just. They had found refuge in a roadside settlement where the horsemen were driven away by the angry villagers. They carried on to Tidegate, and after a few days arrived there and were hailed at the gates by Maricari soldiers. They had taken full control of the city and were awaiting orders from Odo on what to do next.

Both William and Eleni were allowed into the city, and there was little argument between Eleni, her father, and her uncle. They were overjoyed to see Eleni safe, and although initially hesitant about giving up a city that had cost them much blood to take, it did not take long for them to agree to come to Stephan's aid. As Eleni had promised, the Maricari were fiercely loyal to family.

Once Eleni had told us her tale, I left her with my friends while I headed outside for some air, and time to think. I walked the walls surrounding the palace and let my mind wander. I hated what I had done, but I could think of no way to give Matilda the apology she deserved. There was nothing I felt I could do to make it up to her.

I paced the ramparts until evening fell, when I heard the sound of heavy feet jogging towards me. Thorry was running my way, and I gave him a wave. He stopped in front of me and caught his breath.

"Good evening, Thorry," I said.

"Good evening, lord," he panted. "How is your arm?"

"It still aches, but it's bearable."

"Thank the Gods for that. I've come with a message for you."

"Oh?"

"Lady Eleni has invited you to a private supper later tonight, with her father, uncle, and possibly Lord William."

"*Possibly* William?"

"He's vanished, lord." Thorry must have noticed the look on

my face, for he chuckled. "Lady Eleni said not to worry. He sometimes disappears to get some time alone, so she does not want to look for him. If he turns up before supper he will be joining you, but otherwise it will just be the Almond Islanders."

I nodded. "I can understand that. I will join Eleni for supper. Walk with me for a bit, Thorry."

"Yes, lord," he said.

He stretched his back, then the two of us continued slowly along the ramparts, looking down at the city in the fading orange light. Calm had returned to the city now, but unlike before the fight at the dock-gate, this was an anxious calm. The city was on edge.

If one forgot the fact we were under siege, the landscape was quite beautiful. Smoke was rising from chimneys and roof holes, and the thousands of windows dotting the cityscape started to glow yellow one by one.

The light of the setting sun caused the Ard to shimmer and illuminated the stone, bestowing upon the city the soothing warmth that comes with summer evenings. The long shadow of the palace was cast over the main street, already shrouding it in darkness.

Soldiers moved through the streets ordering people back into their homes, and this time folk were eager to obey. A cat howled, and a dog began barking soon after. Thorry let out a quiet chuckle.

"I used to own a cat," he said. "She was blind, but that didn't stop the bitch from clawing you when she got the chance. I still loved her, though."

I smiled. "What happened to her?"

"Oh, she passed a few years ago. Held a funeral for her and everything. Have you ever owned any animals?"

"My family in Winterhome had a cow, a dog, and a few sheep. I also used to own two hounds, until recently."

Thorry sighed. "They're great things, animals. They bring us joy, comfort, security, asking for little in return. They can be our greatest companions in even the darkest of times. They know nothing of the troubles of the world, and I envy them for that."

"You wish you were an animal?"

"Oh, yes," he chuckled. "I would want to be a boar. King of the woods!"

I laughed. "Thorry Boar-Heart, fiercest of warriors." I stared down at the city. "You are right. They are a reminder of the innocence we have lost. The beasts live entirely as the Gods wish them to, never straying from their own law. Something men forgot long ago."

"Perhaps, lord, it's within Man's nature to forget. To be free to choose obedience to the laws of the Gods, or otherwise."

"Perhaps," I mumbled. A flock of sparrows caught my attention as they flew west over the city. They passed over our heads, then turned to watch them disappear over the roof of the palace. It must be nice to be a bird, especially in times such as this.

"What are they saying?" Thorry asked.

I shrugged. "Birds do not often say things worth translating. Those sparrows are just speaking nonsense. 'Lights. Ladders. Log.' They're just telling each other what they see."

Thorry and I jolted to the sound of a horn in the distance, coming from the New City's wooden wall. It sounded again, and the beacon atop the Old Fort's watchtower burst into a sudden blaze. The horn blew again, three times.

Warriors, the birds said. *War*.

A sharp chill ran up my spine. Lord Edric had begun his assault.

13

Assault

Horns were blaring. Bells were clanging. Panic caught the Capital once more.

Thorry and I raced back to the palace, pushing past the soldiers hurrying to the eastern wall. We made it to our rooms, where we began dressing for war. I pulled on my mail and helmet, threw my cloak over my shoulders, and buckled my sword belt.

I took my shield and met Thorry again in the hallway. He too was now dressed for war in the armour Stephan had given him. He had no sword, but held a fierce-looking axe along with his shield. He seemed formidable, but I could see the fear in his eyes.

"You'll live to see tomorrow, my friend," I said.

He gave a nervous smile. "I hope so."

"Just remember what Dughlas has taught you, and don't forget to block. Let's go."

We made our way down the corridor and out of the palace, then found Dughlas and Philip waiting at the gate. They were both ready for battle, though Philip's mail appeared a little too big for him.

"Philip, what are you doing?" I asked.

"I am going to fight."

"No, you're not."

"What are *you* doing?" Dughlas asked me.

"I'm going to fight."

He laughed. "Not with that arm of yours, you're not."

"My arm is fine."

"Lift your shield then."

I did as he asked and then without warning he swung his sword. A surge of pain shot through my upper body, I gave a yell, then stumbled back. Dughlas chuckled and shook his head.

"You even winced when you lifted it. Sit this one out, boss. There will surely be more to come," he said.

"What am I supposed to do, then?" I asked.

He shrugged. "Protect the women."

Philip smirked, and I grumbled. "Fine, but I won't let you command me next time. Philip, come."

"Oh, let him fight. He's ready, and he needs to see combat one day. Why not let his first time be with the advantage of a wall?" Dughlas said.

I looked down at him and thought. He looked back up at me, a certain fire in his eyes, and I remembered how eager I was to fight when I was his age. Dughlas was right; I could not keep him from battle forever. I sighed. "Alright, but you two better defend him as if he were my own son. If I hear of Philip's death, I want to hear of yours as well."

Philip grinned, and Dughlas patted him on the shoulder. I nodded to him, and he nodded back. "We'll see you soon, Edward," he said.

"Good luck," I said. "The Gods are with us tonight." I hoped.

Dughlas smiled. "Course they are, we'll have a Godspeaker praying for us."

The three of them made their way out of the gate with the rest of the city's warriors. I stood back as a party of horsemen rode through the crowd, led by Stephan and his son. The king noticed me and waved, while his son only glared.

My arm still throbbing from the blow of Dughlas's sword, I made my way to the palace's main hall, where a number of women, children, elders, and a few wounded soldiers were waiting. There was a sense of unease hanging over the room, and hardly anyone spoke more than a whisper. The muffled, distant sound of horns echoed from outside.

Eleni and Arlette hurried over to me, frowning. "Why are you not with the men?" Eleni asked.

"I took an arrow earlier this morning," I said. "I can hardly lift my shield."

"William has gone to the wall with his oathmen, along with my father and uncle," said Eleni.

"Gods, it seems everyone is going that way," I said.

"Should they not be?"

"It's a big city." I looked around the hall. "Where is Matilda?"

Eleni turned to Arlette, who shrugged. Eleni shook her head. "We have not seen her all day."

"Shit," I breathed. I pushed past them and headed for the corridor leading to our rooms. Eleni called my name. I ignored her. I knew exactly where Matilda was, but I held on to a sliver of hope.

I broke into a sprint when I reached the hallway, bowling past a servant, and within moments reached Matilda's room. I threw the door open, ran inside, and looked around.

It was empty.

I searched the room for her armour or sword, looking under the bed, pulling open her drawers and cupboard and finding nothing but ordinary clothing. I opened the chest at the foot of her bed, but that too held nothing of note.

I kicked the chest and yelled. It was as I feared.

And it was all my fault. I should have been kinder to her, and given her the love she deserved. Perhaps then she would not have been so eager to rush into battle with no knowledge of what she would face. The vision I received during Winterlow, of Matilda standing in dirty mail as blood poured from her eyes, mouth, and fingers, flashed before my eyes.

I threw down my shield, pulled off my helmet, and sat down

on the bed with my head in my hands. My eyes watered. I lay down on her pillow and closed my eyes.

I took a deep breath. The pillow smelled like her. Tears dribbled from my eyes.

I put my hand under the pillow and felt something — a piece of folded parchment. I unfolded it to find a note scrawled in Matilda's handwriting.

Edward,

I do not know how to say these things to you, but I cannot keep it inside, so I write it down to let it go. I would never have the courage to give you this letter, but a part of me hopes you will stumble upon it someday.

I suppose in you I found the love story I always dreamed about, but Gods, the stories do not nearly show how much it hurts. Ever since I first laid eyes on you, on that bitter Firstsnow night, I felt something drawing me to you. Was it the Gods? Your Gift? Love? I do not know.

What I do know is that I love you, Edward. I know you know in your mind but I fear you do not feel it in your heart. Every day your mere existence rips my soul in two, but your smile and the sound of your voice never fails to mend it and make it whole once more.

I hate that I love you. You break me. I do not know myself anymore, nor do I know what I feel. There are days when you make me feel like a queen, and others when I feel like nothing. It tears me apart just to see you greet another woman, but at the same time I cannot help but love when they make you smile. I am so confused.

What do I mean to you? How do I make you feel? You told me Wynflaed is nothing to you — yet if you give more love to one who means nothing, I must matter even less.

I just want clarity, Edward. I want to know who I am. I thought I found the answer to that question in you, but now I am not so sure. I have spoken to Lady Eleni and even Dughlas about this, and they both tell me you care deeply. They say that because of who you are it is difficult for you to show it. Why? Just give me an answer.

I have collected some insects I found around the palace. It keeps me sane. I want to show you, but I fear I will just end up in tears again. I hide from you because I do not want my heart to break anymore.

I hope one day you see in me what you see in Solvi, and Wynflaed, and my sister. If you cannot love me, at least let me be your whore. Perhaps then I can feel like I mean something.

Matilda.

I let the note fall to the pillow and stared up at the ceiling. A tear ran down my face and I sighed. I still have that letter to this day.

"Edward?" Eleni said. She had appeared in the doorway with a concerned look on her face. She looked around the room. "Matilda has gone to fight?"

I nodded. "Neither her armour nor sword is here. Gods, why did I give her that damned sword?"

"You wanted to keep her safe."

I grunted. "Matilda has been speaking to you about me."

"I promised her I would not tell you." Eleni came and sat on the bed beside me, then took my hand. "I understand you, Edward. You fear your feelings for her. You love her, but fear the pain you might bring her if you let your feelings be real."

"What do I do, my lady?"

"Let yourself love her."

"I do not know how to love. I was never taught."

Eleni smiled. "Yes, you do. I have seen it, in the short time I have known you. Now come, the people in the main hall will feel better if Ardonn's famous Godspeaker is with them."

I smiled. "You go. I will be there soon."

Eleni curtsied, then left me alone in the room. I pocketed the letter and hoped Matilda would not mind me taking it — if she even survived the battle. My heart told me she would, yet Fate was more unpredictable than she had ever been, and the Gods told me little.

I made my way over to the writing desk by the window and picked up the tray atop it. It displayed a variety of insects that

Matilda had stuck on tiny pins. They were nothing too unusual, but there were many I had not seen before.

I did not often take notice of the world's smallest creatures, so Matilda's interest in them had always intrigued me. Where most would see a spider, beetle, or fly, Matilda saw just one of a multitude of different species. She showed this great variety with her jars and pin-trays. I have never met anyone else with such an obsession. I sighed, placed the tray down, then headed back to the main hall.

I waited in the hall with Eleni, William's mother and his sisters for hours. I often paced, but Eleni would tell me to sit back down. If I made it clear I was worried then others would worry too.

After some time, the queen entered the hall with the ageing High Priest at her side and wandered around talking to those most clearly afraid. That was the first time I had seen Queen Bebbe, and I understood why. Rumour told that she spent most of her time in her quarters, for whenever she met with strangers she often fell terribly ill soon after.

Those rumours proved true, for the poor woman seemed so frail and sickly that the slightest breeze might knock her over. Her nose was bright red and her eyes bore dark rings, which contrasted sharply with her pale skin. She was not an old woman, but her condition made her appear far beyond her years.

She did not approach us. We would have been strangers to her, faces she had never seen before, and likely avoided us on purpose. She did not spend long in the hall. After speaking with a few people she hurried to the back door and headed for her quarters.

I leaned close to Eleni. "Queen Bebbe's father is the Lord of Winterhome," I said, my voice hushed. "His eldest daughter was married to the late King Edwin, so Lord Wulfstan was able to take a position of neutrality during the Usurper's War."

"William told me Wulfstan of Winterhome betrayed Edwin," she whispered.

I nodded. "Edwin's wife died when the Capital fell to the Usurper. Wulfstan immediately marched in support of Wim, saying a true king should be able to protect his wife. Shall I tell you something I probably shouldn't?"

"You have to, now that you have caught my interest."

"Some say that Edwin's wife was killed by one of her housecarls." I lowered my voice. "And that Wulfstan himself gave the order."

Eleni gasped. "Why would he do that?"

"He may have seen that Edwin's reign was doomed, and sought to benefit from aiding the Usurper. And benefit he did."

Eleni said nothing, which was probably wise of her. I admit, it was probably unwise of me to be spreading such rumours then, especially so soon after I had been charged with treason.

I spoke no more of the subject anyway, for almost as soon as I said that, Crawmaer entered the hall. He saw me, glared, then went to sit in the chair beside the throne and brood. His beady eyes flicked back and forth as he glanced around the hall. The air in the room had grown foul.

Soon after he sat down, the palace doors burst open, and in marched Lord Tripho and his brother. Odo came with him, his arms drenched in blood up to the elbows, and spots of red dotting his face and hair.

"The Maricari ships burn on the docks!" Odo shouted.

Crawmaer showed no concern. "Do they assault the gate?"

"Not yet, Minister."

"Were you not forbidden from entering the Old City?" He waved a hand. "Bah. What would you have me do?"

Tripho spoke in his own language. He was stern, assertive, but seemed desperate. Odo translated for him. "Lord Tripho would sally forth from the gates to defend his ships."

"Only the king has authority over the gates in times of war."

"You hold the king's authority, damn you!"

It was then the Gods revealed to me the enemy's plan. Their true target was not the eastern wall.

"Crawmaer," I barked. Eleni grabbed my arm, but I pulled it free. The First Minister glared at me. "First Minister, they *want* those gates opened. They know the Maricari will want to defend their ships. They will cross the river and—"

"Silence!" Crawmaer said.

"Edward," Eleni hissed.

"Damn the ships," said Odo. "If they take the docks, we lose river-borne aid."

Crawmaer nodded. "That is true. Fine, the Maricari may defend their ships. But I will not hear of Ardish blood being spilt."

Odo spoke to Lord Tripho, then he nodded and bowed to Crawmaer. The three men marched from the hall.

Eleni knew what I was thinking. She stood and grabbed my wrist. "Edward, stay."

"Most of the men will be at the main gate. Your people will need all the help they can get. And Matilda…I cannot sit here while she is Gods know where."

"I understand. Edward, go with your Gods, and keep my father alive." Eleni smiled and brought my hand to her mouth, kissed it, then bowed her head.

I joined the gathering Maricari and went with them to the dock-gate. My heart was racing. My knees were weak. Yet on I went. I knew the fight there would be savage, but I had a duty, and I preferred the heat of battle to the uncertainty in the hall. In battle, all things are certain.

A few soldiers stood on the walls above the gate, but there was nothing they could do. A burning orange glow radiated above them, turning the night into day, and a great black pillar of smoke rose up to the clouds. Beyond those gates the docks burned.

The warriors amassed before the gate, and I pushed my way through the crowd to find Odo. "How were they not seen?" I shouted.

"They used the cover of darkness," Odo said. "And the distraction at the main gate. I believe this was their real goal."

"Bastards."

Odo nodded, and then pointing at me spoke to Tripho in Maricari. The Sealord nodded to me, and I nodded back, before he turned to face his men. He gave a speech, and they gave cheers, and together they beat their shields.

An order was given. The gates began to creak. The roar of fire and the drumming of shields drowned out all other sounds. I could smell it — the stench of burning wood and cloth. My arm ached. I was terrified.

"There will be no place for cunning here," Odo said to me. He snorted. "Or for honour. This will not be a typical battle. You kill or you die; that is the only rule in a street fight. There will be no formation, no strategy, no mercy. All we must do is go out there and slaughter whoever we find."

"You know this from experience?"

He nodded. "As a boy I fought with King Edwin's father in his efforts to drive the Erilans from Swelenda's Hand. I became an animal that day. Never was the same after that."

The gates began to open. Slowly. Heat blasted through the gap, and the roar of the fire reached a crescendo. The ash stung my nostrils.

"Are you ready?" Odo asked.

I shook my head. "I don't think I am."

He laughed. "Nor am I, Godspeaker. Nor am I."

The gates were almost open. We could see clearly the carnage before us. Edric's men noticed us too, and began turning away from their destruction to assemble a shield wall in the street ahead. I closed my eyes and whispered a prayer.

"The Maricari will move to defend their ships first," Odo said. "But you and I have another task. We must find their commander and send him to the Pits, else his men will burn the dock-town to ash. We cannot lose the docks."

"How will we know him?"

Odo only laughed. A horn was blown, the Maricari gave a resounding cry, and we charged. I was possessed by a sudden fury and roared. I ran with the warriors towards the half-formed shield wall. I ran to my death.

Yet before I could die, Odo grabbed my collar and pulled me back. The horde of Maricari raced past me and crashed through the enemy line. That is when the slaughter — the screams — began.

"This way!" Odo shouted.

Tripho was barking orders in his own language, but Odo and I ignored him. I followed Odo away from the battle and down a side street. Behind me the enemy shield wall collapsed and Edric's warriors were cut to pieces, but still many were spread throughout the dock-town or on the docks themselves. The Maricari ran to hunt them down.

Odo and I ran too, through alleys and back streets. I did not know where he was taking me but I had no choice but to trust him.

Soon we were faced with three Beglen warriors. Their cloaks were blood-red, their mail gleaming in the orange light. Three against two. They grinned, and believed they had victory.

Odo would not give them that. He lifted his axe above his head and before they could even reach us he hurled it towards them. It went spinning through the air at blinding speed, then with a crack and a gasp it buried itself in the skull of the leading man.

I simply watched in horror. Odo snatched my shield from me and held it before him, drew his shortsword, then charged the other two. I picked my target and charged with him.

Odo was right. The fight was savage, and conjured impulses I never knew I had. Instead of blocking, my opponent punched at me with the rim of his shield. It made contact with my shoulder and I felt the wound in my arm rip open again. I screamed, pain surging through me, but within a moment that pain was replaced by a cruel bloodlust.

I fell to a knee and the warrior swung his axe down at me. I swung my sword up and the blade met his wrist. It cut right through, just below the mail sleeve, and sent blood squirting over my face. The man screamed and recoiled and then Odo, who had just finished with his opponent, tackled him into the brick wall beside him.

I stood and thrust my sword with both hands at the enemy's gut. It pierced his mail's links and he lurched forward. I pulled the blade free, then brought it up to his throat and sliced. I growled as the man vomited blood and collapsed.

I spat on his corpse, my chest heaving. Odo grabbed my arm. "They are not men, but monsters. Remember this and you may yet survive."

We carried on through the streets and encountered similar skirmishes at every turn. We came around a corner and bumped into two Begleners, but none of us took a moment to think. We simply put them down like butchers would cattle. The fights were short and brutal. The walls of the dock-town were painted red that night.

We met another on his own. He tried to run, but Odo was faster. The man had his hamstring cut in two by Odo's axe, then Odo pinned him down and held his dagger to his throat.

"Who leads you?" Odo growled.

The man only screamed, so Odo pressed the tip of his blade beneath the man's jaw.

"Answer me!"

"Earl Merric," he sputtered.

"Where is he?"

"He's captured the fishworks. Lord, please—"

Odo thrust the knife up through the man's jaw and his eyes rolled back. He stood and pressed his boot against the man's face, pulling the blade free. We carried on, cutting ourselves a path through the streets to the fishworks. Both Maricari and Beglener corpses alike littered the alleys.

"He'll be guarded," I said.

"I know."

Did Odo even care? I do not know. All I knew was that Odo sought redemption. He sought a way to clean the reputation of his house. If it took the death of an earl to achieve that, Odo would have killed a thousand.

I had little time to prepare myself for the coming fight. We were at the fishworks soon enough; as I predicted, they were swarming with Merric's housecarls. Odo grabbed my collar again and pulled me into an alley. He peeked back around the corner. "I know Merric," Odo said. He did not need to hush his voice, for the sound of battle and wrathful fire would deafen Merric's men. "I know how he fights, and I know how he wins. That is how we will beat him."

"I have never heard of him."

Odo snorted. "That's because he's a fameless coward. A looter. He sends his men against farmers and traders, then scurries off like a cockroach in the light when warriors come. There is no glory in slaughtering the weak."

"How will that knowledge help us?"

"Because we will shine the light on the roach." He reached for the horn at his belt.

"You knew Merric would be leading this assault?"

"I suspected it. Who else would be better at burning an undefended town than Earl Merric? All he needed to do was cause terror until the next wave comes."

"We must defeat him before then."

Odo nodded and brought the horn to his mouth. "His warriors will abandon him the moment they sniff defeat. Let us give them a whiff of it. Follow my lead."

Odo sounded the horn, letting out one long, loud drone. It filled the alley and the surrounding streets. Odo blew for as long as his lungs would let him, and the drone was followed by shouting and the thunder of boots on wood and stone. He turned and smiled at me. "They are monsters, not men."

At that he yelled, and charged from the alley. He ran towards the fishworks, axe in both hands, and I followed. We both shouted, cursing them, and Merric's warriors panicked. A few came at us, but most ran into the fishworks.

Odo struck the first blow. One moment the housecarl was screaming, and the next his head rolled. Odo swung at the next man, but this one had the sense to block. His shield was split in two, he pulled his blade back to lunge, but I sliced at his hamstrings. With a cry he fell to his knees, then Odo silenced him.

Another came at me and I swatted the thrust of his spear with my shield. A stupid weapon to use in such a fight, but he learnt that too late. I thrust at the gap between his mail and helmet, and the fool tried to parry with his spear. It was an awkward and clumsy move, the weapon far too long, and so instead my blade met his flesh.

He died fast, just as Odo split the helmet and skull of another man. A few more came at us and we slew them easily enough.

These were men adept in rape and murder, but had little experience in combat against real warriors. I was starting to understand now how Merric's deeds would be his downfall.

The sound of a Maricari horn echoed triumphantly from the ships. The fires were dying down and Beglen's men were diving into the river or fleeing to their rafts. Odo responded with his own horn, and that was enough to drive the rest of Merric's men into the fishworks.

Then we saw him. A man with a rich, red cloak and a gilded, red-crested helmet emerged from the building in a panic. His mail was shining and bore not a drop of blood. In his hand he clutched a silver hilt around which curled a bronze snake, and from the open mouth of that snake stretched the sword's long, clean blade.

"Merric!" Odo growled. "Face me, coward."

The earl turned, startled, and a half-dozen housecarls put their shields up around him. Odo strode forward, and I followed.

"Kill them both, kill them!" Merric barked. His voice quivered. All six of his men moved forward as one, but Merric wailed. "No, not all of you. Two of you, go."

Four inched back to their master while the two at the front moved forward. I could see their eyes behind their visors, and in them I saw fear. Odo laughed and held out his arms. I held my shield in front of me. Then Merric yelled and the two men charged.

They stood no chance. Odo feinted and knocked his

opponent's shield to the side, leaving his torso exposed. He lunged and winded the man, who keeled over. I could not watch the coming slaughter, for I had my own man to deal with. I killed him fast after a few clashes of sword and shield, cutting his throat open. As he collapsed, Odo was pulling his axe free from his man's ribs.

The remaining four still surrounded Merric. Odo and I slowly walked towards them, and they inched back.

"Defend me," Merric sputtered. He pushed two men forward.

"Do you really wish to die for a stinking fish-shed?" Odo said. "Abandon this honourless wretch, or tell your forefathers tonight why you join them."

The men dropped their shields and ran for the rafts. The other two followed suit, and after a brief moment of disbelief, Merric ran too. Odo bolted after him. The earl was too slow. He was snatched like a dog by the scruff of his neck and thrown to the ground. I came to stand over him and held my blade at his throat.

Merric held up his hands while Odo picked up the snake-hilt sword. The earl looked from me to Odo, then from Odo to me, again and again. "Remove his helmet," Odo said. I did as he asked and revealed an ugly, red-faced old man. His eyes begged for mercy.

"Stand back, Edward," Odo said.

Merric stammered, sputtering out nonsense. Without a word, I let Odo stand over the earl. His face betrayed no emotion.

"Oh Gods, Lord Odo. Please, I beg you—"

"Are you afraid, Earl Merric?"

He nodded. Frantically. Odo held the blade up to his face and admired it.

"Warrior's blood has never stained this blade, has it?" Odo pressed the tip of the sword against Merric's throat, and the man gasped.

"This night shall not change that fact. Open your mouth."

Merric seemed confused. Odo shrugged, then turned and stomped on Merric's knee. The earl let out a mighty wail, and I just stood by and watched. The fires were dying now, but the sounds of clashing steel could still be heard echoing around the docks as Maricari fought against Beglener.

"Open your damned mouth, you shit-eating bastard," Odo barked. Merric obeyed that time, and then Odo gently rested the end of Merric's own sword on his tongue. Tears were streaming down the earl's face and he was trembling. "Beg for your life, and I may spare it."

Merric tried to speak, but cut his lips against the blade and moaned.

Odo laughed. "I cannot hear you! Speak properly, man."

"Lord—" I stepped forward, but Odo held up his hand.

Merric tried to speak again but his words were incomprehensible. Odo roared with laughter — a terrible, maniacal laughter — and Merric groaned and cried. I looked away, and with the sound of steel scraping against tooth and bone, Merric was ferried to the Pits.

The earl's death was witnessed. Men began shouting, crying out for retreat. It was just as Odo had planned. With Merric's death, the assault on the dock-town had failed. A few courageous warriors remained to fight their final stand, but the bulk fled, piling onto their rafts or simply discarding their mail and weapons and braving the currents of the Ard.

"One day, Edward, if you have daughters, you will understand why I showed him no mercy. Now, get back to the keep," Odo said. He was stripping Merric's corpse of valuables, then pulled a silver chain from his neck with a gold talisman of a two-headed axe, the symbol of Hildafol. He chuckled, then tossed it at me. "It seems the God of Strength gave none to Merric. Go, tell the First Minister what happened here. The Islanders can clean up."

I nodded and put the chain around my neck, then tucked the talisman beneath my mail. I headed back to the city, passing dead or wounded warriors from both sides. Some were being carried on stretchers or dragged back into the city.

The rush of battle died and the pain returned to my arm. It was throbbing, aching, and I could feel blood dribbling down my arm from the reopened wound. I was somewhat dazed. My mind had not yet processed all that had happened or recovered from the savagery of that fight.

I did not even feel the relief of victory, for although we had driven the Begleners back over the river, the status quo had not changed. I was afraid. I still did not know where Matilda was, nor did I know what had happened at the main gate.

When I arrived back at the palace, Capital soldiers were assembling outside the keep. They were elated, cheering and singing, and that gave me some hope. I entered the main hall where Eleni and Arlette came to greet me. The former embraced me. "What happened?" she asked.

"We won," I said. I did not care to say much more, for there was only one thing on my mind.

Everyone in the hall cheered at the news, and Eleni smiled. At that a trumpet was sounded. The men gathered outside parted, and in came King Stephan. He was a mess, his mail stained with blood, and behind him followed his limping, bruised son. The two were followed by several dozen warriors. Stephan strode to his throne and sat down beside Crawmaer. Wim sat in the chair to his left.

"You are safe now," Stephan said to those gathered in the hall. "Go back to your quarters. There is time to rest while the dog at our gates licks his wounds."

Crawmaer began speaking to Stephan. I breathed a sigh of relief, and the people started to disperse. Soon, William entered the hall. He looked ragged, but was grinning. He pulled off his helmet and ran over to us, hugged Arlette, kissed his wife, then nodded to me. "You missed a good scrap, my friend," he said.

"Was Matilda there? Did you see her?" I asked.

William frowned and shook his head. "Was she not with you? That was no place for a woman."

"No."

I glanced at the door as Dughlas, Thorry, and Philip strode in. Dughlas and Philip wore a proud look, both covered in blood and eyes blazing, but Thorry seemed distant. He carried half a shield and appeared not to notice those around him.

I raced over to them and we greeted each other fondly, but Dughlas frowned at the sight of my bloodied mail. "What in the Heavens happened to you? You were to stay in the keep."

"I can tell you later. I need to know Matilda's whereabouts. She was not here and I fear she went to the wall."

Dughlas shook his head. "Gods…"

I looked around the hall, hoping desperately to see her, but all those dressed in mail were men. "What was it like? The fight?" I asked.

"We won, and at little cost, too. Hardly a skirmish," Dughlas said. "I think Edric just wanted to test us. I'm sure Matilda—"

"I'm going to find her. You three get yourselves a strong drink."

Before Dughlas could protest, I pushed past them and headed out into the courtyard. Warriors were gathering there, boasting and laughing about their victory. This was the promise of hope we all needed, but I did not feel it. If Matilda had died I felt it would have all been for nothing.

I ran from the palace and headed into the Old City, jogging along the main street as I called Matilda's name again and again. I looked left and right, but saw no sign of her. My heart was beating faster than my footsteps.

I broke into a sprint once I entered the New City, moving as fast as my legs would take me. If she was wounded or had died, she might still be at the wall. I needed to know her fate. Gods, the uncertainty was worse than anything I had felt before. I thought I would collapse and be consumed by panic.

I reached the New City's wooden wall and looked around. Healers were rushing to tend to the wounded, while others collected the dead. Some soldiers still sat up on the wall, though they were weary and leaned on their spears or against the palisade, huddling around braziers.

A few of them were shouting down at the enemy, taunting them, daring them, asking when they would send their *real* men. Down below, a man sat over the lifeless body of another and wept. I saw a man talking to himself, muttering at the wall. Another man was singing a cheerful song while downing a bottle of mead.

Yet no matter who I asked, or which bodies I checked, I could not find Matilda.

I gave up. It was hopeless. If she was alive I should have seen her; she should have returned to the palace. But if she was dead she was not on the city side of the wall. She would be among those piled in the corpse-yard on the other side, left to feed the ravens and dogs.

I felt as though the ground had opened up beneath me. I did not even have the strength to weep. I simply turned and wandered back up to the palace, staring blankly at nothing. My mind was empty.

I did not even go through the main hall. I did not want to see anyone. I did not want to speak. I went through one of the palace's side doors near the back and followed the corridor to my quarters.

I stopped outside my door and glanced at Matilda's. I sighed, remembering her scent on the pillow and the tray of insects — those small pieces of her that had been left behind. I went over to the door and leaned my head against it, then pushed it open.

And there she was.

She was in her bath, and with a gasp she rushed to fold her arms over her chest. I stood there agape. A servant girl who had been combing her hair stared wide-eyed. "Forgive me, My Lady," the girl said. "I forgot to lock the door."

She stood to hurry me from the room, but Matilda shook her head. "Worry not, I know this man," said Matilda. "Leave us, please." She frowned at me and sunk so that only her head was above the water. The servant hurried past me and I shut the door.

"I thought you were dead," I mumbled.

"Why would I be dead?"

"I know where you went."

Matilda said nothing, then pulled her head under the water. All I could see now was a mess of floating black hair. Her belt, with Idris's sword and sheath attached, was hung over the bedpost. I walked over to it, then Matilda popped her head back up out of the water.

"Leave it," she snapped.

I ignored her and pulled the sword from its sheath. The blade was clean.

"I did not fight," she said. "I just wanted to find you."

"Why?"

"I wanted to keep you safe."

I laughed. "I didn't even go to the eastern wall. Gods, Matilda, what is wrong with you?"

She bowed her head and pulled her knees up to her chest. "I know, Dughlas told me," she muttered. "I just wanted to be worth something to you."

"*Dughlas* told you? You saw him?"

Matilda nodded. "He was at the wall too. I asked him where you were, and he said you were at the palace because of your arm. But…why are you such a mess?"

I scowled and shook my head. A ripple of pain went through my arm. "That lying bastard. What did you do then?"

"I did not fight, I swear. Dughlas told me he would not tell you I was there if I waited below the ramparts."

"What happened to your warrior blood, eh? Your noble spirit?"

Matilda flinched and stared down at her knees. She mumbled something.

"Pardon?"

"I said stop yelling at me," she barked.

I took a deep breath, then sat down at the foot of the bed. "Do you know how worried I was during that assault? Do you know how it felt knowing you were at the wall? I fought through smoke and fire tonight, and as I looked men in the eyes while my sword drained their life-blood, all I could think about was them doing the same to you."

"I am sorry," she said.

"I found your letter, by the way. The one under your pillow."

She raised her eyebrows and stared up at me. "That was private."

"Well, it was addressed to me." I took it from my pocket and unfolded it. "*At least let me be your whore*," I read.

"Edward, I—"

"You want to be my whore? Come on, then." I shuffled over. "Lie down and let me make your dreams come true."

Matilda just stared at me, her mouth slightly open. I stared back, waiting for some kind of response. The silence must have been too much for her to bear, for after a while she spoke. "Why are you doing this to me?"

"Because that's just who I am," I said. I stood, and Matilda flinched. "Since you have clearly changed your mind, I'll just find someone else to play the part."

Matilda's lip quivered. "Please."

"Please what?"

She put her hands to her face and sobbed. I rolled my eyes, headed for the door, and left her alone. Gods, what a fool I was. I was filled with a rage that had come from nowhere. Why was I so angry, so frustrated? Why was I losing control of myself so easily?

I went to my room and found Wynflaed inside. She had prepared a bath for me and was stoking the flames in the hearth. She turned and gave me a small smile when I entered, then stood and curtsied. "Is everything alright, lord? I heard shouting."

"Just fine," I said. I closed the door behind me and strode over to her. I loosened her hair and began to untie the bodice of her dress, but she pushed my hand away and shook her head.

"Not tonight, Edward. I'm still shaken by all that's happened today," she said.

"Then leave," I said.

Wynflaed frowned. "I wanted to ask if you would come with me to the shrine of Wynn. I thought to pray for peace and victory before I retire to bed."

"No. If that is all you intend then I have no further use for you. My bath is warm and fire hot, so leave me be."

"*No further use*?" Wynflaed retorted. "I am not your slave."

Wynflaed glared at me for a while, and I stared back. I let out a sigh. "Forgive me, this day — this city — has taken its toll. Shall we visit the shrine?"

"No, I've changed my mind. Goodnight, Grave-Knocker."

Wynflaed thrust the poker into the flaming logs and stormed from the room. I turned to follow her but was met with the slamming of the door. I thought it best to just let her go, so instead went to sit by the fire.

"Gods, Edward, what has become of you?" I whispered.

I thought of my old master, Brendan, and what he would think of me now. There was no doubt he would be ashamed. The man I had been in those days at the Capital was not the man Brendan had raised me to be.

I removed my mail and shirt, then peeled off the dirty bandages around my arm while the poker warmed in the fire. The gash caused by the Maricari arrow was healing, but not fast enough. I took a deep breath and bit down on my belt, then took the poker and pressed it against the wound.

I muffled the scream as best I could and curled my nose at the smell of burning skin, then threw the poker to the ground. The searing pain was almost unbearable, but I felt a sense of relief. Still dizzy, I slumped back down and stared at the ceiling.

That city was weighing on me. Ever since I passed through those gates when we arrived I had felt a cloud of dread in my mind. It was a dark place, ripe with intrigue and ill-intent, where the seeds of betrayal could bloom. I was letting it get to me, but I should have been strong. I needed to resist the impulses that every breath of the city's foul air planted in my mind.

I felt isolated and alone behind those walls. There were few I could trust, and every day I felt my friends and companions growing ever distant. I could not trust Matilda nor Wynflaed after how I had treated them. I could not trust Dughlas, as I had just learned. Could I trust Thorry, a merchant-turned-assassin? Philip, a foreign child?

And what of William? I believed he was my friend, but since

being reunited with his family I felt something unsettling about him. He had done no wrong, and was his usual jolly self, but my gut told me to keep an eye on him. Just as I had noticed his housecarls keeping an eye on me.

I felt everyone was plotting against me, but perhaps that was just the city and the siege taking its toll. Such thoughts were foolish, based on nothing, but I could not shake them. They nagged at me, a burden on my mind.

I called out to the Gods and my ancestors for comfort and for answers, but they remained silent. Had they abandoned me? Was I helplessly waiting there, doing nothing while the Capital's doom approached?

It certainly seemed so.

I could not bear to hide behind the Capital's walls any longer. I felt choked. Suffocated. I needed to get away from this city, but how? The gates were locked, and Emrys's men patrolled the riverbank.

Yet there was another way out of the city. A hidden way, known only to the King of Ardonn and his family.

And me.

14

Flight

The first to notice my disappearance was Wynflaed.

She went to my quarters a few hours after our quarrel to apologise for her bitterness, though in truth it was me who should have apologised. Still, she went to my room but found it empty. The bloody poker still lay on the floor and my weapons and armour were gone.

She thought little of it at first. She knew I was prone to wandering in the late hours of the night and reasoned I had gone to visit a temple, or perhaps an alehouse to seek what I could not get from her.

Then the riots began.

It started small. A petty tavern brawl erupted between some Maricari soldiers and Stephan's men, presumably over a working girl. Nobody knew who started it.

Soon after the brawl began it spilled out onto the streets. Both Maricari and Ardish soldiers nearby saw only one thing — strangers speaking a strange language assaulting their countrymen. That was enough to have the whole street in uproar.

The tensions, fear, and anger ignited by the day's drama had erupted into a blaze.

It did not take long for the brawl to become a city-wide riot. By the time the New City was in chaos, the tavern the brawl started in was cinders. Men slaughtered each other in the streets, looted stores, and burned down the barracks and inns. It was madness.

The palace erupted into a panic. None quite knew what was happening. Did the enemy breach the walls? Was the city infiltrated from within? Rumours spread and the fear took hold.

King Stephan and Lord Tripho rode out with their personal guards to restore peace and order, despite Crawmaer and Queen Bebbe urging them to keep the Old City gates firmly shut. None knew exactly who they rode out to face.

It took until dawn for the violence to cease, and even longer for the fires to be quenched. The final death toll was immeasurable. Hundreds had died, mostly soldiers, and the streets of the New City were littered with their bodies. Many more were wounded, among them Lord Tripho himself, who returned to the palace with a broken leg and a bleeding skull. The healers said he would mend, but would need weeks of bedrest.

It would have taken Lord Edric numerous assaults on the city's walls to equal the damage done by a few drunkards and a whore. Cracks were forming in the city's defences, and Edric saw an opportunity to widen them. At dawn, while the city's soldiers struggled to put out the blaze and with the rising sun in the eyes of the weary defenders, Edric attacked.

He hit the city hard and fast. His men scaled the eastern wall while a heavy ram hammered at the gate, putting the strength of its hinges, bolts, and bars to the test. Fireballs and pots of oil were launched over the wall to fuel the flames within.

The defence was weak at first. Those who defended the wall were few in number, for many raced through the streets to fight the fire, and it did not take long for a section of the wall to be captured by Edric's men.

This contingent of warriors was led by Edric's second son, Tatric, who triumphantly waved the red banners of Beglen over the wall's southernmost bastion. Obeying his father's command to give no pause to his attack, he pushed the advantage further by penetrating the city's south-eastern quarter.

That was when reinforcements arrived. Men from the Old City had come at last, along with a large number of those who had beaten the blaze. Tatric's men found themselves engaged in a bitter melee against more warriors than they anticipated. Tatric chose to fight rather than flee.

Beglen's hero was cut down in the streets of the Flood Quarter by none other than William — his first heroic deed as the new Lord of Everlynn. Tatric was given the chance to yield, but yield he would not. I am told he fought bravely.

With the arrival of reinforcements Edric's men retreated, but not before inflicting a heavy toll on the defence. We were fast running out of time.

After the city had calmed down, Wynflaed began to worry. She searched the palace for me and instead found Dughlas with Philip, Thorry, and William hanging about in the kitchen. They were watching a new chef struggling with the baking of bread, and had to keep stifling laughter whenever he made a mess of the dough.

Wynflaed curtsied. "Lords. You are Edward of Oldford's oathmen, yes?"

Dughlas turned and smiled. "All that's left of them, anyway. Oh, and this is William, the new Lord of Everlynn. How can we help?"

"I'm looking for Edward. He's not in his quarters. Have you seen him?"

"Who's asking?"

"My name is Wynflaed. I'm the servant who has been tending his room."

Dughlas sighed. "I've heard about you, though not from Edward. We haven't seen him all day. He wasn't at the battle this morning and I figured he would be resting."

"He likes to wander the walls," said Thorry. "And visit the temple."

"I'll look there. Thank you, lords." Wynflaed curtsied, then headed out of the palace to find me.

Yet find me she could not. She searched the temple but the priests and priestesses had not seen me. She walked the entirety of the palace walls and found no trace, and even asked the guards at the Old City gate if they had seen me.

Wynflaed sighed, then headed back to the palace. There was only one other person who might know where I would be, she thought, but hoped she would not have to ask. Someone I had told Wynflaed to avoid.

She came to Matilda's door, took a deep breath, and knocked three times.

"My Lady," Wynflaed said. "I'm a servant. May I enter?"

"Of course," said Matilda.

A few seconds later Wynflaed heard the lock sliding in the door and then it opened. Matilda stood there smiling, but that smile quickly became a frown. "Oh, it is you. What do you want?"

Wynflaed curtsied. "My Lady, I am wondering if you've seen Edward recently. He seems to have gone missing."

"Missing? I have not seen him since last night. I assumed you would know. Is that all?"

"Um, I guess so, My Lady. Thank you."

The door slammed shut and the lock clicked.

Wynflaed went back to my room, still empty, and sat own on the bed. *Is this my fault?* she wondered. Worries entered her mind. *Have I killed him? Does he lie dead in some stinking alehouse?*

She continued her search of the palace and the surrounding streets. As evening drew near Dughlas, Thorry, and Philip joined in, and after a meeting with the king, Eleni helped too. They all searched but none could find me.

The next morning, William reported my disappearance to Stephan. He did not care much, and assumed I was just keeping to myself somewhere in the city, so did not want to waste men and resources scouring the city for one missing Godspeaker. He did issue a decree, however, ordering anyone with any information to report it to the nearest soldier.

The decree yielded nothing. My friends waited days for news of my whereabouts, searching the streets and asking around in the meantime, but nobody knew anything. They grew distressed. I often disappeared for short spaces of time, just to be alone with myself and the Gods, but it was unusual for me to be gone for days without warning.

Eventually Eleni promised a reward for any who knew where I was, using wealth her father had given her. Even Stephan started to concern himself with me, and he added a few extra pounds of silver to Eleni's reward.

The promise of coin was probably a bad idea. It was not long before folk flocked to the palace with rumours that I had been seen. "I saw him in the tavern," some would say.

"He was at the guardhouse," said others.

"He frequents the temple."

"I've been hiding him in my cellar!"

All were false, of course. A few of the claims made by folk who seemed sincere were checked, but yielded nothing. Stephan had to put Dughlas and Thorry in charge of receiving reports, for there were so many seeking the reward it was taking up too much of his time.

Matilda was rarely seen in those days. Dughlas caught her leaving the palace some mornings and returning late in the evening, but he did not ask her where she had been. She clearly did not want anyone to know.

One evening, while Thorry received false reports from the city folk, Dughlas and Philip went to the Old Fort to see if I was there, or if Odo knew where I was. When they arrived they discovered they were not the only ones searching for a missing man.

The fort's hall was guarded by Odo's oathmen, who refused to let my friends inside, so they snuck in through the cellar. While creeping through the empty kitchen Dughlas and Philip heard muffled shouts coming from the room above them.

Two people were arguing, and Dughlas soon realised it was Odo and his daughter Anora. He looked down at Philip and put a finger to his mouth, then stood still and listened.

"I told you once, and I will tell you again. I do not know!" Odo yelled.

"I do not believe you," said Anora. "I know you want him dead. That is why you had me defend him during his trial, is it not? So you could kill him yourself?"

"No. *She* wanted him alive. Besides, there are more powerful forces at work here. The Gods do not seem to desire his death either."

"Since when have you cared about the Gods?"

"Since I watched a horde of immortal warriors slaughter hundreds of panicked men like pigs," he shouted.

There was silence for a moment, before Anora spoke again. "I still want him dead."

"Did you make him vanish, then?"

"No. My insolent little brother suspects something, so has his warriors keeping an eye on him. My man cannot reach him."

"William is my only son. Do not speak of him that way."

Anora snickered. "You have always preferred him over your daughters. That is why I must now marry that rat, and why the Corpse-Whisperer had you on your knees ready to suck his cock if he so demanded."

There was a resounding slap, followed by hurried footsteps and a door slamming shut. Dughlas grabbed Philip by the arm and pulled him into the pantry, then listened as Anora strode past. They waited for a time, and once they were certain she was long gone they slowly emerged back into the kitchen.

"What was that about?" Philip whispered.

Dughlas shook his head. "Pretend you heard nothing. I think we're done here, let's go."

They returned to the palace unsuccessful. There they continued their wait, hoping for any news of my possible whereabouts.

And the next day, Lord Wulfstan of Winterhome arrived.

My friends searched the city in vain, for by the time Wynflaed discovered my quarters empty I was miles from the city.

How did I know the location of the Capital's secret escape route? Carol. He told me about it when he considered sending an assassin to end Stephan's line, but ultimately decided against it. The risk of letting that secret be known by some rogue was far too great.

He trusted me with that secret, though, as the Royal Godspeakers had always known of the route. It was part of the ancient complex, built for unknown reasons long before our people came to this land. It was an immense tunnel system, though it had only three exits. Known exits, that is. The tunnels formed a vast maze beneath the city, connecting the palace to the Old Fort and a small, hidden cave just east of the city.

The exits were not guarded, as that might draw attention to them. They were hidden in plain sight, and the complexity of the maze meant that any who wandered in by mistake would never return to the surface to reveal its secrets.

Only those who knew how to navigate those dark, narrow passages could have any hope of seeing daylight again. Fortunately, I remembered Carol's instructions. They were simple enough, and after hours of carefully following the path through the dank corridors I reached the exit.

I crawled through the tight hole at the back of the cave, then emerged beside a small pool concealed by a grove of beeches. There was no doubt folk had been to that cave, but any foolish enough to squeeze through the small hole at its rear would be doomed to die in darkness. I occasionally encountered what remained of some of those poor souls.

There was some time left before dawn. I needed to make haste lest the light betray me. Emrys and Edric's camp was so close I could not only hear the men there, but I could smell it. Horses and smoke. I needed to hurry.

But I also needed a horse, for I could not simply walk from that place. However, the only place I would be able to find a horse was the siege camp. I prayed the Gods were on my side that morning.

I crept from the grove, bent low and taking care not to make too much noise. Perhaps I could act normal and walk through as if I were one of Edric or Hakon's warriors? No, it was too risky. The last moments of darkness before dawn were all I had.

I snuck up to the camp and ducked behind a tree stump. Sharpened stakes had been driven into the earth surrounding the camp to prevent an attack from any reinforcements Stephan called, but they were far enough apart that I could creep past them. The light was turning grey now, and I could see a little easier — though that meant I would be spotted easier too.

Two soldiers stood slouching at the entrance to the camp, and to their left stood a makeshift stable where several dozen horses were tied. They were fine beasts, too. I just needed to take out the two guards, then I would have a clear run.

I whistled. They looked around and mumbled something to each other, then one shook his head. I whistled again, and this time they peered in my direction. One of them pointed, then they strode across the field to the stump I hid behind.

I waited, my heart racing. They drew nearer. I could hear their footsteps. I clutched my knife in both hands and held my breath.

They stopped, standing no more than a yard away from me. I did not move.

"See, must've been a bird," one said. "Nobody's out here, it's just an empty field."

The other grumbled. "Whatever. Come on then, let's get back to our posts."

They turned and headed back to the camp entrance. Now was my chance. I silently prayed they would not make a noise.

I leaped over the stump and sprinted at them. Before they could turn, I grabbed one man's face from behind and sliced my blade across his throat. He wheezed, then crumbled to the ground.

The other man spun around and gasped, but before he could shout I tackled him and plunged the knife into the underside of his jaw. His eyes bulged and the life left them. He died with barely a sound.

I had no time to move the bodies. The grass was long enough

to conceal them anyway, at least until the sun rose — by then I would be gone. I moved with quiet haste to the horses, a fire surging through my veins. Gods, it felt good to finally be free of that city. I almost smiled.

I ducked behind a barrel and peered at the horses. Then I felt the point of a sword at the back of my neck.

"Come to steal a horse, have we?" said a voice.

I raised my hands. "Perhaps I can buy one." I slowly turned my head, and when our eyes locked the man — the boy — raised his eyebrows.

"Godspeaker?" he hissed.

"Godwald. I am glad to see you alive."

Godwald lowered his sword, and I turned. "I have you to thank for that."

"How about thanking me by letting me go?"

He glanced over his shoulders and crouched down. "Why are you here?"

"I'm fleeing, and you should, too. Only death awaits you here."

"I cannot flee. I would dishonour my family."

"Your family was dishonoured the moment they betrayed their king."

"Gods, there are so many kings these days. Which one is true?"

"Carol Eomundson. Come with me, and restore your family's honour in his service."

He pursed his lips and looked down at the dirt. He shook his head. "I cannot, but I will help you. You do not want any of these, though. Follow me, you can take my brother's horse."

"What if someone recognises me?"

"Wear this," he said, then removed his cloak and handed it to me. I threw it over my shoulders. "You will look like one of my guards. Keep your head down and nobody will suspect a thing."

He had a nervous look in his eyes, and I smiled at him. "I'll trust you. Let's go."

Godwald stood, and I followed. We walked side by side through the camp. The darkness was fading now and I could see the first faint rays of sunlight edging over the city to the west. It was then I noticed the great plume of smoke rising above it.

"What in the Heavens is happening in there?" I asked.

"We suspect a riot," Godwald muttered. "There has been fighting within the city and a great fire has raged through the night. We will be attacking soon, while they are weak."

"Gods, I did not know…"

"Forgive me, Edward."

I clenched my jaw. My friends were in there, and I had abandoned them — but it was too late to turn back now. I had to do this.

I tried to act normal as we walked to avoid arousing suspicion, but fear was gripping my heart. Every man that saw us I worried might recognise me. There were men in that camp who certainly would.

Then someone gave a yell, a horn was blown, and a small

group of men ran past us in the opposite direction.

They must have found the corpses I left. My heart felt as though it would burst through my chest. There would be no escape for me if something went wrong, or if Godwald betrayed me. That could have been my final morning in this world.

Yet betray me he did not. Fate had other plans. Godwald brought me to the corral where a dozen or so stallions were kept, then showed me his brother's. It was a gorgeous, light brown Erilan with powerful legs. It would serve me well.

"His name is Rapid," Godwald whispered. He stroked the horse's mane while I mounted. Rapid shuffled his feet a bit, but Godwald calmed him.

"Thank you, Godwald," I said.

He nodded, then frowned as I drew my sword. He spun around and saw the man who had caught my attention.

It was Hakon.

"Edward of Oldford!" gasped Hakon. He was standing there, his sharp eyes wide, flanked by two warriors dressed in black. Our eyes locked, and he snarled. "Aided by Godwald of Beglen, the traitor. Take them."

"Oh, Gods!" Godwald cried. The two men drew their swords, Godwald threw himself up into the saddle of his own horse, and I grabbed Rapid's reins and kicked his sides. I charged forward, swinging my sword down at one of the men as I passed. The blade connected with his mail and he fell back with a cry.

I sped through the camp, Godwald close behind me. Horns

were blowing and men were shouting, and a few arrows whistled past us. I sheathed my sword and then snapped the reins.

"Ride, Godwald!" I shouted. "With me."

Rapid's name was fitting. Gods, he was fast. We shot past the tents towards the camp's eastern exit, but were faced with four men standing side by side, spears and shields in hand.

"Do not falter!" I yelled. "Ride through them."

I feared Rapid would rear, cowed by the spears, but the courageous beast did not fail me. We charged through their pitiful wall, a spear only just missing my leg. The men were thrown back and I looked over my shoulder to see Godwald race past them. I punched the air and caught him smile.

But it was far from over. The warriors I feared had come. Horsemen, decked out for war, with their leaf-bladed swords glistening in the rays of the early sun.

Godwald noticed them too, and he cracked his reins. The immortals rode hard and fast, and I feared they would catch us, but Rapid was faster. We rode on, beating the poor horses as though the world depended on it. It certainly felt like it did.

"Godspeaker, they are coming!" Godwald cried.

"Gods damn them, just ride."

Our horses thundered forward, moving like lightning. I could hardly hear their hoofbeats over the sound of air rushing past me.

Then a horn sounded. I looked over my shoulder to see our pursuers rear their horses and turn around to ride back to camp.

"They are retreating!" Godwald shouted.

"Keep going!" I yelled. "We don't stop until we reach that patch of woodland."

We raced onward as if the men were still behind us, but every time I checked over my shoulder they were nowhere in sight. Whatever that horn signalled must have been more important than Godwald and I. I thanked the Gods for it and carried on.

We reached the treeline, and only then did I give Rapid a break. Godwald was close behind, his horse skidding to a stop. He fell forward and hugged its neck, panting. I took a deep breath.

"We're alive," I sighed.

Godwald looked up at me, his eyes red from the wind. "That man—"

"Hakon. We know each other well."

"Gods, why did I flee?"

"Fear, perhaps? You were right to."

"My father would have forgiven me."

"Your father may have, but there are powerful men in that camp who would not. Why did you help me?"

Godwald climbed down from his horse and sat on the ground. "Because you spared me, on the day that we met." He started massaging his legs.

"I meant on that day. Why warn me?"

He shrugged. "Fear. I do not like this war one bit, and I hate those cursed horsemen. They are unnatural. I could not let Idris slay the Hero of Tillysburg. I was afraid of what would happen if he did."

"You are a brave young man, Godwald," I said. "Now mount up. I want to be as far from the Capital as possible before nightfall."

Godwald nodded, then struggled to his feet. He climbed back into his horse's saddle and the two of us headed off.

We went east.

For miles the land was scarred.

As Godwald and I rode, we passed scorched fields and the charred remains of abandoned villages. The earth was black, and a grey haze hung in the air. Scavengers, both man and beast, picked through the ruins of what was once a prosperous country, now a wasteland. Ravens circled overhead or tore at the singed, rotting corpses strewn about. The stench in some places was sickening.

Emrys and his men had been busy, and I could not help but blame myself. I had played a part in unleashing this horror upon the land. True, I had been unwilling and bound by the whims of Fate, but even so I felt responsible. If only I had left my sword in Tillysburg, things might have been different.

That is why I left the Capital. I was not fleeing, but acting. I needed to put an end to this chaos.

Thus, I rode for Carol.

Why Carol? I asked myself the same question. Carol's men

were still recovering from the battles during winter and he owed no loyalty to a usurper's bastard. There were other lords loyal to Stephan with larger, fresher forces, but while their priorities were to their own lands first, Carol was the rightful defender of all Ardonn. He would have the chance to prove himself worthy of that title in the coming days.

Carol also trusted me, and I him. It might have been more pragmatic to make the shorter ride north and seek the aid of Lord Wulfstan, but history had shown that man to be loyal to none but his own ambition. If he had not already marched south, there was no way I would convince him.

I did not tell Godwald I hoped to return to the Capital with an army. He truly believed we were abandoning the city to its doom, and although he cursed himself for betraying his father and brothers, he knew there was no turning back. He could have betrayed me and perhaps earned Emrys's forgiveness, but the boy had a good heart, and I knew I could trust him.

We encountered several small groups of refugees along the way, as well as some who travelled alone. They begged us for food or money, though we had little to give them that we did not need ourselves.

Some asked to come with us, desperate for the protection of Ardish blades. We allowed those with horses to follow, but those on foot we left behind. They would only slow us down. The longer our journey took, the more refugees Emrys would make.

As we moved east, the days grew brighter, life returned to the fields, and the number of scorched and ruined settlements thinned. We had reached the limits of Emrys's destruction around the Capital.

We reached Tillysburg not long after that. Godwald and I sat on our horses agape at the sight. Before then I had only seen Tillysburg once after Emrys burned it to the ground, on the day after the battle while the town's ruins were still smouldering.

Now, however, Tillysburg was cold. Dead. Nought remained of it besides its crumbling walls, the stone fort, and the cracked, blackened framing of what was left of its stronger buildings. Even the old bell tower had collapsed. What remained was merely a ghost, a shell of the town's former self.

We did not say it, but Godwald and I both knew that would be the Capital's fate if Emrys were not destroyed. I could only hope that Carol would listen to me, and that we would not be too late.

The day was darkening, but we did not stop. I could not bear to be anywhere near that cursed town. We rode for hours through the cold night, only stopping once Tillysburg was far behind us. It did not take long for it to be out of sight, but for miles I could feel it. An unseen shadow hung over that place.

A week later, we stood before the gates of Giant's Rest.

Wynflaed was sweeping the hallway in the guest wing when she was grabbed by the arm and turned around. She gasped, and found herself face to face with Matilda.

"Where is he?" Matilda demanded.

"Who?"

Matilda scowled. "Edward. I know you saw him before he disappeared."

"I do not know where he is, my lady. I assure you I am just as worried about him as you are."

"I can assure you that you are not. You have no idea where Edward has gone?"

Wynflaed shook her head. She tried to pull away from Matilda, but the lady gripped her arm tighter.

Matilda looked up and down the hallway. "Follow me." Matilda pulled Wynflaed before she could protest and led her through the corridor to the lady's quarters. Wynflaed was thrust inside, and then Matilda shut the door behind her.

"My lady?" Wynflaed said.

Matilda unsheathed the sword leaning against her bed and stood between Wynflaed and the door.

"My lady, I—"

"I know you were the last to see him," Matilda hissed. There was a fire in her red-wreathed eyes. "I have asked everyone. None saw him since he left the great hall after the assault on the docks. His friends know not where he is, none of the guards at the gate have seen him. Did you see him that night, after the assault?"

Wynflaed nodded. She wanted to speak, but the sight of the sword caught her words in her throat.

"What have you done with him? He would not just disappear like that, not without letting anybody know. Have you killed him?"

"My lady, I swear. I haven't seen him since that night. I did not spend much time with him, we only fought, and then I went to pray alone. He was gone when I returned."

"You fought?"

"Yes—well, no, I mean. It wasn't much of a fight, my lady. We only had a disagreement, and neither of us was in a pleasant mood."

Matilda lowered her blade. "You have been spending time with him, intimately, have you not?"

Wynflaed nodded.

"Has he captured your heart too?"

"I…Yes, my lady. I suppose he has."

"Then I pity you."

They were interrupted by a hurried knock at the door.

"Who is it?" Matilda asked.

"Lady Eleni, my lady."

"Oh. Come in."

The lady entered while two of William's housecarls stood by the door. She looked from Matilda to Wynflaed, then glanced down at the sword, and her eyes widened. "Goodness me," she gasped. "What is happening here?"

"Never mind that," Matilda said. "You look flustered, my lady. What is it?"

"You're needed at the east gate."

"Why?"

"My husband's uncle wishes to speak with you."

Hakon. Matilda's stomach dropped. At this news she felt that something was not right.

Eleni led the way through the palace and to the gate.

"Did he say what he wanted?" asked Matilda.

"No," Eleni said. "But Lord Wulfstan has come, and now the armies of Winterhome stand on the field waiting to do battle with Emrys. Hakon has come to parlay with a message from his lord, he says, but he will only speak to you."

"I feel I will not like what he has to say."

Eleni said nothing. They carried on, mounting horses outside the palace before making their way through the Old and then the New City.

"I have not seen you in some days, my lady," Eleni said. "Have you been well?"

"As well as I can be in a time and place like this," Matilda said. "I am beginning to think it might have been better for me to remain in Henton."

Eleni laughed. "If I had not married I would at this moment be sipping wine and baking under the open sky in a sun-kissed courtyard, a gentle breeze keeping me cool while I watch the waves crash against pristine shores without a care in the world."

"Yet here you are."

"Yet here I am. It is funny what paths our lives lead us down."

Eleni shifted in her saddle and straightened her back. "Now I am the Lady of Everlynn, and my duty is here."

"To your husband?"

"To my family. Since the sudden loss of our primary Ardish import we relied more on piracy, and the battles between Cavoucari pirates and Ardish sailors cost many lives. The alliance forged by my marriage came with the hope for peace between our peoples."

"And you still work for that peace even now, while we fester in the bowels of war. I admire you, Eleni."

"I do, and I am proud of it. My people have a love for both peace and war. It is not unusual for us to find ourselves embroiled in both."

"But which do you prefer, my lady?"

Eleni sighed. "I pray only for peace for my people." She turned to smile at Matilda. "And for my friends."

Matilda smiled back. It was not long before they reached the east gate, where the pair were greeted by a contingent of the Royal Guard. Stephan was with them, as was William. Upon seeing Matilda the king strode forward. He had a grim look about him.

"Thank you for coming, my lady," said Stephan.

Matilda curtsied. "I am happy to be of service, though I know not what use the second daughter of a forest earl might be."

"I have my suspicions. Come, let us go and speak to the bastard."

The view from the eastern wall presented a scene of both hope and horror. The stench of death wafted up from the corpse-yard below where the already-decaying bodies of fallen warriors lay, their eyes staring blankly up at the blue sky.

Columns of dark smoke rose up over the hills, painting the horizon with streaks of black. A haze hung over the fields where fell the ashes of Ardish homes. To the north, stretching across an open meadow, stood the brave men of Winterhome. They were lined up, shields and spears and bows at the ready, awaiting the coming bloodshed.

Their number was considerable, but it would not be enough to defeat Emrys alone. The warlord's army, reinforced by Beglen and what remained of Everlynn's warriors, outnumbered Wulfstan's by nearly two to one. Their only hope for victory was for Stephan to march from the city's gates and meet his ally on the field of battle.

"They cannot win this," Matilda gasped.

"No," muttered Stephan. "They cannot. That is why we parlay with Everlynn's rat."

Odo spat. He stood beside Stephan on the wall, glaring down at the lone black horse that stood before the gates. In its saddle was Hakon.

"It is good to see you, my lady Matilda!" he called.

Matilda said nothing. She only glared down at him.

"It has been too long. When last I saw you we marched north — as friends."

"Your men tried to kidnap her, uncle!" William shouted.

Hakon only smirked.

"Why have you summoned me?" said Matilda.

"I have come with a gift," said Hakon. "One befitting the beauty of a daughter of Henton."

"A gift?"

"Indeed. And in exchange for this gift, I would urge you to convince your bastard king to open these gates, kneel before Lord Emrys, and avert the coming slaughter. For if he does not we will have no choice but to destroy his allies, burn his city, and send his people to the Pits."

"I may be a bastard, Hakon," barked Stephan. "But at least I am a bastard with a crown. What are you?"

Hakon laughed. "Does the false King of Ardonn lose his nerve?" He tutted. "Enough of this. Bring me the lady's gift."

At that a man came forth bearing a wooden box. He held it up to Hakon, who opened the box and reached inside. What he pulled from within made some on the wall gasp while whispers and murmurs ran up and down the line. Matilda froze and her blood went cold. She said nothing.

"What mockery is this? Have you come to taunt us?" Stephan said.

The bastard only smiled. He held the bruised, bloodied head up high for all to see. Wet, brown hair covered its battered face and blood dripped from its open jaw. "There is no mockery here, Stephan. I thought only that the Lady of Henton would wish to see her Godspeaker one last time."

Matilda gripped the hilt of her sword. Eleni squeezed her arm. Her blood was now running hot. Her heart was racing, her face burning. She could not conjure the words to voice the anger she felt.

"Have you missed him? We caught him some days ago attempting to flee."

"Archers!" Stephan shouted. The men along the wall drew their bows, and at Stephan's command they loosed a volley at Hakon. He reared his horse and backed away, the arrows only just missing their mark. He tossed the head towards the gate before turning to ride back to his men.

One of Stephan's housecarls shook his head. "The Godspeaker has foreseen our doom," he muttered.

"If he has fled," said another. "We ought to flee too. There is no hope."

"Silence," barked Stephan.

A horn was blown out in the field. Drums began to rumble. The two forces outside the city advanced on one another.

Eleni turned Matilda to face her. "Matilda, I am sorry—"

"He lies. He hopes to lead us into despair," hissed Matilda. A tear ran down her face. "He hopes to leave us without our Godspeaker."

At first, the man at the gate did not believe I was me.

"Edward's dead!" he shouted to us. "He disappeared weeks ago."

"*I* got into some trouble, but am still very much alive!" I yelled.

The guard grumbled. "Look, I want to believe you, but we've been ordered to be wary of strangers and let none through the gate we do not expect."

I scowled and turned my horse, then another man called out. "Wait!"

I looked over my shoulder and saw a large warrior standing above the gate. He waved down at us. I knew that man. "Arne, it's me!" I called. I turned my horse and rode up to the gate.

"Godspeaker, is that truly you?"

"Yes, sir. I need to see the king at once."

Arne peered down at me for a few moments, then shook his head. "By the Gods, it is you. Guard! Open this gate right away, the Hero of Tillysburg has returned."

Godwald came up beside me, and soon the gate eased open. We rode inside, the few refugees still with us close behind. We dismounted at the stable by the gate and Arne strode over to us, his arms wide. "You are certainly full of surprises, Edward," he laughed.

I smiled, and the two of us embraced. "You'll not believe the tales I have to tell," I said.

"Regardless, you can tell us where you have been later. The king will want to see you right away."

"How is he?"

"He has not been himself lately. He is troubled greatly by the events to the west, and he refuses to accept your death."

"Did you think I was dead, Arne?"

He chuckled. "I've met children with more strength than you."

"I'll take that as a yes."

"I was wrong though, was I not? And who is this?" He nodded to Godwald, who performed a short bow.

"I am Godwald, lord. Son of Lord Edric of Beglen," he said.

Arne frowned. "You probably should not be here."

"Godwald wishes to swear to Carol. He does not approve of his family's treason," I said.

"I see. Well, you two best come to the keep."

"And what of these folk? They flee the destruction Emrys has wrought upon the land, and seek the king's protection."

"They can wait here," Arne said. "I will have Carol send men to look after them."

We left the refugees and followed Arne through the ancient fortress to the great hall. It had changed a lot since I was last there, and only then did I realise how much time had actually passed.

The city did not seem so much like a ruin anymore, and had many wooden homes built among the stone buildings, many of which had been repaired with thatch and timber. Carol's people had settled in Giant's Rest quite nicely, and many now called it home.

We climbed the steep steps to the great hall, and once we reached the top the keep's doors opened up. And there he was, in his finest clothes and with the iron crown atop his head. His hair was longer than when I last saw him, and he had grown some messy stubble, but he still looked youthful. He grinned and raced over to me.

"Edward, my dearest friend," he cried. Clodild ran from the hall after him.

I went down on one knee and bowed my head. "Lord King, I have returned."

"Get up, you fool, get up," he laughed. I stood, and he put his hands on my shoulders. His smile filled my heart with a hope I had not felt in a long time. "Thank the Gods. Everyone said you were dead, but I knew better. I knew!"

"I knew too," said Clodild. She beamed up at me.

"But tell me, where in the Heavens have you been?"

"I went to Emrys, as I promised, but I failed to cure his curse in time. I've just come from the Capital—"

"The Capital? But that is where…"

"Yes, Emrys and Edric have besieged it, as well as Odo's brother with Everlynn's men. I can tell you the whole story later, but there is only one thing I need to tell you now: we must go and save the city."

Carol's mouth hung open. He stared at me for a while, processing what I had said. I could feel the surge of emotion rushing through him, and the confused thoughts. Queen Amalie emerged from the hall, alongside her father, a dozen warriors, and Solvi. Solvi's jaw dropped when she saw me. She stepped forward, but Amalie pulled her back.

"Edward, you must tell me everything. I want all the details, from the moment you left this fortress until now," Carol said at last. His smile had gone now, and his brow was furrowed.

"Of course, Lord King, but we have little time."

"Yes, yes, I can see that. You would have me break the siege."

"And destroy Emrys for good. Let Ardonn know the name of her true king — Carol Eomundson."

Carol nodded, and flashed a half-smile. "Get yourself cleaned up. Your old quarters are still vacant. Once you are ready and rested you, Lord Sigg, and I will discuss this properly."

"Lord King," Godwald said. He was on his knees, and Carol turned to him with a frown. "Lord King, I wish to swear an oath of fealty to you and redeem my family's name in your service."

"That is great news, but who are you?" Carol asked.

"Godwald of Beglen, Lord King. Son of Lord Edric."

Carol took a deep breath, then sighed. "You have chosen kingdom over family."

"Yes, Lord King."

Carol nodded. "Very well. Arne! Take Godwald to a comfortable room. Once I have spoken with Edward, he can swear his oath."

The king turned to me, nodded, then marched back into the palace. Clodild grabbed my hand and smiled at me while Arne's men took Godwald by the arms. Sigg followed the king into the palace, and his daughter went with him. Solvi gave a small wave, but I just looked past her.

None of this felt real. I could scarcely believe I had reached Carol. Now all I needed to do was convince him to march west. Then, Ardonn's fate would be in his hands.

And while we spoke, Winterhome's men were slaughtered.

The battle between Wulfstan and Emrys was terrible, from what I have heard. The Lord of Winterhome and his men came marching from the north and positioned themselves on the grassy plane outside the city. They were proud warriors, made tough by the bitter cold of their northern country.

Emrys, Edric, and Hakon marched to meet him. Two great shield walls were formed, they smashed together, but the two sides seemed evenly matched. Winterhome had locked the enemy in place, and all it would have taken for Stephan to defeat them was to march from the city and outflank them, crushing them from two sides.

Yet Stephan's men did nothing but watch helplessly from the New City walls. Even when Emrys brought his horses round to Wulfstan's flanks, Stephan did nothing. While the Immortal Horde rode through Wulfstan's men, Stephan did nothing. When the fields outside the city were made into a grave for Winterhome's warriors, Stephan did nothing.

The histories blame Stephan for his inaction. I knew, however, that Crawmaer was truly to blame. Stephan was a weak king, no doubt, but he was a man of honour and by no means was he a coward. If he had his way he would have marched from those gates ahead of his army the instant Wulfstan arrived. I used to believe Stephan's weakness implied cowardice, but my time with him had taught me otherwise.

If Carol had heard about Stephan doing nothing while the loyal men of Winterhome were butchered like cattle, I suspect he would have stayed in Giant's Rest. However, for good or ill, news of the slaughter did not reach Giant's Rest. If it had, things may have turned out differently.

It was not long after I arrived in Giant's Rest that I met with Carol, Sigg, and to my surprise Amalie in a small, private meeting room. The king and queen sat on a wide seat opposite me, while Sigg leaned against the fireplace.

I told them everything, though admittedly left out some personal details. I told them of the Lakelanders' attack on Oarsley and the journey down the River Aed. I told of our kidnapping in Beglen, and my subsequent meeting with Emrys. I recalled our journey to Wilere's cave and my experience within that Otherworldly realm. Sigg was most fascinated by that part of the tale, and could hardly believe I had been gone an entire month.

I then told the tale of my journey to Henton, to Everlynn, and finally the Capital. I spoke of the skirmish with Idris and

Godwald, the massacre outside Everlynn's walls, and the events that unfolded after we reached the Capital. Amalie wanted to see the stump of my finger, and then cringed when I pulled off my glove. Carol smiled, however, and praised my staunch loyalty.

I finished with an account of my escape and flight from Emrys's camp, and the journey to Giant's Rest. Once I finished, Carol looked blankly ahead, his hand on his face. Amalie picked her fingers. Sigg stared into the fire, twisting the ends of his beard.

"If we march, and defeat Emrys, the world shall know who the Gods favour," Carol mumbled.

"And if you are defeated?" Amalie said.

"Then the Gods have abandoned the Eomundson kings," grunted Sigg.

Carol nodded slowly. "I am being tested."

"You will have victory, My King," I said. "I am sure of it."

"Have the Gods told you this?"

"The Gods have not revealed anything to me in a long time. I am trusting my gut."

Carol chuckled. "What is it they say about the gut of a Godspeaker?"

"*Wiser is the gut of the Gifted than the mind of a king,*" I said.

"That is why you are here, my friend," Carol sighed. "If what you have said about numbers is true, I will not be able to defeat Emrys alone. Stephan will have to leave the safety of his walls."

"Will he?" Sigg asked. "I have heard the bastard is softer than a virgin's c—"

Carol grimaced and raised his hand. "Please, Lord Sigg. Stephan may be weak, but he is no fool."

"Nor is he a coward," I said. "He will march."

"If he does not, Ardonn is lost. Can we risk it?"

"The same can be said if you remain here."

"The Wightman is right," Sigg said. "March now, and you will win the hearts of many. Lords across the land will see you for the king you claim to be. I may come from foreign lands, but men are men wherever you go. Your support will be earned not by blood, or by law, but by deeds."

"I suppose…" Carol muttered.

"Your ancestor, Eomund, became King of Ardonn not by right, but by conquest. He took an army and made this land his own," I said. "And did Carol the Great, whose name you bear, not earn the fealty of many petty kings and lords by defeating Emrys?"

Carol smirked. "With Godwin Godspeaker at his side."

I stood. "Let us march, My King. Together, even if it is to death, for Ardonn."

"Aye, Lord King," Sigg said. "My warriors are with you. Let us see if Northern blood still flows through Ardish veins."

Carol took a deep breath, then stood. I saw a fire burning in his heart, and passion raging in his eyes. He clenched his jaw. "Invoke the Gods, Edward. I think it is time to give them a battle to sing about."

And so it was. At dawn the next day the men in Giant's Rest

were assembled, and the army of the Pretender — the true Lord of Ardonn — rode for war. To victory, or to death.

15

The Grey Dog

The air was still. The sun was hot. The only noise was the snorting of horses and shuffling of men. Someone down the line coughed.

We stood facing south on the gentle slope before Lord Edric's shield wall. The slope was our only advantage that morning, for we certainly lacked the numbers. The Lord of Beglen had his finest warriors, his elite household troop, in the centre of his shield wall. They all wore rich mail and fearsome helmets, and their bright blades glinted in the sunlight.

I glanced up at the wall of the Capital, so close yet so far. I could almost make out the faces of the men who watched us silently. Would Stephan open the gates? Would he join us, or would we be doomed? The remains of Lord Wulfstan's army lay strewn about to our west, their rotting corpses serving as a reminder of what might happen should we fail. The stench was powerful, though in recent times I had grown used to the smell of death.

Carol would not let me stand in the shield wall. He had me at his side behind the wall atop Brand, with whom I had been reunited in Giant's Rest. I had done enough fighting, he said. I was more valuable alive, inspiring his men rather than dying beside them.

The king — the true king — wore a gilded helmet adorned with a crest in the shape of a golden griffin. His sword hung at his side, and the sunlight ignited his shining mail. He wore a deep purple cloak pinned at the shoulder by a golden dragon brooch. His crown he left in Giant's Rest with Clodild. He refused to let Emrys take it from him if he were to die that day. If we lost that battle, Clodild was the Eomund dynasty's last hope.

Godwald was at my side. He was shaking, and clutched his sword in his hand. He kept fiddling with the clasps of his helmet, and it was getting on my nerves.

"Calm down, Godwald," I hissed.

He took his hand from his helmet and grasped the reins. "I have never been in a battle such as this before."

I reached over and put a hand on his arm, then nodded. "Trust in the Gods, my friend. There is nothing to fear."

I lied, of course, for I was dreadfully frightened. Not for my own life, but for Matilda. I could not take her off my mind that morning. I could not stop picturing her face, her eyes, her smile.

I was afraid of what might happen should Emrys defeat us. Her fate and the fates of all behind those walls were in our hands. I feared the prophecy, the vision of suffering and death I had seen that Winterlow, and I hoped that our victory here could prevent it coming to pass.

"Remember who we are, warriors of Ardonn!" I shouted. "Do not fear the men who stand before you, for they have betrayed their king and their gods, and the Gods hate traitors above all others. It is they who should be afraid. Do not forget why we are here. Tell me, for whom do we fight?"

"For Ardonn," cried one man.

"For Carol," cheered another.

"For the Gods!" yelled Carol.

Soon the whole line was shouting. *For Ardonn. For Carol. For the Gods.* That is what we all cried, but in my heart I knew I did not flee the Capital and come back with an army for my king, my kingdom, or even the Gods.

I fought for Matilda.

I fought so that she would no longer need to live in fear behind that damned city's walls, tormented by the thought of what the next day might bring. I fought because I was afraid that she would die without knowing what she meant to me, so to show her I had brought Carol's warriors — the Mountaineers — to war. I fought, and would likely die, for Matilda.

Our men chanted and beat their shields, battle-fury bubbling up within them. They were ready, but I feared their enthusiasm would not be enough. We truly needed the Gods on our side that day, for the might of mere men could not bring us victory. Yet I had acted on nothing more than hope. I was desperate for a sign from the Gods, but they were silent.

And then, their silence was broken. The Gods were about to reveal their favour. They were watching.

Godwald gasped when the warrior stepped forward. Though his visor concealed his face, Godwald recognised him. He was tall, with a beautiful sword and a crested helm, and a rich red cloak draped over his shoulders. He pushed through the enemy shield wall and strode forward several paces, thrust his sword into the dirt, and held out his arms.

"That is my brother," Godwald said.

"I, Redwin of Beglen and heir to Lord Edric, do challenge your false king to single combat!" the man shouted. "Face me, Pretender, and prove your right."

Carol grunted and nudged his horse forward, but I grabbed the reins. "No, Lord King. Don't be a fool," I said.

He turned to me, then back to Redwin. "I can slay him."

"I do not doubt that, but I doubt that our enemy will accept it."

Carol sighed, but before he could do anything more, our own shield wall parted. Sigg, who had been standing in the vanguard, marched forward. An aventail covered his face, but we could recognise him from his immense stature and the heavy axe he carried in one hand.

Redwin walked to meet Sigg, and the two stopped several feet away from each other in the centre of the field. The men on both sides were silent now. They held their breath, praying the Gods would grant their champion victory.

"King Carol does not stain his honour by facing traitors," Sigg said. "But if you are so desperate to be slain by a king, Redwin, I suppose I can humour you. I am Sigg, son of Felagi, and King of Frostmarch."

"And I am your doom, Sigg son of Felagi," said Redwin.

They went three paces back. Then, the men charged.

The songs that tell of that day sometimes describe a great duel, a test of arms lasting long enough to bore those watching. Bards sing of how the noble Redwin clashed with the mighty Northern lord, of how sparks flew from their swords and scorched the grass beneath them, and of how even the Gods cheered when victory was claimed.

The songs exaggerate, however. Sigg wielded a heavy axe, not a sword, and it was with that axe that Redwin's head was sliced clean off only moments into the fight, before the poor man even had time to lift his arms to block. Redwin's body crumpled to the side, while his severed head rolled down the slope back to his father's shield wall.

Godwald lurched forward and vomited, and I put a hand on his back. "He is with your forefathers now, boasting of how he faced the mighty Sigg without fear. Few can make such boasts," I said.

Godwald sat back up and wiped his mouth. "He was always foolishly brave."

"Forgive me, Godwald," said Carol.

"There is nothing to forgive. My father's treason is to blame," Godwald sighed. "I was never close with Redwin, but he was my brother."

Sigg strode back to the shield wall, axe raised triumphantly over his head, still dripping with Redwin's blood. Our men all cheered, but his men cheered even louder. They began to sing a song in their own tongue, and started to beat their shields. Soon, the whole line had joined in. I noticed some of Edric's men shuffling. They were afraid now, but that fear would not last long.

"Carol, we should strike now," I said.

"And yield the advantage of the hill?" Carol said.

"Yes. The Gods have given us a chance. Let us not waste it."

Carol thought for a while, then he drew his sword and raised it. "Forward, men. We shall hit them now, and hit them hard. Wipe the miserable toads from this world. Forward!"

Horns sounded, and drums thundered. Our men cheered and the shield wall inched forward. It moved as one. Edric's men were anxious, but they held their ground. Emrys and Hakon's men waited behind them.

Perhaps we did have a chance of defeating Edric's wall, but I doubted we would be able to overcome Emrys and Hakon too. Our only hope was that Stephan and Lord Tripho would march from the city to support us.

The only question was, would they? We would soon find out. I glanced up at the city's walls, but saw no signs of movement. The soldiers just stood there, spears pointed to the sky, watching us.

The gate remained shut.

Our men continued their slow march, and Carol's cavalry moved to its flanks. I stayed atop Brand with Godwald and Carol beside me, accompanied by a few of Carol's old commanders. We were out of the range of Edric's archers, but in a moment our shield wall would not be.

Soon enough, the arrow rain began to fall. Hundreds of iron points shot up into the sky, arched over Edric's shield wall, then whistled down upon our own men. The men in the back rows raised their shields, but some arrows got through the gaps. So died the first of the many who would fall that day.

Our men moved faster, hastened by the threat of that sharp hail. The hissing of arrows and the shouting of men was deafening. Soon the thundering crash would come. I glanced at the city's wall again, but still there was no sign of movement. Had I led these men to their doom?

It was too late to turn back now. With a resounding roar, the shield walls collided. The beating of steel on wood had begun. Screams of pain and terror and the cries of bloodlust and fury were the songs of the day.

The two walls pushed against one another. Those of us watching were tense. We said nothing, but did not need to. We all knew what we were thinking. Would we win? Or would

Ardonn fall to the Immortal King? One thing was certain: Ardonn's fate would be decided that day.

I looked at the city again. The gates were shut. I thought of Matilda, and of the dream I had during Winterlow, and a shiver crept up my spine. The images of her and of the dead king in his hall flashed through my mind.

"Edward," Carol said. He had opened his faceplate, and his eyes were red. "If we should lose this day, swear to me you will do all you can to protect my sister."

"My king?"

"Swear it."

I nodded. "I swear it."

"Good. I will not abandon my men to these savages, and will die with them if I must. If that is so, you will marry Clodild when she comes of age, and rule Ardonn alongside her. I trust none other with this."

"It will not come to that."

He opened his mouth to speak, but before he could we heard the sound of horns. Edric's left flank was wavering, and our men were beginning to press that advantage. Emrys's horsemen then began to move.

My heart dropped. For too long they had been waiting on the edge of battle. Watching. Biding their time until the perfect opportunity presented itself.

"It's a trap," I said.

Carol nodded, and shouted orders. A horn was blown and our

cavalry unit rode to counter Emrys's. The horn kept blowing, Emrys's men hastened towards our flank, and our own cavalry rushed to intercept them.

They clashed. It would not take long before our cavalry would be overwhelmed and routed, but it would give us some time. I could not stop shifting in my saddle.

Then another horn sounded, this time from afar. Three times it blew, long and low. Some of Emrys's men turned and rode westwards, and Hakon's forces began to move.

The gate was opening.

I could not help but smile.

Hundreds upon hundreds of men on horse and foot poured from the city's gates. They raced to join us, to aid us, and crush our enemy's flank.

Emrys and Hakon rode to meet them, while several hundred immortal horsemen kept our cavalry busy. The first of Stephan's men to emerge formed a shield wall outside the gate, which swiftly grew in size as more and more men ran from the city. Even the Maricari came, lining up behind the shield wall with their bows at the ready.

Carol blew a horn, and our men pushed harder against Edric's. We could see some weak points in Edric's wall now, but it was not yet breached. The morale of our own horsemen, however, was on the brink of collapse. I drew my sword and grabbed my reins. I knew what I had to do.

"Where are you going?" Carol demanded. He held up his hand.

I pointed to our cavalry engaged in a losing struggle. "You wanted me to inspire your men. If our cavalry is routed, our warriors will be outflanked."

Carol hesitated, then finally nodded. "The Gods are with us today. Show them, my friend."

"I will follow you, Edward," said Godwald.

I turned to him and smiled. "Is there a girl you fancy, Godwald?"

The boy smirked and gave a sharp nod. "Yes."

"What is her name?"

"Alice. She is only a kitchen maid in my father's hall, but no lady is more beautiful." Godwald looked down and blushed. "I promised I would marry her once I returned from this damned war."

I laughed. "Keep her in your mind. That promise will do more to keep you alive than skill or luck."

Godwald nodded, then I turned and snapped the reins. I drove Brand towards the battle and heard Godwald close behind me. "For Alice!" he cried.

I smiled. "For Alice!" I shouted. I called the name of Godwald's girl, but thought only of Matilda, and pushed aside the fear that gripped my heart. She would have been afraid, so I could not be. If I could inspire our cavalrymen to continue their fight until Edric's wall crumbled then Matilda might have a chance of surviving that siege.

Even if it meant I had to die.

We entered the fray, and the flame of battle-rage inside me erupted into a blaze. It was chaos. Men came at me from all sides, and it was more luck than skill that allowed me to dodge or block most of their blows as they rushed past. I swung or lunged my blade at any who came at me, and even came close to slaying a few Ardish men on several occasions.

"Men of Ardonn," I called. "Hear me, and hear the Gods call your names. Your ancestors are betting on your victory. Do not fail them. Fight, fight for your families, your country, and your gods."

I heard a few cheers and yelled again. Whenever I had the chance I would raise my sword and rear my horse, calling out to the horsemen around me. I spotted Godwald not far from me slice through the neck of another horse, sending its rider tumbling forward to crumble into dust. "Alice!" he cried.

And that is when the spear came.

He yelled once more, but Alice's name was cut short by the cruel, cold tip of an ancient spear. In a flash a horseman charged past and Godwald was thrown back from his horse. He landed in the dirt with a broken spear protruding from his chest.

Fury washed over me and I gritted my teeth. "Slaughter them all!" I screamed. I kicked Brand's side, making him bleed, and charged for the man who had downed Godwald. I ducked under an axe swung at my face. I was gaining on him. He was close.

Closer. Closer.

I cut down at his horse's back and its legs buckled. The horseman tumbled forward and rolled, but I did not stop and trampled him with my horse. By the time I turned to see him he was a mangled mess of bones. My presence had rallied Carol's men, and they were slowly pushing Emrys's cavalry back. Soon enough, the chaos had moved away from where Godwald lay, and I raced back to him.

I pulled Brand to a stop and threw myself down from the saddle. Godwald lay among the many who had fallen, jerking and coughing. Blood bubbled from his mouth and he looked up at me with wide, fearful eyes. I knelt down to him and grabbed him by the shoulders.

"Get up, lad!" I shouted.

"Am I dying?" he gasped. He fumbled for the spear deep within his chest, but I took his hands and held them between mine.

"Dying?" I shook my head and chuckled. "No, you fool. A warrior never dies."

"I do not feel too good, Edward."

"Just breathe, Godwald. Take in the air."

He took a deep breath and winced before spitting up more blood. I looked up to see the enemy cavalry retreating further from our own, but to my left Lord Edric's shields were pressing ours back up the slope. We needed to hold on until Stephan's forces could reach us, but we were running out of time.

Godwald groaned. "Edward, what happens to us when we…after?" He was deathly pale, and blood dribbled down his chin.

"We are welcomed into a vast, mighty hall, with a roaring fire over which roasts a delicious giant pig," I said. "There the dead meet their ancestors, and fallen warriors feast at Alcyn's high table, knowing neither pain nor sorrow."

Godwald smiled slightly, then grimaced. "What happens then?" he muttered.

I smiled. "You are reborn into this world, or if you are lucky, join the Gods in the Heavens."

Godwald nodded and closed his eyes. His mail was stained a dark red, and he trembled.

"The horses are moving away, Godwald," I said. "We are winning."

"Really?"

"Yes, so just wait with me a little longer and we can get you to a healer. I know a woman who can stitch you right up. Then you can boast of your first scar!"

Godwald shook, his teeth chattering. Tears streamed down his face and he stared up at the clear sky above. "Edward, I feel cold."

"Just breathe, and keep your eyes on the Heavens above us. Hefencyn has cleared the clouds for you."

"I am scared," he mumbled, then squeezed my hand. "Please do not let go of me."

"I've got you, Godwald."

I wish I could say that Godwald's last words were something noble, and I am sure the poets have made some lie about them, but in truth he said nothing after that. I watched the life leave that young man's eyes, and though I barely knew him I could not shield myself from the pain of grief.

I closed Godwald's eyes and kissed his forehead, then the grief turned to rage. Emrys's cavalry had been reinforced and was now pushing our men back again. Our shield wall still groaned against the pressure of Edric's. I took Godwald's sword and left him lying among the corpses, mounted Brand, and galloped back to Carol.

"Pretender!" I shouted as I approached. His housecarls raised their swords, then lowered them when they saw it was me. "Carol, Lord King, pull the wall back."

He nodded, and one of his men blew a horn. I reined my horse in beside his. "Thank the Gods you are alive. I was holding out until I was certain you were safe, but the men were getting itchy," he said. "Can we still win this?"

"We lost Godwald."

"Oh."

"I think I can ensure his death was not in vain. I need to speak to Lord Edric."

"Now?"

"Yes."

Carol hesitated. His men were pulling away from Edric's,

giving them some well-deserved respite, and the enemy let them retreat. They moved a few paces towards us, and then reinforced their wall as they braced for another clash. Carol nodded. "I hope you know what you are doing."

I did not wait. I rode down the slope to our wall and shouted for the men to part. They did, I raced past them, and then reared the horse in the space between the two walls. "Lord Edric of Beglen!" I shouted.

I waited for silence. Bows were drawn and spears were readied. There was muttering behind both walls but I could not make out what was being said. The screams of men and horses still filled the air, but the men in the walls were hushed.

"Lord Edric, I am Edward of Oldford, Royal Godspeaker to Carol of Ardonn. I wish to speak with you."

There was no response for a few moments. The battle still raged to my right, but here the armies stood still. Then Edric's wall shuffled, and the Lord of Beglen strode forward, clothed in his war-gear and drenched in the blood of his enemies.

"You wish to surrender, Edward?" he barked.

"No, but I offer you the chance to surrender instead."

He frowned, and a few of his men laughed.

I held up Godwald's sword. "Yield, lord, before yet another of your sons loses his life."

Edric took a step back, his eyes wide. He mouthed the word "no." His men were silent.

"Godwald was slain by an immortal rider. He died honourably,

347

fulfilling his duty to his king and his people. Redwin died nobly out of loyalty to his family. Edric, I beg of you, do not let your misdeeds cause the deaths of more good men.”

Edric said nothing for a few moments, then he let out a deep breath. “Give me my son’s sword.”

I climbed down from my horse, and then with Godwald’s sword in my hands I stood before the Lord of Beglen. He stared at me, his eyes resembling smouldered fire. I pitied him, and knew then that he did not want this war. He simply did what he thought would be best for his people. I held the sword out to him and he took it with trembling hands.

“Thank you,” he said. “Godwald was the last of my sons to be born, and the last to die. My line is now broken.”

“But Beglen still stands. You are her lord — do not lead her into doom.”

Edric nodded. “I have brought shame to my house. I will not bring us further dishonour by kneeling to this…this *tyrant*.” He pulled a warhorn from his belt and blew into it, filling the air with its long, deep groan. “Men, we march east, to Beglen. Move.”

The line murmured and did not move. A great confusion washed over the men, but soon more horns were blown, drums were beaten, and the shield wall was dismantled. The red-cloaked men of Beglen simply turned and marched away.

I returned to Brand and threw myself into the saddle, then drew my sword and raised it high. I saw Carol, standing on the hill, raise his sword in response. His men blew their horns and our shield wall also turned — to the west. The Mountaineers ran, charging towards Emrys's horsemen still engaged with our own. I reared my horse and rode alongside them. Carol cried for his men to go forth and destroy their enemies.

And destroy them they did. Emrys's cavalry saw the danger too late. Our horsemen circled around to their west, while our footmen came at them from the east. Many escaped and fled to join the rest of their comrades, but many also died, with no choice but to fight until death. It was a slaughter, and the screams of dying men and horses remain scarred in my memory even today.

Yet the battle was far from over. We had won the first round, a victory given to us by the spear of an immortal warrior, but the majority of Emrys and Hakon's forces still hammered at Stephan's shields — and they would soon be reinforced by the few horsemen who escaped Carol's wrath.

Though instead of moving forward, a tight shield wall was forming. Carol had been unhorsed and his men amassed around him.

"Edward!" I heard him yell. "Edward, to me."

I pulled my sword from an enemy horseman and turned, saw his banner waving side to side, and rallied with the rest. His men parted for me, and I brought my horse up beside the king. "Lord King, are you hurt?"

"My heart is pained by the loss of my charger, but otherwise I am fine."

"Take Brand. You need a horse more than I."

"No, I need you seen. In a moment we shall take them from the rear, but I want you to lead the horsemen and sow discord amongst them."

I nodded, and then Arne pushed through the crowd to meet the king, covered in blood and dirt. "The men are with you, My King," he said.

"Good. Let us finish this, and save the bastard king once more." Carol handed me a warhorn, which I slung over my shoulder. The king smiled. "Blow thrice, my friend, short and sharp. The horsemen will follow you."

"Gods be with you, Carol. I will see you at the end of this."

I turned Brand and charged toward the battle. I blew the horn, then raised my sword, and Carol's horsemen rallied behind me. "To me, men!" I cried. "Ride, ride, and live forever!"

The men roared with passion. Emrys's horsemen turned, more horns were blown, and then the slaughter resumed. It all seemed so easy. Both Emrys and Hakon were trapped between us and Stephan, like a piece of soft iron beaten against an anvil. In only a matter of time Emrys, the king who had for centuries evaded his enemies, would be destroyed.

I tried to find him as we fought his men, harassing them before swiftly retreating, only to rally again for another charge. Then Carol came with his shield wall, leaving them with nowhere to run. I rallied the cavalry and led them to Carol's flanks, then as a single unit we closed the jaws on the enemy. It was so easy.

Too easy.

For as we engulfed Emrys's cavalry, I felt a sudden urge to flee. Something was not right.

But the urge came too late. Out of the woods to the south emerged several hundred horsemen. They were dressed in ancient armour and wielded ancient blades. They charged, driving their wedge formation at the rear of Stephan's wall.

And at their head, with his snarling wolf-faced helmet, was the Immortal King.

So many died in the ensuing chaos. The morale of Stephan's men collapsed immediately, and the shield wall fell apart. I do not blame them. They had spent weeks living in fear of Emrys, and now they found themselves surrounded by his men. No shield wall can withstand an attack from the rear. Men let instinct take over and they turn to defend themselves, abandoning their formations.

Emrys had been hiding in the forest with his best horsemen, waiting for the perfect moment to strike. We had given him that moment. Carol's wall remained intact, but it was forced to retreat and abandon Stephan's men to their fate. The Maricari fled, with many discarding their gear and diving into the Ard to swim for safety. Emrys simply ignored them.

Some of Stephan's brave men stood their ground and fought

till their final breath, but without the wall it was hopeless. The cowards fled to the city's gates and beat helplessly against it while others, as the Maricari had done, dived into the river — but unlike the Maricari, they could not swim. Of their dreadful fate I need not speak.

The clever ones gave up the fight and fled to Carol's wall, where they swiftly regrouped. I charged forth with the horsemen to cover their retreat, and though we saved many, it merely prolonged our defeat. There was no way we could defeat Emrys in battle now. We never had the advantage of numbers, but the chances we had of outmanoeuvring the enemy were lost in that slaughter.

One moment I glanced behind me, and the next Brand crashed head on into another horse. Amid screams and flailing hooves I was thrown from the saddle. The wind was knocked out of me and I lay gasping while a few of Carol's horsemen circled me.

I was picked up by two of Stephan's men and managed to get back on my feet, then alongside Stephan's fleeing forces I ran back to Carol's wall. I turned to call for Brand but saw him lying motionless in the grass.

That was the last I saw of Brand, my loyal companion. I could only hope that he did not suffer much. Regardless, I knew that he would find peace in Eocyn's shining green meadows where go all faithful steeds who fall in battle. There he enjoys a life galloping saddleless in the light of the sun, a crisp breeze flowing through his mane.

Yet there was little time for me to mourn. Things were to get even worse.

I met Carol and Sigg behind the wall, and then the warriors who had rescued me removed their helmets. They both grinned — a man with one eye, and a merchant from Beglen. I threw my arms around them and kissed both their cheeks. "By the Gods, it is good to see you again."

Dughlas had tears in his eye, and Thorry could not stop smiling. "I'm crying because I lost a bet," said Dughlas.

"Hakon told us you died fleeing. Dughlas reckoned he spoke true, but I knew otherwise," said Thorry.

I laughed. "I could not stand waiting any longer. I had to do something."

"Well, you've certainly arranged a beautiful show here," said Dughlas.

Another warrior, his deep blue cloak stained red, grabbed my arm. His hair was a mess, but his eyes full of joy. "Edward, you are alive," he exclaimed.

"William," I said. We embraced, then I held his head in my hands. "I am glad you are here too. Forgive me, my friends. For everything."

Dughlas shook his head. "There's nothing to forgive. Now, shall we go meet our ancestors?"

I nodded, my eyes wet. "Let's. Matilda, is she okay? And what of Philip?"

"They're in the palace, ready to flee with Stephan's family

should the city fall."

"Good. Then we shall at least give them time."

Emrys's men were rallying, banners flying in the breeze, while Everlynn's forces formed a shield wall that slowly came to meet ours. Carol and Sigg began shouting orders and the men moved into formation. There would be no retreat without slaughter, so we would make one final stand. If we were all going to die, we would die well.

Emrys must have known it would be a vicious fight. His numbers overwhelmed us, and though he would have eventually defeated us, he would lose many. Emrys's power lay in the fear of his horde, but without his horde he was nothing. Instead of sending his men in a mighty clash against ours, his line halted just beyond the range of our archers.

Then the Immortal King strode forward atop his horse. He held something in his hand, and all could see his face, for instead of his helmet he now wore a bejewelled golden crown. The crown of Ardonn.

He raised his arm, and all could see what he held.

"Your king is dead," he proclaimed. His men cheered, and we stared in disbelief at the limp, bloody head of Stephan. His jaw hung open, and blood dripped from his neck. Emrys tossed it towards us and it landed in the grass with a thud. "Yet the crown he wore is not mine. Where is it?"

He spoke our language, though clearly with difficulty. Nobody spoke, and I sensed Carol tense up beside me. We moved to the front of the shield wall.

"I offer all of you life, if one of you sacrifices your own," he said. "We shall duel — man to man, horse to horse. I would like to face my descendant, Carol, if he is here. But in the end I do not care who it is. Fight me, one of you, on your kingdom's behalf. We decide here and now Ardonn's fate with only one final death."

"I will not give him what he desires," Carol muttered. "I do not trust his men."

"Nor should you," Arne said.

"Neither do I wish to forfeit Clodild's claim should I fall."

"Let them all come. I will drench these fields," declared Sigg.

Carol gave no orders. He did not reveal himself, and did not answer the challenge. All were tired and ready to die. Emrys knew he had victory, but he wanted to make a show of it. A duel would be little more than a humiliation. Nobody was brave or foolish enough to face him.

Except for one. A young man, a nobody, stepped forward from the shield wall. He was short, with an oversized coat of mail and a helmet covering his face. He had no horse, and carried a faded shield, though his sword was deftly crafted. I thought he must have taken it from some warrior's corpse, or inherited it from a noble ancestor he was eager to impress.

Regardless, that young man walked forward a few paces and stood still. His long black hair flowed loose down his back from under his helmet, and he shuffled into a fighting stance.

Emrys laughed. "So this *boy* is the bravest, mightiest warrior Ardonn has to offer? I am disappointed, but I will keep my word. Somebody lend him a horse."

I could see the frustration in Carol's eyes, but nevertheless he turned and nodded to one of his horsemen. The warrior dismounted and brought the horse over to the brave young man who thought he could save our kingdom. The boy climbed into the saddle with the horseman's help, then took a deep breath.

"I do not mock you, boy. I mock only the kingdom you will die in vain to defend." Emrys bowed his head, and our boy nodded.

Then Emrys charged.

Our young warrior kicked his horse and sent it forward a few paces, but with lightning speed Emrys rushed past. The boy let out a short yell and held up his shield in time to block the blow from Emrys's blade, but his first strike was little more than a tease.

Emrys circled the boy and stopped a few yards away. "What is your name, young man? I promise you your bravery will be remembered in stone and song."

The boy mumbled something, and Emrys frowned.

"Forgive me, I did not hear. Your tongue is still quite new to me. Tell me your name, boy," Emrys said.

"Matilda of Henton."

I lurched forward, but Carol, William, and Dughlas all grabbed hold of me. I shouted, but Dughlas put his hand over my mouth.

"Ma-til-da," Emrys pronounced. "The Last Champion of the Exiles."

He kicked his horse forward again, and the young warrior — Matilda — kicked hers. I bit down hard on Dughlas's hand and he pulled it away, and I tossed and turned to try to escape their grip. "No!" I yelled. "No, Emrys, take me instead."

He would not have heard me, and even if he did it would not have mattered. Dughlas and William held me tight, while Carol stood before me and took my face in his hands. He was shouting to me, but all I could hear was the beating of hooves. *Look at me*, his lips said. *Look at me.*

I think I spat at him, though I do not remember those moments well. My vision was blurred and I could not bear to watch the fight in front of our wall. I felt like I was going to melt. The world seemed to slow, and then came the scream of a wounded horse.

Carol slapped me across the face. "Come to your senses, Godspeaker," he barked. "You swore to me. Clodild needs you."

Matilda came crashing to the ground as her horse collapsed. She rolled and rolled, then lay still. Emrys reared his horse and turned. In his own tongue he shouted, "Ardonn is mine!" then lifted his sword and went for another charge.

Carol and I looked at each other, and he saw the despair in my eyes turn to rage. I threw my head forward and smashed it into his face, and he fell back with a gasp. I twisted away from Dughlas and William's grip, drew my sword, and pushed through the men.

I burst from behind the shield wall to see Matilda climb to her hands and knees. Her shield had been thrown a yard away, but she had her sword in her hand. I froze for a second, Matilda stood, then turned to the warlord storming towards her. She held her sword in both hands, put her foot back, and braced.

"Matilda!" I cried.

I was too late. Emrys's horse ploughed into her and she was trampled under a flurry of hooves. It let out an unholy screech and skidded to a stop, bucking and thrashing. The dust settled to reveal Matilda lying in the grass in a broken heap.

And the sword of Idris was buried to the hilt in the chest of Emrys's horse.

The Immortal King was losing control of the beast. He kicked it and pulled the reins this way and that, cursing it and the warrior responsible. I looked from him to Matilda, then back to him, then once more back to Matilda before fury overwhelmed me.

"Emrys!" I shouted. "Cursed king, come to me and face your mortality." I snatched a spear from the footman behind me. Emrys spotted me and snarled. I held the spear out in front of me, roared, and charged.

Then came the yells from Carol and Stephan's men. Some of them burst from the wall and ran with me. "Godspeaker," they cried. "Edward!" More and more men broke from the wall, horsemen began to charge, and eventually the horns were sounded. Carol's army rushed forth for Ardonn, for death, and for me. I ran for revenge.

Emrys saw his danger. Arrows whistled past him and landed in the earth by his mad horse. One bounced off his shoulder. His horse saw the danger too, and Emrys whipped its reins and finally managed to regain control. He turned and raced back to his line as fast as his bleeding horse would take him, our men hot on his tail.

And all the while, that little grey dog remained in his saddle.

I knew what I had to do. Emrys's cavalry stampeded, but Emrys did not rally them. He rode past, away from the fight. I shouted for a horse and one man dismounted for me. I mounted, kicked as hard as I could, and pursued the fleeing king. I could not let him escape. Not this time.

Emrys leaped over Hakon's shield wall and they, seeing the warlord fleeing, broke apart. I burst through the gap, and soon the battle was behind me. The shouts of men and clashing of swords grew more and more distant. My eyes, like those of a hunter, focused on nought but my prey. I was snarling, growling like a dog. Emrys kept glancing over his shoulder.

We rode along the river. His horse was slowing while mine was gaining on him. My heart seemed ready to burst from my chest. I could hear the heavy breathing of my poor, tired horse, but it was not as loud as the gasping of Emrys's. He was fleeing for a group of trees up ahead, hoping he could lose me there. Yet I did not think about what he might do. I thought only of ending this, once and for all.

As I drew nearer, Emrys would turn his head to see me, and each time he whipped the reins and kicked his horse's sides. Stephan's crown had tumbled off and his long grey hair flowed out behind him. I could see the puppy sitting in his saddle, peeking its head out to watch me. I met its eyes for a moment. It barked.

I was gaining on him. I held the spear tight under my arm, ready to thrust it into my enemy's back once I was near enough. Yet the trees were getting closer, and it was then I realised I might lose him. I could not let that happen. If Emrys escaped, we would not get another chance for perhaps another century.

I put the spear over my shoulder now and squinted at the horseman moving swiftly toward the trees. A wolf he had once been, with his grey mane and silver mail, though now he was a dog fleeing for his life. I whispered a prayer. I gripped the shaft tight. I focused. I held my breath. Time seemed to slow down.

And then I threw it. I jerked my arm forward and opened my fist, and the spear hurtled ahead of me. It whistled through the air. I watched it cut through the wind, my heart racing, and held my breath.

Then, with a loud thud, Emrys's horse fell forward. It rolled and rolled, I heard the spear snap, and Emrys tumbled into the grass.

I pulled my reins and the horse skidded to a stop. I threw myself down from the saddle, drew my sword, and sprinted over to the king who now lay in the grass. The end of the spear protruded from his chest, and blood was pouring down his front and dribbling out from his mouth. A man of flesh. He had touched the ground, yet dust he was not.

I stood over him and touched the tip of my blade to his neck. He looked up at me, his eyes heavy, and grinned. The puppy skipped over to him, yapped, then reached up to lick the blood from his chin. Emrys stroked its head. "You won," he coughed. He then let out a pained chuckle. "*Should the grey dog dismount…*"

"*…this curse shall be broken,*" I finished.

"You knew," he said.

I nodded. Emrys realised the answer to the riddle the dwarf had given him, though too late. The curse was broken, but Emrys's wound would be fatal. He winced and then held his hand up to me.

"Take it off," he groaned. "My glove."

I glared at him, and pressed the point of my sword harder against his throat. He gasped.

"Please, Edward. I am defeated. Must we still be enemies?"

"You killed my friend."

"The brave young warrior? He lives."

"*She*. How do you know she lives?"

Emrys smiled, his teeth stained red. "I know all too well the difference between life and death. Please, Edward, give an old warrior his dying wish."

My heart jumped. Something told me he was telling the truth. The pain — the rage — within my heart seemed to subside and I could now enjoy the taste of victory on the air. I had a strong urge to go find her, to hold her in my arms and never let her go, but I had business with Emrys first.

I pulled my sword away and knelt down beside him. I removed the glove from his trembling hand. He nodded and then lowered it to the grass. The king ran his fingers through the soft, cool blades, gripped them tight, and then dug his fingers into the soil. He pulled some dirt up to his face and took a deep breath.

"As sweet as I remember," he sighed. Emrys wore a soft smile, and for the first time since I had met him he appeared content. I put my arm underneath him and helped him to sit up. He gazed out at the river, which now glistened in the low afternoon sun. He sighed again. "It is beautiful."

"It always will be, long after this kingdom passes and men are gone from this world."

Emrys nodded. "You truly are Godwin's heir, my friend, but you remind me also of another."

"Another? Who?"

"Carol."

"The Pretender?"

He laughed, then grimaced. "No, no. The one you call *the Great.*"

I said nothing, then he pointed to his feet. I understood. I removed his boots for him, then he curled his toes and planted his feet in the grass. He sighed once more. "You have done as you promised, Edward Godspeaker. I can now be at peace and join my forefathers in the land of the dead at last. I can hear them now, calling me home."

"You are long overdue that visit," I said.

He chuckled. "Indeed. And when you too reach that welcoming hall, you and I can share a drink."

"I will look forward to that."

"And I will look forward to hearing of your mighty deeds."

He then groaned and put his hand on my shoulder. I put my arm around him, then slowly raised him up, supporting him as he stood on his two feet. His toes curled and uncurled, scrunching in the grass, and he stared once more at the calm, sparkling Ard.

"The sun. I can feel her warmth. No longer do I feel the chill of the unliving," he said. He whispered something in his native tongue, though I did not hear what it was, before he let out a long, deep breath. His body went limp. I lowered him down and then laid his head once more in the grass.

I picked up my sword and looked around for the puppy, but it was nowhere to be found. Emrys's horse had climbed back to its feet and trotted off into the woods. I looked back to the battle, which still raged on outside the city's gates, but once the horsemen realised their curse had been broken they fled to preserve their new mortality. They were chased down, but many escaped. The men of Everlynn fled too, but many were surrendering to their countrymen. The day was won.

I knew the men would know Emrys as little more than a savage warlord, as an enemy to be destroyed and vilified. They would have mutilated his body if they found it, so while the remnants of the horde and their allies were defeated, I laid Emrys on one of the makeshift rafts Edric's men left on the bank.

I put his sword in his hands, put Stephan's crown on his head, and then pushed him out into the river. It floated gently with the current, and would eventually find its way to sea. I said a prayer for him and sung a hymn to the Gods. The Immortal King, Emrys of Ardonn, sailed off to meet his ancestors.

And Ardonn, a kingdom once again torn apart by war, found peace.

We burned our dead that night on three mighty pyres outside the Capital's walls. Carol and his men were not allowed inside the city, by decree of Prince Wim — though I knew it was Crawmaer who gave the order. On the bright side, Crawmaer and his new puppet made no indication they intended to wage war against the Pretender. At least for now.

The decree did not stop many men and women from within the city from leaving to bring gifts and food to their saviours. Warriors who had met on the battlefield united once more, while others came out to mourn their short-lived brotherhoods. The smell of the burning bodies was powerful, but not as powerful as the joy of victory.

Carol, Sigg, and I had each lit a pyre and stood back as they ignited into a blaze. We watched, while priestesses sung mournful songs that echoed on the breeze. A slow rumble came from the drums, and horns were blown.

I shed a tear as the smoke went up, for many men I had once known lay on those pyres. Both Godwald and Redwin were cremated that night, and Arne — that brave, loyal commander of Carol's elite — burned with them.

I held the piece of amber I had found beneath Godwin's shrine, turning it over in my hands. The light from the pyres made it glimmer like fire.

"The seas will be calm again, for a time," Carol said to me as the pyres burned. "But our respite will not be long. Stephan was a man of peace, but I fear his son may be different."

"Wim is weak. Crawmaer will rule Ardonn now."

"Indeed. We must prepare. Will I have you by my side?"

I smiled and bowed my head. "As always, my friend. I am not dead yet."

Carol chuckled. "My kingdom rejoices at that." He put a hand on my shoulder. "Soon the tempest will return, and the waters shall churn once more. I will need you then. I am sorry for sending you away, Edward. Please, forgive me."

"Lord King, if you had not sent me away, we would not have gained this victory."

"That is true." He smiled. "You have seen enough death. Go, find your friends. They need you more than the dead do."

I pocketed the amber, bowed, then pushed back through the crowd. I made my way to the camp that had been erected outside the city's gates, then walked through the maze of tents to the place my companions waited. Dughlas and Thorry had survived the battle, though Thorry was gravely wounded. He would be fine, though, for his mail took the worst of the axe's blow.

Emrys did not lie. Matilda, too, had survived. I opened the flap of the tent and poked my head in to see Dughlas and Philip engaged in an arm wrestle, while William refereed. Two beds sat by the little fire. Thorry sat up in one of those, a jug of ale in his hand, and in the other lay Matilda. Her head was propped up by pillows, and a bandage was wrapped over her eyes. Eleni sat beside her, holding her hands, and she smiled when she saw me.

Everyone went quiet when I entered, and Dughlas bowed his head. William stood, raised his arms, and cried, "Edward Godspeaker, the Hero of Tillysburg, and Bane of the Immortal King. Hail, friend!" He lifted his tankard and took a big drink of ale. Dughlas, Philip, and Thorry clapped, Eleni laughed, and Matilda lifted her head.

I walked past Philip and ruffled his hair, then went to stand beside Thorry. I tapped his belly. "Does it hurt?" I asked.

"Hardly felt it, lord," he said.

"Bollocks. You squealed like a pig," Dughlas laughed.

I smiled, then went to stand beside Matilda. Eleni nodded, then stood up and ushered the men out of the tent. William and Dughlas helped Thorry out of bed, and soon Matilda and I were alone. I knelt beside her and took her hand. We said nothing to each other at first.

"How are you?" I said at last.

Matilda took a deep breath and cringed. "Not good."

Her voice was soft and frail. I felt my eyes beginning to water. "The healers say you'll have no lasting injury."

She nodded.

"Matilda, I do not know how to beg for your forgiveness. I put you in danger, I broke your heart, and I watched you face Emrys alone."

She smiled somewhat. "I hated you, even before you abandoned us," she said. "At least, I thought I did."

"You were right to."

She shook her head. "I always had hope you would return. I knew you were not dead. You never can disappoint me, and I cannot seem to hate you for long. Messing around with servant girls is trivial when compared to the fact you brought an army to die for Ardonn."

A tear ran down my cheek. "I didn't."

"Sorry?"

"I did not bring Carol and his men for Ardonn. I brought them here for you."

She smiled properly then, and a drop of blood trickled down her face from beneath the bandage.

I stood and frowned. "Matilda…" I said. I wiped the bloody tear away with my finger.

"Let me see you, Edward," she said. "Let me know you are here."

I reached forward and slowly lifted the bandage from her eyes. She looked up at me. The whites of her eyes were a deep crimson red, and another tear of blood ran down her cheek. She smiled and squeezed my hand.

"The healer assures me it will not last. At first I could see nought but blackness, and I bled from my eyes and nose, and coughed up blood. I am broken. I was so afraid. Someone pulled me from the battle, and I drifted in and out of a dreamless sleep," she said.

"I have seen this before."

"Really?"

I nodded. "In my dream last Winterlow. I saw you standing beside a dead king, bleeding from your eyes. I am so sorry."

"It is not your fault. It was my choice. I was so angry. He took almost everything from me, from us, and I wanted to show him how much I hated him." She winced again, and I put a hand on her head. She closed her eyes.

"You fought well, and bravely. I am very proud of you," I said.

Her eyes went wide again. "Edward, I am so sorry."

"Why?"

"I lost the sword you gave me. The ancient blade."

I laughed. "Good, you've caused nothing but trouble with that weapon. Did nobody tell you what happened?"

She shook her head. "I only knew we won, and that you killed

Emrys."

"*We* killed Emrys. You thrust the sword through his horse's chest, and without that wound I never would have slain him. The horse bolted, but is probably dead in the woods by now."

Matilda said nothing. She closed her eyes again and sighed. Drums and flutes were playing cheerful songs outside while the sound of laughter and cheer echoed softly around us, and the small fire crackled in the pit.

Then Matilda smirked. "I suppose I should get the most credit, really," she said.

I laughed. "We can take half each."

She grinned and squeezed my hand. "I am glad we made it to the end."

I knelt down again and looked at her bruised, scratched face. Her nose was broken and her lips split, but beneath all that I could still see the sweet, adventurous girl I had met in Henton during winter. I stared at her, and she opened her eyes and looked back at me, her brow furrowed.

"What is it?" she said.

"I love you, Matilda."

She closed her eyes and took a deep breath. A small smile appeared across her face, and she sighed. "I thought so," she said.

I put her hand to my face and held it there. She was cold, but alive, and for that I was grateful. My heart skipped a beat when her hand went limp, but she had only gone to sleep. Her breath was short, but she was at peace. I lowered the bandages back over her eyes and sat with her for a while, and soon the others came in.

Carol was right — war was on the horizon. I could feel it. I could smell it. Already the rats in the city were plotting their next moves, scheming for ways to take more and more power from soon-to-be-king Wim. The Pretender was given a night to burn his dead and rest his men, but he was still a rebel and an enemy to the men in the palace and council hall.

Yet that would be something to dwell on another time. That night, my only concern was for Matilda and my friends. I was glad they had lived and that we were all together once more. The next morning, William and Eleni would return to the city and their families, and the rest of us would march east.

We had won the first in a long series of wars. The Hostess was making her tables vacant, for the coming years would bring many new guests to her hall. The storm Emrys brought was over, but clear weather never lasts.

Especially not in Ardonn.

Epilogue

Edith's toys were little more than a distant memory by the time I finished telling the story of Emrys, and how he was defeated. She was fixated on my words, and even though the night was late and the fire barely more than a few crackling embers, she was wide awake.

The dogs had come to curl up beside her and a servant brought us both our supper. Edith sat at my feet staring up at me with the same deep blue eyes her mother had. When I finished telling the tale as best as I could remember it, Edith smiled wide.

"What happened next?" she asked.

"Haven't you heard enough?" I sighed.

She shook her head. "I want to know about the kings, and who wins, and I want to know more about your friends, and you and Ma."

I chuckled. She was like me, in many ways, but she was also very much like her mother. I could not blame her for her curiosity, and it would be cruel for me to keep her longing unfulfilled, but it was getting late and I was growing weary. "Perhaps another time. You should rest now."

"Sleep is boring," she protested. "I want to hear your stories."

I stood up. "Come on, if you go to bed now I promise I will tell you the rest tomorrow night."

She smiled and clapped, then stood up and raced off to her room. The dogs followed and I went over to stoke the fire. My tales brought joy to Edith, but to relive those memories sometimes troubled me. To Edith, they were stories from a distant past, or perhaps even another world, and she would not have grasped their reality. But they were real for me. I had little sleep that night.

Instead, I stayed in my chair by the fire until dawn, contemplating the events succeeding Emrys's defeat. The story was far from over, of course. Emrys was merely the stone dropped in a pool, which sends ripples far beyond it.

As Carol had predicted, there was peace for a short time. Hakon managed to flee the battle once he realised it was hopeless, and nobody knew where he went. Some suspected he took a boat across the sea, while others thought he went south. He was declared a traitor and marked for death, and had a bounty placed on his head. His forces, leaderless, were pardoned by William, the new Lord of Everlynn.

On the full moon following our victory, Prince Wim was crowned King of Ardonn in the palace temple. It was a fabulous ceremony, so I heard. I was not able to witness it for the day after the battle I went with Matilda, Dughlas, Philip, and Thorry to Giant's Rest. There, we regrouped and recovered, preparing for the imminent war.

There were many others that came that had not been with us before — citizens of the Capital whose love and gratitude Carol had earned, and who were driven away by the fear of their new king. Wim was a weakling and a coward, but he had a reputation for callousness, and few loved the First Minister whose grip on the throne only tightened. Wynflaed was among those who came with us to Giant's Rest, though we spoke little on the journey there.

Soon after Wim's coronation he and Anora of Everlynn were married, as Odo had promised, and so Ardonn had a new queen. Both Odo and William swore oaths of fealty to Wim, securing the peace between them.

Carol, threatened by such a union, sought allies wherever he could find them. He first reached out to Lord Edric, but Edric refused to take a side. He sent envoys to the southern lords, but they too remained neutral. They would not act until Lord Adalbert did.

Then the following spring, King Wim declared war.

The armies of north-western Ardonn marched on Beglen. They laid siege to the city and demanded Edric's surrender, but Edric kept his gates shut. He sent a messenger to Carol, who after much deliberation decided to send a force south to "see what all the fuss was about."

There was no battle. Wim went to Beglen as a show of force, and had no intention of wasting his men on the city's gates or in a shield wall. He withdrew from the city, raided the wine-country for a few weeks, then went back home to enjoy a summer on the coast.

Edric still refused to swear fealty to Carol, but the two men agreed to peace. It was not an alliance, but it allowed both men to focus on their western borders, where Wim's forces began carrying out raids. The warmer seasons meant skirmishes along those borders between the north-eastern and north-western lords, but never open war.

To settle disagreements among Carol's lords about my position at his side, the king granted me a noble title at last. Soon after we returned to Giant's Rest I was officially made an earl, and given lordship over a small settlement in the hilly country south of Carol's fortress.

So, I moved there with my companions and a dozen or so young men who wished to swear as my oathmen. Carol visited when he had the time, but never stayed long. He was a busy man in those days — not least of all because he and Amalie had their first child. The birth of the princess was welcome and joyous news throughout the land.

Then one year, after the snows melted, the king came to me

with a request. "I would not ask this of you if any else could do it," he told me. "But I fear I have need of you once more."

Carol had made an agreement. A secret pact, with a prince from beyond the eastern mountains. Tensions were growing and the petty incursions and raids along the border were escalating into more than mere skirmishes. The pieces on the board were shifting, and the players were making their move at last.

And I, bound to the strokes of Fate's cruel pen, would need to play my part.

*Edward's saga, and that of all Ardonn,
will soon continue…*

The Noble Families of Ardonn

The Eomundson Kings

Family currently headed by **Carol**, known as *the Pretender*, who was married to Princess Amalie of Frostmarch, daughter of Sigg, son of Felagi.

Who is the son of King Edwin of Ardonn, known as *the Fifth*, who was married to Lady Elfswith of Winterhome, daughter of Lord Wulfstan of Winterhome, and also fathered Clodild.

Who was the son of King Edwin, known as *the Fourth*, who also fathered Lady Alhilda, wife to Lord Adalbert of Oldford.

Who was the son of King Francis, known as *the Feeble*, who was married to Elain, known as *the Weaver*.

Who was the son of King Ermenwulf, who was married to Lady Eadburg.

Who was the son of King Edwin, known as *The Third*.

Who was the son of Carol, who passing one year before his father never reigned over Ardonn.

Who was the son of King Edmund, known as *the Child*, who was married to Lady Melisende of Everlynn.

Who was the son of King Francis, known as *the Second*, who was married to Lady Hemma and who also fathered Queen Hemma, known as *the Traitor*, wife to King Tanred of Erila; and

Cwenhild, Clodild, and Edwina.

Who was the son of King Francis, known as *the First*.

Who was the son of King Carol, known as *the Great*, who unified the Twin Kingdoms, who was married to Lady Aleanor and also fathered Carol, known as *the Younger*, who was married to Edith, Godwin's daughter.

Who was the son of King Edgar.

Who was the son of King Edbert, known as *the Strong*.

Who was descended from Queen Clodwig, known as *Deathsbane*, who defeated the Immortal King.

Who was descended from King Edwise, known as *the Lost*, who defeated the Immortal King yet succumbed to his wounds.

Who was descended from King Emming, known as *the Hopeful*, who defeated the Immortal King when he first returned.

Who was descended from King Adalwulf, known as *the Good-Healthed*.

Who was the son of King Edwulf, known as *the Spurned*.

Who was the son of King Edwin, known as *the First*.

Who was the son of King Edward, known as *the Ardborn* for he was first of the Eomundson kings to be born on Ardish soil, who was murdered early in his reign; who was succeeded by his wife, Queen Clodild *of the Ard*, who crushed the Crisan Revolt, and who was daughter of King Eomund *the Nephew*, son of King Eored *the Exile*.

Who was the son of King Adalric, known as *the Artist*, who built the Hall of Legends in Ardonn.

Who was the son of King Eomund, founder of the Eomundson dynasty, who was the first King of Ardonn from among the Exiles, and who married Lady Eirwen of Ardonn, descendent of King Emrys; and who legend tells was the son of Lita, the daughter of Morenlea and Hefencyn.

Who was the son of Adalwer, King of the Black Coast, who also fathered Eored, founder of the Eoredson dynasty, who was the first King of Aedonn from among the Exiles.

Who was the son of Cynric, King of the Black Coast, known for his mastery over the seas.

Who was the son of Godwer, known as *Gehalgod*, who legend tells slew the wyrm of Fyrdun and became the first King of the Black Coast, and who married Oswifa.

The Eoredson Kings and Lords of Oldford

Family currently headed by **Lord Adalbert of Oldford**, who was married to Lady Alhilda and who fathered Lady Ecwyn.

Who was the son of Lord Godred, known as *the Mild*.

Who was the son of Lord Elwin.

Who was the son of Lord Godred, known as *the Lesser*, who also fathered Earl Adalstan, known as *the Cowherd*, who fathered Lady Alia, who was married to Earl Odhelm of Henton, who fathered Earl Harold, who was married to Eleanor and who fathered Gunn, Alia, and Matilda.

Who was the son of Lord Godred, known as *the Oathbreaker*, self-styled King of Aedonn.

Who was the descendent of King Godheart of North-Aedonn, later Lord of Oldford, known as *the Kneeler*, for it was he who yielded the Kingdom of Aedonn to King Carol *the Great*.

Who was the son of Queen Aelda of Aedonn, known as *the Fair* and *the Cruel*, who was married King Godheart of Beglen and who also mothered King Elwulf of West-Aedonn, known as *the Coward*; and King Cured of South-Aedonn, later Lord of Beglen, known as *the Hammer*.

Who was the daughter of King Elwulf, known as *Wolfsbane*, who married Lady Hilda of Bullhorn.

Who was descended from King Eomund, known as *the Nephew*, who fathered Clodild *of the Ard*, wife to King

Who was the son of King Eored, founder of the Eoredson dynasty, who was the first King of Aedonn from among the Exiles, and who fathered the shieldmaiden Bladswith; and who legend tells was the son of Lita, the daughter of Morenlea and Hefencyn.

Who was the son of Adalwer, King of the Black Coast, who also fathered Eomund, founder of the Eomundson dynasty, who was the first King of Ardonn from among the Exiles.

Who was the son of Cynric, King of the Black Coast, known for his mastery over the seas.

Who was the son of Godwer, known as *Gehalgod*, who legend tells slew the wyrm of Fyrdun and became the first King of the Black Coast, and who married Oswifa.

The Usurper Kings

Family currently headed by **King Stephan of Ardonn, previously Lord of Tidegate**, known as *the Bastard*, who is married to Lady Bebbe of Winterhome, daughter of Lord Wulfstan of Winterhome, and who fathered Lord Wim of Tidegate, known as *the Young*.

Who was the son of Lord Wim of Tidegate, later King of Ardonn, known as *the Usurper*, who remained unmarried until death.

Who was descended from Cedwin, who was the first Lord of Tidegate from among the Exiles, known as *the Tidebringer*.

The Lords of Everlynn

Family currently headed by **Lord Odo of Everlynn**, who is married to Lady Eadswith and who fathered William, who married Lady Eleni, daughter of Sealord Tripho of Cavoucara; and Anora, Arlette, and five other daughters.

    Who was the great-grandson of Lord Elmore of Everlynn, known as *the Peacemaker*.

    Who was descended from Richard, known as *the Foreign-Lord*, who was the first Lord of Everlynn from among the Erilans and who also fathered Lady Melisende, wife to King Edmund *the Child* of Ardonn.

    Who was the son of King Rubert of Erila, who also fathered King Tanred of Erila, also later King of Ardonn, who married Queen Hemma *the Traitor* of Ardonn.

The Lords of Everlynn

Family currently headed by **Lord Edric of Beglen**, who fathered Redwin, Tatric, Bedric, and Godwald.

Who was the son of Lord Edwald of Beglen.

Who was the son of Lord Edric of Beglen.

Who was descended from King Cured of South-Aedonn, later Lord of Beglen, known as *the Hammer*, who was defeated and yielded to King Carol *the Great*, who made him Beglen's lord.

Who was the son of King Godheart of Beglen, who married Queen Aelda of Aedonn and who also fathered King Elwulf of West-Aedonn, known as *the Coward*, and King Godheart of North-Aedonn, later Lord of Oldford, known as *the Kneeler*.

Who was descended from Lord Elfric of Beglen, later King of Beglen, known as *the Liberator*, who for a time freed the Shires of Beglen from Ardish overlordship.

Who was descended from Godric *of the Hills*, who was the first Lord of Beglen from among the Exiles.

Acknowledgements

Firstly, I'd like to give acknowledgements to my number one
fan and supporter: my wife. Throughout my journey as an
author, Sophie has been unshakeable in her confidence and faith
in my ability, has constantly offered her advice and feedback,
and helped me to keep going whenever I felt it was hopeless. I
can safely say that the love Sophie has given me while writing
this book, *the Immortal King*, and my numerous short stories is
what made it all possible.

I'd also like to extend gratitude to my family for their support
and encouragement, allowing me to turn my dreams into a
reality. Each step of the way they have provided the
encouragement and help I needed to put this story to paper, as
well as challenging me to make the right decisions about it. To
my mum, dad, my brothers Harrison and Samuel, my
grandparents, and to Talitha: thank you.

I thank my friends (you know who you are) for their constant motivation, interest, and inspiration throughout the writing of this book, and their eager impatience for *the Grey Dog*'s release, which drove me to put in the effort and quality this novel needed. You helped me to do the best I could do, and for that I'll always be grateful.

A special thanks should also be given to my fans and supporters, both online and offline, who read my writing, engage with it, and help to share it around. I write these stories for you all, and I hope that this book has proven just as good as the rest of my writing. If you've come this far, thanks heaps!

I also want to acknowledge my editor, Nick Hodgson, and my cover artist, Lena Yang, for their fantastic work in making this book publish-ready. I think it's obvious what an astounding job they've done.

As with *the Immortal King*, gratitude must be given to the goddess Frīge, my divine patron and muse, who provided the inspiration for this story and all others I have written. Once again, it cannot be said that these stories are my own — I am merely the pen with which their true author writes.

Enjoy the Immortal King?

Consider leaving a review on Amazon!

If you want to read more tales from Ardonn, you can read my
free short stories at these addresses...
www.patreon.com/jasoncmalone
www.buymeacoffee.com/jasonc.malone